YOU AGAIN

What Reviewers Say About Aurora Rey's Work

Twice Shy

"[A] tender, foodie romance about a pair of middle aged lesbians who find partners in each other and rediscover themselves along the way. …Rey's cute, occasionally steamy, romance reminds readers of the giddy intensity falling in love brings at any age, even as the characters negotiate the particular complexities of dating in midlife—meeting the children, dealing with exes, and revealing emotional scars. This queer love story is as sweet and light as one of Bake My Day's famous cream puffs."—*Publishers Weekly*

"This book is all the reasons why I love Aurora Rey's writing. It's delicious with a good helping of sexy. It was a nice change to read a book where the women were not in their late 20s–30s…"
—*Les Rêveur*

The Last Place You Look

"This book is the perfect book to kick your feet up, relax with a glass of wine and enjoy. I'm a big Aurora Rey fan because her deliciously engaging books feature strong women who fall for sweet butch women. It's a winning recipe."—*Les Rêveur*

"The romance is satisfying and full-bodied, with each character learning how to achieve her own goals and still be part of a couple. A heartwarming story of two lovers learning to move past their fears and commit to a shared future."—*Kirkus Reviews*

"[A] sex-positive, body-positive love story. With its warm atmosphere and sweet characters, *The Last Place You Look* is a fluffy LGBTQ+ romance about finding a second chance at love where you least expect it."—*Foreword Reviews*

Ice on Wheels—*Novella in* Hot Ice

"I liked how Brooke was so attracted to Riley despite the massive grudge she had. No matter how nice or charming Riley was, Brooke was dead set on hating her. A cute enemies to lovers story."—*Bookvark*

The Inn at Netherfield Green

"I really enjoyed this book but that's not surprising because it came from the pen of Aurora Rey. This is the kind of book you read while sitting by a warm fire with a Rosemary Gin and snuggly blanket."
—*Les Rêveur*

"[Aurora Rey] constantly delivers a well-written romance that has just the right blend of humour, engaging characters, chemistry and romance."—*C-Spot Reviews*

Lead Counsel—*Novella in* The Boss of Her

"*Lead Counsel* by Aurora Rey is a short and sweet second chance romance. Not only was this story paced well and a delight to sink into, but there's A++ good swearing in it and has lines like this that made me all swoony because of how beautifully they're crafted."
—*Lesbian Review*

Recipe for Love

"*Recipe for Love* by Aurora Rey is a gorgeous romance that's sure to delight any of the foodies out there. Be sure to keep snacks on hand when you're reading it, though, because this book will make you want to nibble on something!"—*Lesbian Review*

Autumn's Light

"Aurora Rey has a knack for writing characters you care about and she never gives us the same pairing twice. Each character is always unique and fully fleshed out. Most of her pairings are butch/femme and her diversity in butch rep is so appreciated. This goes to prove the butch characters do not need to be one dimensional, nor do they all need to be rugged. Rey writes romances in which you can happily immerse yourself. They are gentle romances which are character driven."—*Lesbian Review*

"[*Autumn's Light*] was another fun addition to a great series." —Danielle Kimerer, Librarian (Nevins Memorial Library, Massachusetts)

"Aurora Rey has shown a mastery of evoking setting and this is especially evident in her Cape End romances set in Provincetown. I have loved this entire series…"—*Kitty Kat's Book Review Blog*

Spring's Wake

"[A] feel-good romance that would make a perfect beach read. The Provincetown B&B setting is richly painted, feeling both indulgent and cozy."—*RT Book Reviews*

"*Spring's Wake* has shot to number one in my age-gap romance favorites shelf."—*Les Rêveur*

"*Spring's Wake* by Aurora Rey is charming. This is the third story in Aurora Rey's Cape End romance series and every book gets better. Her stories are never the same twice and yet each one has a uniquely *her* flavour. The character work is strong and I find it exciting to see what she comes up with next."—*Lesbian Review*

Summer's Cove

"As expected in a small-town romance, *Summer's Cove* evokes a sunny, light-hearted atmosphere that matches its beach setting. ...Emerson's shy pursuit of Darcy is sure to endear readers to her, though some may be put off during the moments Darcy winds tightly to the point of rigidity. Darcy desires romance yet is unwilling to disrupt her son's life to have it, and you feel for Emerson when she endeavors to show how there's room in her heart for a family."—*RT Book Reviews*

"From the moment the characters met I was gripped and couldn't wait for the moment that it all made sense to them both and they would finally go for it. Once again, Aurora Rey writes some of the steamiest sex scenes I have read whilst being able to keep the romance going. I really think this could be one of my favorite series and can't wait to see what comes next. Keep 'em coming, Aurora."—*Les Rêveur*

Crescent City Confidential—*Lambda Literary Award Finalist*

"This book blew my socks off... [*Crescent City Confidential*] ticks all the boxes I've started to expect from Aurora Rey. It is written very well and the characters are extremely well developed; I felt like I was getting to know new friends and my excitement grew with every finished chapter."—*Les Rêveur*

"*Crescent City Confidential* is a sweet romance with a hint of thriller thrown in for good measure."—*Lesbian Review*

Built to Last

"Rey's frothy contemporary romance brings two women together to restore an ancient farmhouse in Ithaca, N.Y. ...[T]he women totally click in bed, as well as when they're poring over paint chips, and readers will enjoy finding out whether love conquers all."
—*Publishers Weekly*

Winter's Harbor

"This is the story of Lia and Alex and the beautifully romantic and sexy tale of a winter in Provincetown, a seaside holiday haven. A collection of interesting characters, well-fleshed out, as well as a gorgeous setting make for a great read."—*Inked Rainbow Reads*

"One of my all time favourite Lesbian romance novels and probably the most reread book on my Kindle. ...Absolutely love this debut novel by Aurora Rey and couldn't put the book down from the moment the main protagonists meet. *Winter's Harbor* was written beautifully and it was full of heart. Unequivocally 5 stars."
—*Les Rêveur*

Visit us at www.boldstrokesbooks.com

By the Author

Cape End Romances:

Winter's Harbor

Summer's Cove

Spring's Wake

Autumn's Light

Built to Last

Crescent City Confidential

Lead Counsel (Novella in The Boss of Her collection)

Recipe for Love: A Farm-to-Table Romance

The Inn at Netherfield Green

Ice on Wheels (Novella in Hot Ice collection)

The Last Place You Look

Twice Shy

You Again

YOU AGAIN

by

Aurora Rey

2021

YOU AGAIN

ISBN 13: 978-1-63555-791-6

This Trade Paperback Original Is Published By
Bold Strokes Books, Inc.
P.O. Box 249
Valley Falls, NY 12185

First Edition: April 2021

CREDITS
Editors: Ashley Tillman and Cindy Cresap
Production Design: Susan Ramundo
Cover Design By Tammy Seidick

Acknowledgments

I got the idea for this book on a bus ride home from New York City, listening to my favorite sad song du jour. I started writing it just as the pandemic took hold and everything about the story softened—even the playlist I created to keep me company as I plugged along. The result is less angsty than I first imagined, but rings true to me and, I hope, to the characters I created. Just like the town of Duchesne, sometimes we have to write the world as we want it to be.

A huge thank you to Jaime and Leigh for the beta read—for keeping me laughing and keeping me honest. Ash, I'm running out of clever ways to say I adore you and you make me a better writer, but both are truer than ever. Cindy, same goes for your grammar lessons and liberal use of the "The More You Know" gif. Rad, Sandy, Ruth, Carsen, and everyone who manages the business of BSB, your passion and attention to detail make me so proud to be part of the Bold Strokes family.

And last but not least, my readers. I'm so grateful you go on these adventures with me. Thank you from the bottom of my heart.

Dedication

For PN

PROLOGUE

Ten years ago.

Sutton wrapped an arm around Kate and pulled her closer. They only had another hour or so before Dad would be home from work. He knew they were together, but it didn't mean he'd be cool coming in and finding them tangled up in bed in the middle of the afternoon. And he most definitely wouldn't be cool finding them naked.

The naked part still felt new. They'd gone from kissing to all the way like six months ago, but it still felt new to her. In that she still couldn't believe it was real sort of way. Magical. Wondrous.

And now she was about to leave and not see Kate for months. Just the thought of it put a knot in her throat. She squeezed Kate tighter. "Maybe I shouldn't go."

Kate lifted her head and gave Sutton the look she'd come to think of as Kate's *don't make me be the adult* face. "Of course you're going. Don't even say things like that."

Her week of orientation at Emory University started in exactly two weeks. Eight impossibly long hours away. The fall semester would start right after. And then she wouldn't be home until Christmas. "But it might not be too late to enroll at LSU instead. Then I could come home every weekend."

Kate sat up fully. "Sutton."

She propped herself on her elbows, only to flop on her back a second later. "I know."

"I'm not saying I'm not going to miss you, but this is a big deal. You got into Emory and got almost a full scholarship. You can't throw that away."

She knew this. All of it. But the more she thought about being so far away while Kate finished her senior year, the sadder she got. Add to it the probability that Kate would end up at LSU or at least somewhere in state. It meant spending the better part of three years only seeing each other at Christmas or in the summer. She wasn't sure she could take it. She sat up and crossed her legs so they were sitting face-to-face. "I'm not saying you're wrong. I just don't get how you can be so blasé about it."

Kate sat up straighter and put her hands on her hips. "I'm not blasé."

The conversation was serious, but Sutton couldn't help but be distracted by Kate's naked torso. She was so soft and feminine and perfect, especially next to Sutton's more angular, androgynous frame. Just looking at her made the idea of wasting time fighting seem like the dumbest thing she could think of. "I know. I'm sorry."

Kate lifted a brow. "Are you sorry or do you just not want to fight?"

"Both." Which wasn't a lie.

Kate shook her head, but smiled. "What am I going to do with you?"

Although Kate was technically a year younger than her, there were moments—moments like this—that made her seem older. She had this way of being practical and down-to-earth in ways Sutton tried to be but wasn't. It was one of the things Sutton admired most about her. That and her ability to make Sutton laugh about pretty much anything. And her body, of course. All that plus the fact that, for some reason she still couldn't quite understand, Kate loved her. "Kiss me?"

Kate's smile grew and took on an air of mischief. It was so sexy and it made Sutton's stomach do this weird fluttery thing. She angled her head slightly. "I think that could be arranged."

She leaned forward and pressed her lips to Sutton's. Sutton's whole body melted. Kate shifted onto her knees and kissed her harder, until they were both lying down and Kate's whole body covered hers. Kate's blond hair fell forward, tickling her shoulders and making a curtain around both their faces. She went from melted to on fire in about five seconds.

Every time they had sex, it seemed to get better. She wondered if that was normal, like learning something new and improving with practice. Or maybe it was unique to them. Sutton was pretty sure they were soul mates and, in her mind, that brought a sort of magic with it that regular love or sex couldn't compete with.

After, they lay under the fan in a tangle of limbs. Kate dozed and Sutton stared at the ceiling. She still didn't want to leave, but knew she would. Because going to college at a place like Emory was a once in a lifetime opportunity. Because Dad had sacrificed so much to save enough to cover her room and board and he would never forgive her if she backed out. And because Kate was the love of her life. Which meant nothing—not even five hundred miles and months of making do with texts and phone calls—would change that.

Chapter One

S utton shoved the final duffel bag into her trunk and slammed it shut. When her phone vibrated in her pocket, she pulled it out, smiling at her father's picture on the screen. "Hey, Dad."

"Are you sure you should be making this drive all by yourself? I don't like thinking about you all alone on the back roads of Alabama."

"I'm great, thanks. How about you?" He never bothered with hellos or pleasantries and she never failed to tease him about it.

"Having second thoughts about you driving."

His stubbornness drove her crazy, but his heart was in the right place. "It's eight hours. I'll stop a couple of times to stretch and go to the bathroom and still be there by dark."

He grumbled but didn't push further. On top of her making a sound argument, he knew better than to pull that woman alone business with her. "You send me updates, you hear?"

She smiled. "Promise. Car is loaded. I need to coax Hugh into his carrier and we'll be on our way."

"Damn cat."

He said it out of habit more than malice. In fact, the last few times he'd visited her in Atlanta, she'd come home from work to find Hugh snuggled on his lap. "He can't wait to see you, either."

"Drive safe, will ya? I don't know what we'd do if we both got laid up."

The idea made her wonder. "We might have to call Mom."

He let out a string of expletives but laughed. "Like I said, drive safe."

Neither she nor her father had hard feelings toward her mother, but they didn't have much use for her either. She'd run off with some oil rig operator when Sutton was ten and, other than gifts for Christmas and her birthday, they never heard from her. Even the gifts had dried up a few years prior and Sutton found herself relieved rather than disappointed. "I will."

She went back inside and did a final sweep of her townhouse. The fridge was empty, the thermostat set. She had a friend planning to stop by every week to water plants and check on the place, but it was otherwise ready to be empty for the next three months.

Three months.

The reality of what she'd signed up for hit her. Not the time off from work or leaving her place for so long. She had a feeling Jay would be calling to tempt her with projects here and there. And as for her place, well, it and everything about Atlanta had started to get on her nerves. So much so that when Dad finally agreed to knee replacement surgery, she jumped at the chance to stay with him for the duration of his recovery. But now that she was doing it—going home—it suddenly seemed like a much bigger deal.

She closed her eyes and took a deep breath. It was fine. It would be fine. She'd get out of the city, get a break from work, and get quality time with her father. She wanted all of those things. As for the rest, she'd keep a low profile and take it one day at a time.

Not terribly impressed with her pep talk, she shook her head and the canister of treats she'd left out to tempt Hugh. As expected, he came running. She gave him a few, then tossed a few more into the crate. He looked at her with disdain. She picked him up and nuzzled his nose, offering words of affection and apology. Then she shoved him—as gently as one can shove a reluctant cat—into his carrier. To his credit, he didn't really fight. He just wanted to make it clear he wasn't going by choice.

"It's going to be great." She picked up the crate and peered inside. "You're going to get to torture Duke to your heart's content."

Hugh let out a meow that might be enthusiasm or might be a "fuck you." Sutton nodded her agreement either way, did one final look around, and they were off. She made good time, singing loudly and eating more junk food than was probably a good idea.

As she crossed into Mississippi, she realized how long it had been since she'd made the drive. She'd mostly convinced Dad to come to her for holidays, especially since he'd retired. And on the few occasions she had to go home, she flew. The drive was pretty, though, and it felt quicker than she remembered, especially with the addition of an audiobook. She managed to stop only once and rolled into Duchesne a good half hour before she expected to.

Not much had changed since her childhood. A chain dollar store had come and gone, but that was about it. Blanchard's Shur-Fine remained the sole grocery store. Clotille's remained the only bar, complete with a trio of old men sitting on a bench out front. A bunch of kids played basketball in the park next to the school. Cormier's Hardware still offered lumber, tools, plumbing, and paint supplies to anyone who couldn't—or didn't want to—head to one of the big box stores in Houma or Thibodaux.

Seeing Cormier's sent a sigh of, well, something, through her, but she didn't linger on it. She'd have plenty of time to linger, or meander down memory lane, in the next three months.

After pulling into the driveway of her childhood home, Sutton cut the engine and sat for a moment. It was funny. She might come home less, but the infrequency of her trips didn't make the place any less familiar, any less home.

She grabbed Hugh's carrier but left the remainder of her bags. Climbing the porch steps didn't feel all that different from when she did it as a teenager. Maybe she didn't tear around quite so fast. Maybe she had a little less wide-eyed wonder about the world and all the potential it held. But home was home and, despite her hesitation over coming back for such a long stretch of time, she was glad to be here.

She opened the door and called out a greeting. Duke bounded into the front hall from the kitchen. She set Hugh on the ground and got down on her hands and knees to greet Duke. "Hey, Dukey. I missed you."

The old hound gave her the once-over, licked her face, then turned his attention to the cat carrier. Hugh hissed and Duke backed up, making it clear who was going to be the alpha of this arrangement.

"Hey, buddy." Dad stood in the doorway, an apron over his jeans and T-shirt and an LSU ball cap on his head.

"Hey, Dad." She got up and went to him, letting herself sink into the bear hug she'd never get tired of as long as she lived. The house had nothing on his hugs.

He let her go and regarded her with suspicion. "You're early. You drive eighty the whole way?"

"Seventy-three."

"Hmpf. Likely story. I just started dinner. You want a beer?"

"Yes, and what are we having?" He'd learned to cook when her mother left and discovered he both liked it and was good at it. And he always made something special when she came home.

"Your cousin Trey brought over some catfish he caught. I figured I'd fry it up while it was fresh."

Sutton's stomach rumbled at the thought. "Please say you're making hush puppies, too."

"You don't make catfish without them, girl."

"I should have known better than to even think otherwise. I want to let Hugh out and make sure everyone is okay."

Dad sniffed. "I'm going to leave you to it."

He returned to the kitchen and she turned her attention to the cat carrier. She opened the door and Hugh strode out like he owned the place. Duke tried to give him a sniff and promptly got his nose batted. He retreated to hide behind her while Hugh sauntered into the living room and perched himself on the back of the sofa. That, it seemed, was that.

Sutton shrugged and went to the kitchen. Dad had started breading the fish, coating the fillets in flour, then egg, then cornmeal. Well, not just cornmeal. He had his own special blend of cornmeal, corn flour, and spices that he refused to share with anyone—his only daughter included. He angled his head toward an open beer on the counter, already nestled in a koozie.

"Thanks." She slid it out far enough to read the label and smiled. "Your taste in beer has improved."

He shrugged but didn't look up. "There's still Bud Light in the fridge, too."

She took a long sip, letting the hoppyness of the IPA play across her tongue. "All about balance, right?"

"Speaking of balance, I need you to be straight with me."

"Dad, nothing about me is, or ever will be, straight."

He brushed flour from his hands. "That's not what I mean and you know it. I'm talking about your work."

She had a feeling that's what he meant, but she didn't want to pass up the chance to tease him. "We've already discussed this. I'm on a leave, so there's no work to worry about. And if I need to check in, I've got my laptop. As long as your Wi-Fi works, I'll be completely fine."

"I called the cable company and upgraded to their fanciest one. Lightning something or other."

The description, and his underlying Luddite tendencies, made her smile. "I'm sure it will be more than sufficient."

"But I'm talking about your time, too. You're going to have to shuttle me around, but I don't want you waiting on me hand and foot."

She never imagined he'd let her do anything even remotely close to that, but she planned to bully him into letting her do more than he probably wanted. "Can you just trust that I've got everything under control? And that I want to be here?"

His shoulders dropped and he turned all the way around to face her. "I know I can be a cantankerous bastard, but I'm glad you're here."

She crossed the room and planted a kiss on his cheek. "I'm glad I'm here, too."

❖

"Seriously?" Kate set the last tub of joint compound on the shelf and turned to face her mother full-on.

"Don't you make that face at me, Katherine Elizabeth."

Kate pressed her lips together, willing herself not to laugh. "You know I used that exact line on Harper this morning."

Mama folded her arms and raised a brow. "I take comfort knowing she's putting you through the paces. But that still doesn't give you the right to sass me. Even at twenty-seven."

She'd been getting lectures, and occasional threats, about her propensity for sass for most of her life. At this point, she was convinced Mama's fussing was more a combination of habit and affection than anything else. "I wasn't sassing."

"Are you truly upset, then? I was worried you might be."

"I'm not upset." She wasn't thrilled, but she wasn't upset. Who got upset at the idea of seeing her high school girlfriend ten years after breaking up? Someone without much of a life, that's who.

Mama's arms remained crossed, but she added an incredulous head tilt to show her skepticism. "The puss you're wearing says otherwise."

"I'm surprised is all. I was pretty sure she'd decided she was too good for Duchesne a long time ago." Despite all their plans, all of Sutton's promises, to come home after she finished college.

"Well, Albin's finally having his knee replacement. Sutton is coming to take care of him. At least that's what Mavis said."

That made sense. She might want to believe Sutton had become too self-important to set foot in her hometown. But even if she had, it wouldn't supersede the bond between Sutton and her father. "How long will that take?"

Mama shrugged. "When your pawpaw had his done, he had six weeks of rehab for each."

As close as Kate was to her grandfather, Harper had been a toddler at the time. And she'd just moved into a place of her own, so she missed the day-to-day of his recovery. "Right."

"Mavis seems to think she's coming for the whole time and not just the surgery itself because Albin is stubborn and won't even consider a rehab facility."

That made sense, too. Her memories of him might be a decade old, but he was a homebody through and through. Although it surprised her he'd let Sutton leave her big fancy job for close to three months to take care of him. Maybe she was such a big deal by now, they let her take that much time off. Not that it was any of her business.

"You know you're probably going to run into her at some point, right?"

Oh, she did. "It's been a long time, Mama. I'm pretty over it."

She expected an argument, or at least disbelief. Instead, Mama looked at her with something akin to sympathy. "I know, honey. Doesn't mean seeing her won't rile things up."

Kate blew out a breath. "Forewarned is forearmed. Isn't that what you always told me?"

Mama let out a chuckle. "Indeed it is."

"I'm not looking to be chummy or anything, but I can be nice. I like my life just as it is. And I gave up pining a long time ago."

"Darlin', your voice has a lick of bitterness in it."

She squared her shoulders. "I am not bitter. I was a sad and brokenhearted teenager and I gave that up a long time ago, too."

Mama lifted her chin and offered a wink. "There's that fire. Just making sure it's still there."

Kate smiled. "I'm pretty sure fire is sass directed at someone other than you."

"Nah. Fire's got some heat behind it. And principles."

"Ah." It seemed like a gray area to her, but getting into a philosophical discussion about it would probably double the time it took her to finish restocking the paint aisle. "Thank you for enlightening me."

Mama pointed at her and made a little circle with her finger. "See, now? That's sass."

She laughed and picked up the now-empty boxes. "Touché."

The bell on the front door jingled and Mama headed up to greet whoever had come in. Kate brought the empty boxes back to the stockroom, breaking them down for the recycling bin. She pulled out the iPad and updated the inventory she'd put out. She noted the next half dozen items that needed replenishing and started gathering them.

Although technically manual labor, stocking shelves was one of her favorite tasks at the store. To be fair, it was more about using the inventory tracking software she'd implemented than the actual stocking. But since she'd been the one to choose it, and justify the expense to her parents, seeing it work was extra satisfying.

She continued with paint brushes and rollers, stopping to chat with a young couple about possible colors for a gender-neutral nursery and a teenager about what spray paint would make the bike he inherited from his sister less girly. Despite what she'd said to her mother, her thoughts kept drifting back to Sutton.

She'd meant what she said about not pining. She'd stopped wasting time on that shortly after Harper was born. She didn't even go down the what-if rabbit hole, except maybe on the occasional summer night when she sat out on the porch alone with a glass of wine.

The truth of the matter was, even if she'd once believed Sutton was the love of her life, life hadn't turned out that way. But she loved her daughter more than anything, along with the little house they called home and the life she'd built over the last ten years. So, even if a tiny part of her wondered—or longed—for the happily ever after she'd imagined, she wouldn't trade it for the very real, perfectly happy life she had now.

Chapter Two

D id you think you were going to get away with not putting them in?" Sutton shook her head. "Or without the doctor mentioning them at your pre-op appointment?"

Dad shrugged and had the decency to look sheepish. "Grab bars are such an old person thing."

She took her eyes off the road long enough to give him a withering stare. "You know what's an old person thing? Slipping in the shower and breaking a hip."

He mumbled something not entirely comprehensible, but Sutton picked up more than a couple of cuss words. "You trying to make me feel even worse?"

She wasn't. Because even though he could be a stubborn bastard sometimes, she knew he'd never had major surgery before and was scared. Scared of the surgery itself but also about what it meant for his life moving forward. "No. But we're still going to get them. We can install them together tonight so they're up when you come home."

More grumbling. "Fine."

They stopped for lunch before heading back to Duchesne, then the grocery store. It was all fine until they pulled into the parking lot of Cormier Hardware, just like she'd done hundreds of times, from the day she got her license to the day she left for college. A hitch of anxiety lodged between her ribs. "How about I wait in the car and keep the AC running?"

"Not a chance. I refuse to be the little old man buying DIY geriatric supplies."

"You're not little or old. When did you get so dramatic?"

He didn't miss a beat. "When I was forced to accept I needed grab bars in my bathtub."

"Fine." Christ, what a pair they were.

She shut off the car and climbed out. Maybe Kate wouldn't be there. They'd run into each other at some point. She wasn't an idiot. But she'd hoped to have a few days to steel herself. To make sure Kate knew she was around and maybe do some reconnaissance on how she was and if she was seeing anyone. Information she couldn't get from her father without seeming too invested in the answers.

The bell over the door jingled just as it always had. And the cool blast of air conditioning welcomed her in, just as it did every hot day she stopped by to kill time and talk to Kate while she worked. Even the smell was the same. The combination flooded her senses and made her the tiniest bit lightheaded.

"Welcome to Cormier Hardware. Can we help you find something today?"

The voice came from someone way too young to be Kate and Sutton felt herself relax. She looked around to see where it had come from and found a little girl perched on a stool behind the service desk. Her hair was in two identical French braids and her T-shirt said Girls Rule. And her green eyes were almost identical to her mother's.

Sutton's stomach clenched and she got lightheaded in earnest. She fought off the dizziness, and the wave of nausea that went with it. She willed herself to get a grip, to act like a sane and rational adult. She swallowed and said nothing. Apparently, dumbfounded was the best she could muster. Better than passing out, right?

"Good afternoon, Miss Harper. Are you in charge today?" Dad asked.

Harper. She'd known Kate's daughter's name was Harper, but she'd somehow managed to block it out. Along with the reality of seeing her at some point, too.

"Hey, Mr. Albin. Mama's in the back, but until she gets back, I'm the boss. She said so herself." Harper turned her attention to Sutton. "I'm Harper. Who are you?"

Sutton opened her mouth, but no words came out.

"This is my daughter. Her name is Sutton and she lives in Atlanta."

Harper hopped down from her stool and strode toward them with that confidence unique to kids who'd yet to experience the horrors of middle school. She stuck out her hand. "It's nice to meet you, Sutton."

Sutton accepted the handshake. "You, too."

Dad asked Harper if her summer was off to a good start and Sutton tried to get a handle on the million or so thoughts racing through her brain. Like what an adorable and precocious kid Harper seemed to be. Like what a good parent Kate must be to have such a kid. But also, inescapably, how Harper's very existence was the reason she and Kate weren't together anymore.

That last thought probably wasn't fair. It was the act that led to Harper's existence that had been the reason she and Kate broke up. And even if that hadn't happened, there was every possibility something else would have. They'd been teenagers, after all. Full of that optimistic and unrealistic belief that love conquered all. That they'd be together forever.

"Hi, Sutton."

Something about the way Kate said her name made all the years and everything that had happened between them melt away. Her heart flipped in her chest like it used to and the dizziness returned. And then she turned and Kate was standing there looking more beautiful than ever and the rest of the world vanished and all that remained were the two of them and the fact that she'd never, not for one single day, stopped loving her. "Kate."

Kate smiled and, if it was possible to fall even more in love in that moment, Sutton did. "Welcome home."

"Um." Speak. Say something. "Thanks."

"Mama, do you know Sutton? She lives in Atlanta." Harper's question yanked Sutton back to the present.

"I do. We were friends a long time ago. We went to school together."

The reply was completely reasonable and appropriate for a child, but it wrenched her heart nonetheless. Still. There was no way in hell she'd let on that was the case. "We did. We haven't seen each other in a long time, though."

"Did you move back? My friend Bailey moved here last year because her mama got a job at LSU."

In addition to looking so much like Kate, Harper had Kate's confidence, her ease with conversation. It reminded her of the first time she met Kate in the fourth grade. When she and Kate were in the same class for the first time and she'd been drawn to Kate like steel to a magnet. It made this whole interaction all the more surreal. "I'm just here for a long visit."

"Until the end of summer vacation?"

"As long as you keep answering, she'll keep asking questions." Kate had folded her arms and looked almost amused by Sutton's discomfort.

"I'm inquisitive." Harper smiled, clearly impressed with her own use of the word. "Besides, good customer service is about getting to know your customers."

"Seems like you're about ready to start running the place." Dad gave her a gentle punch on the shoulder. The fact that he didn't reserve the gesture for boys made Sutton smile.

"What am I? Chopped liver?" Kate lifted her chin, but humor danced in her eyes.

"My apologies." Dad bowed with a flourish of arms. "Ladies, we need a couple of pull bars because it seems I cannot be trusted to get in and out of the shower without them."

Kate pointed at him. "Safety first, Mr. Albin. Safety first."

"This way." Harper marched down aisle three, not waiting to see if everyone followed because, of course, they did.

They got what they needed. Kate rung them out and Harper wished them a good day. Back in the car, Sutton cranked the AC to full blast and tried to wrap her head around what just happened.

She was pretty sure she hadn't drooled, but had she stared? Had she looked as uncomfortable as she felt?

"That Harper is something, isn't she? Spitting image of her mother."

Sutton nodded, not quite trusting herself with words.

"Growing like a weed, with a vocabulary to match. She's gonna be a handful for her mama before long."

For the last ten years, she'd gone out of her way to avoid asking questions or keeping tabs on the girl—woman—she'd once had every intention of marrying. But seeing her, getting this tiny glimpse into her life and who she was now, made that strategy feel hollow if not foolish. "Is Kate raising her by herself?"

"And doing a damn fine job of it. Oh, she's got her parents, of course, and Bryce, but she never did get married."

There could be a million reasons why Kate remained single. Chances were high none of them had anything to do with Sutton. Still, Sutton couldn't help but wonder if she was happy with that choice. If she ever wished for a partner to share her life with. And, if she was being completely honest, if Kate ever, even in passing, thought about Sutton that way.

❖

Harper climbed back on to her stool. "Sutton seems cool. Why aren't you friends anymore?"

"Because she lives far away." A tiny fraction of the reason, but not a lie.

"Will you be friends again now that she's back?"

Leave it to her daughter to cut right to the quick. "I'm not sure we have much in common anymore."

Harper nodded. "But she probably doesn't have many friends. Like Bailey when she moved here."

Of course Harper would remember the talk they'd had about befriending the new kid. Kate bit back a groan. "Well, we'll see."

"Maybe we should invite her over for taco night. Everybody likes tacos."

She loved that she had a child who was both razor sharp and compassionate. Really, she did. "I think she'll be busy taking care of Mr. Albin for a while, but it's nice of you to suggest that."

She knew better than to think Harper would forget, but for now, she'd settle for buying time.

Harper's eyes lit up. "We should bring tacos to them! I bet Mr. Albin would like company while he recuperates."

"Maybe. We'll see."

Harper frowned. "You always say 'we'll see' when you mean no but don't want to say no."

She laughed in spite of herself. "You're right. How about, let me think about it?"

Harper narrowed her eyes, as though weighing whether or not to press the matter. Eventually, she shrugged. "I just think it would be a nice thing to do."

It would be. And even if she wasn't sure she wanted to spend time with Sutton, it was one of those cases of putting her money where her mouth was. "You're a good egg, H."

"I know."

"You about ready to go home? Cliff should be here any minute."

"Can I stock the cooler first?"

For some reason, Harper's absolute favorite chore at the store was restocking the Coke cooler at the front register. She loved counting how many of each drink was needed and didn't mind pulling out whatever was there so the newer bottles could go in the back. Kate hated doing it so much, she gave Harper a dollar each time, but it probably wasn't necessary. "That would be great."

Harper hopped down and grabbed her notepad. "On it."

In addition to having the task done, it would distract Harper for at least a few minutes and give Kate the chance to strategize. Should she put her foot down? Attempt to explain why it was probably not the best idea? Or should she give in? She was the one who'd gone on and on to her mother about not being bothered by Sutton's return. What better way to prove her point than to bring dinner over while Mr. Albin was recovering?

Assuming, of course, Sutton would accept her offer. She'd seemed kind of shell-shocked when they ran into each other. Which might have made sense had it been anywhere but the hardware store. She had to know Kate still worked there, that the chances of seeing each other were high.

Not her problem. And even though she could say the same about whether or not Sutton had friends, she did want to set a good example for Harper. And if she could prove she was the bigger person—the one who'd stayed behind but moved on—well, that wouldn't be so bad either.

Harper finished with the cooler just as Cliff arrived for the closing shift. She gave Harper her well-earned dollar and they started the walk home. The afternoon thunderstorms had held off, leaving it hot but less humid than it would have been otherwise. She wasn't in a hurry for Harper to go back to school, but July and August were so brutal, she couldn't help but long for fall. Would Sutton still be around in the fall? Mama had said something about three months, but that could be more gossip than reality. Not that it was any of her business.

Harper skipped ahead of her, then back, covering at least twice as much ground over the ten minutes it took them to get home. Once they did, she let Frances into the backyard and sent Harper to wash up. In the kitchen, she put leftover fried chicken in the toaster oven to warm and started chopping vegetables for a salad. As she always did, she said a prayer of thanks that Harper loved raw veggies as much as she did. It saved them arguments, to be sure, but it also meant she didn't have to turn on the stove or the oven a few nights a week.

By six o'clock, they sat at the little table in the corner of the kitchen. Despite telling herself she wouldn't, Kate replayed the conversation with Sutton in her mind. Was it wrong to take satisfaction from the fact that the meeting seemed to affect Sutton more than it had her? Not that she was looking to gloat or anything, but it was nice to think she could hold her own.

Especially since Sutton was more gorgeous than ever. Her face had lost the final traces of baby fat, making her features not sharp, but refined. She'd settled into her body, too. No longer the tomboy with a chip on her shoulder, she now looked every bit the confident butch. Exactly the kind of woman who would catch Kate's eye, assuming of course, there wasn't a whole mess of history to throw a wet blanket on everything.

"I think we should bring Mr. Albin and Sutton tacos on Tuesday because Tuesday is taco day."

Harper's comment pulled her from thinking about the way Sutton's shoulders filled out her shirt. Which was good, really, since that was the last thing she needed to be thinking about. "I said we'll see."

Harper frowned. "Do you not like Sutton anymore?"

Kate blew out a breath. "It's complicated."

Harper dipped a carrot stick in ranch dressing and took a bite. "That's what you say when you don't want to explain something."

Much like Harper's assessment of "we'll see," it was more observation than sass, her way of learning to navigate subtext. Harper was on the bookish side, but she also had this way of reading people that made her seem far more mature than her nine years. It backed Kate into a corner now and then, but it was a skill she wanted to encourage. So, like before, she said, "You're right."

"Did you have a fight? Is that why she moved away?"

How could she be truthful without burdening Harper with things she would probably understand but shouldn't have to yet? "We had a fight after she moved away. And neither of us is still mad, but it was a long time ago and we haven't talked or seen each other, so it would feel weird to hang out."

Harper nodded, her brain clearly turning over this new information. "I think you should make up and be friends again."

In addition to smart, her daughter was kind. She liked to think she modeled that for Harper, nurtured it. But the truth of the matter was she had an empathetic streak all on her own, maybe even more innate than Kate's. It made her chest do that proud parent swell. "I'll think about it."

"Good." Harper finished eating and carried her plate to the sink. "Can I go to Lily's house?"

She loved that Harper was old enough to visit her friends in the neighborhood unaccompanied and young enough to still do it spontaneously. "Home before the street lights come on. And let Frances in before you go."

Harper nodded. She opened the back door and Frances loped in, happy to be back in the air conditioning. Harper went out, pulling the door behind her. "Bye, Mama."

Kate washed the few dishes they'd made and tidied the kitchen. She contemplated taking a glass of wine onto the porch, but decided to spend an hour or two in her studio instead. She flipped on the light in the small bedroom she'd converted to her workspace, settling at the table and pulling out beads she'd made the week before. The swirl of blue and purple glass made her smile. She unspooled some wire, picked up her pliers and snips, and got to work.

When her thoughts drifted to Sutton, she didn't try to stop them. Now that Harper had taken an interest, avoiding Sutton without being obvious would be a tall order. Besides, she'd accepted a long time ago that trying not to think about things usually made her think about them more.

CHAPTER THREE

I could pay Gus to come and do that, you know. I didn't send you to college so you could come back here and do grunt work around the house."

Sutton didn't bother to hide her eye roll. "You raised me to be self-sufficient. That includes basic DIY."

"I'm not saying you shouldn't know how. I'm saying it's not the best use of your time."

Satisfied the anchors were secure, she grabbed a Phillips screwdriver and started securing the metal plates that would hold the bar in place. "Would you rather I sit on the couch and stare at you?"

He let out a dismissive sniff. "You know what I mean."

"I know my job pays me well enough to take three months off to be here with you, so maybe I turned out okay after all."

He scowled.

"You're still irritated about that, aren't you?"

"Three months is a quarter of a year. That's a long ass time not to be making any money and taking care of an old man."

They'd had this argument a few dozen times, starting the day his doctor put bilateral knee replacement on the table. They'd discussed him staying with her or going to a rehab place, but despite his grumbling promises he'd do whatever, she knew better. His need to be home would win out and he'd wind up in the house alone doing more than he should sooner than he should and jeopardizing his recovery.

The reality was, her work as a systems implementation consultant was flexible. Her projects typically ran anywhere from two weeks to two months and clients scheduled her services as much as a year in advance. Her salary bordered on ridiculous, at least in her opinion. Not that she didn't negotiate for pay bumps and promotions like her male counterparts. And her boss valued her enough to want to keep her happy.

Taking three months to take care of the man who'd raised her, pretty much on his own, felt like a tiny attempt at repaying all he'd given her. Besides, she was kind of lousy at taking vacations and she'd convinced herself this was a vacation of sorts. Because her father, even at his most invalid, was pretty damn low maintenance. She had plans to read books and do some projects he'd been putting off around the house. And there was the matter of catching up with people she'd hardly seen in ten years—friends and cousins and, whether she'd allowed herself to really think about it or not, Kate.

Dad cleared his throat, pulling her back to the fact that she sat, perched on the edge of the tub with a screwdriver in her hand. She secured the second screw and turned her gaze to him. "Maybe I want to take care of my old man."

He opened his mouth, but closed it again. Sutton raised an eyebrow at him, waiting for the comeback, either about being taken care of or calling him her old man. But when he did reply, all he said was, "I'm glad you're here."

Knowing how much he hated getting sentimental, she leaned over to elbow him lightly. "Not even qualified with a 'you're a pain in my ass, but.' I'm impressed."

He let out a har-har before asking if she needed anything else. She waved him off, finished installing the bar, and cleaned up her mess. By the time she emerged from the bathroom, the aroma of onions and garlic and bell peppers wafted through the house.

"What's for supper?" She pulled a pair of beers from the fridge before realizing he already had one. She put one back and opened hers.

"Thought I'd do a pork roast so you'd have something to eat on while I'm stuck in the hospital."

Her mouth watered at the thought, but that didn't mean she couldn't give him a hard time. "You're probably going to be in the hospital one night."

"Then you can feed it to me when I get home." He turned from the stove long enough to wink at her.

"You're going to have to eat my cooking at some point. I learned from you, if you recall. I'm not half bad."

"But you're so into vegetables."

"Without bacon fat, even. The horror." She took a swig of her beer, then joined him at the stove and slung an arm over his shoulder. "I promise I'll throw in some bacon fat, just for you."

"It's called comfort food for a reason, young lady. It provides comfort. I'm going to be in need of comfort."

"I got you, old man. I got you." She kissed his cheek. It wasn't like she'd turned into some health nut. It was simply that reasonable standards for healthy cooking and old school Cajun standards were a Venn diagram with only partial overlap.

"Good. How about you get the rice going, then?"

She measured water into the rice pot and got it on the stove. "It's nice to know you trust me with something."

They puttered around the kitchen side by side, ate in front of the TV with a ball game on, and both called it a night early. Sutton read for a while, not a night owl but unable to shut off her brain before ten. Even if they did need to leave by five the next morning.

She told herself it was silly to worry, that Dad was in good health and a good candidate for joint replacement. Not that telling herself not to worry and actually not worrying had much to do with each other. She could let herself obsess about Kate instead. Worse for her in the grand scheme of things, but perhaps slightly better in the moment.

She was beautiful, more now than ever. More than that, though, she looked happy. The last few times Sutton had seen her, well, that hadn't been the case. There'd been tears and yelling, on her part as much as Kate's. Seeing Kate all grown up and seemingly content with her life made her—what?

That was just it. She didn't know. Happy but also sad. Relieved but unsteady. All with a haze of regret she'd never managed to shake completely.

Okay, enough. She was being ridiculous. It had been good to see Kate, even if it had thrown her. They'd probably never be friends, but maybe they could be friendly. That would be nice. It killed her that the person she'd been closest to for so many years felt like a stranger now.

Did Kate feel the same? Even a little?

She fell asleep sometime after midnight and dreamed of sitting on the catwalk of the water tower on the edge of town. She and Kate were teenagers, giggling like they used to. But Harper was there, too, and in danger of falling. Sutton reached for her, leaning farther than her balance would allow, until she woke with a start to the sensation of falling.

Since her alarm was set to go off in a few minutes anyway, she showered and dressed and got ready to drive Dad to the hospital. He teased her for not being a morning person and she let him. Better that than owning why she hadn't slept well.

Dad proved chatty on the drive to New Orleans. She'd forgotten nerves did that to him. They got him checked in and into the prep area. She worried about having to wait for hours, but by some miracle, everything seemed to be running on time. She spent the time he was in surgery reading, pacing, and scrolling through the news on her phone. Thinking about Kate and telling herself not to.

Dr. Braverman's voice cut through the fog of her thoughts. "He'll be groggy, but he's in recovery. We'll get him to a regular room and you can see him in a bit."

She sat up straight, then stood. "He's done? Everything is okay?"

Dr. Braverman smiled. "Everything went perfectly. His joints are shot, but he's got good bones."

Sutton chuckled and the tension she pretended she hadn't been holding melted from her shoulders. "Thank you."

"I'll swing by his room tonight and again in the morning. Otherwise, let's do this again in six weeks." Dr. Braverman offered a playful lift of her chin.

"I'm sorry, is that orthopedic surgeon humor?"

She smirked, then lifted a shoulder. "Too soon?" Sutton shook her head. "Nah. I'll take it."

The doctor went on her way, leaving Sutton to text the handful of family and friends who'd want an immediate update. She thought about texting Kate, but didn't have her number. Which was probably for the best. Bumping into her at the store had gone okay, but it didn't mean they were back in friend territory, or any territory that included chatting over text.

Eventually, she got word that Dad had been moved to a room on the sixth floor, so she made her way there. She found him zonked out, probably from a mixture of exhaustion and anesthesia. The other occupant of the room was blocked by a curtain, but their television was tuned to a telenovela. She smiled. Dad spoke enough Spanish that he'd probably be able to grumble about the far-fetched storyline.

When he started mumbling, she pulled up a chair and took his hand. "Hey, Dad. It's me. Sutton."

Opening his eyes seemed to be a struggle, but he squeezed her fingers. "Am I dead?"

"Not yet, old man. Not yet."

"Good." He nodded feebly. "It would suck if this was heaven."

He remained a more devout Catholic than she was, but he was never stodgy about it. "Just the hospital. I'd offer to sneak in a beer, but I don't think it would mix well with whatever drugs you're on."

"I don't feel a thing." He smiled slightly, then drifted back off.

She waited for the doctor to make rounds, got assurances everything had gone as well as possible, and let herself be shooed out. Despite the leftovers she knew waited for her at home, she stopped for an oyster po-boy because some things were simply better in Louisiana. It felt strange to be alone in the house and made her think of the afternoons Kate would come over and they'd make out while pretending to study.

A lifetime ago. She expected the memories to hurt more than they did. Instead, she found herself smiling. So, even though it was probably a bad idea, she let herself sink into how amazing those afternoons had been. And maybe, just a little, wonder what it would be like to kiss Kate again.

❖

"So, how's it going?" Bryce sipped his Canebreak and angled his head. He'd heard about Sutton coming back to town from their mama and had been needling Kate about it ever since.

Kate took a swig from her own beer and fixed him with a bland look. "It's fine."

He pulled the bottle from his lips, his expression changing from playful to stern. "Come on. I know you have feelings."

"Of course I have feelings. All sorts of feelings. About all sorts of things. It's kind of how being human works."

He scratched his eyebrow. "Are you going to make me drag it out of you?"

"You could accept that it's not a big deal and leave it at that." She knew better than to think he would. She'd mostly gotten Mama to stop harassing her, but Bryce was a different animal. For all his stoic masculinity, he could be relentless when he decided his sister needed to talk about something.

"Really?"

"Really."

"Okay, so don't tell me how you feel. Tell me what you're going to do."

She made a face. "I'm not going to do anything."

Bryce rolled his eyes. "Of course you are. Because doing nothing is something. Are you going to make nice? Go out of your way to ignore her? Be aloof and detached but seethe on the inside?"

"I don't seethe."

"Sure you do. Remember when I got Harper that ant farm?"

Enough time had passed that she could laugh about it. At the time, when Harper had tipped it over and had several hundred ants crawling around her room, she'd come pretty close to seething. "You should have known better."

"Sorry." He shrugged, clearly not sorry.

"Whatever." Kate shook her head. "I'm not going to seethe and I'm not going to avoid her. I've already bumped into her."

"You have?" His voice was a mixture of incredulous and offended.

"She came into the store with Albin to get a grab bar for his shower."

"Aha. And y'all talked?"

"Yes, because it's a place of business and we're both adults."

"Hmm." He took another swig of beer. "And how was it?"

She often lectured Harper on rolling her eyes, but since Harper wasn't out on the porch with them, she indulged. "It was fine. I'm not hung up on her. You of all people should know this."

His eyes softened. "I do. But I also know it's one thing when you never have to see the person and it's another when they come sauntering back into your life."

She thought about the look of discomfort on Sutton's face, the way she warmed right up to Harper in spite of it. "She didn't saunter."

"So, what did she do?"

"Looked uncomfortable, then fell under Harper's chatty spell." The memory made her smile, even if she didn't want it to.

"She met Harper?"

"Met might be a bit of an understatement."

Bryce raised a brow. "Did Harper give her the customer service special?"

She laughed. "Something like that. And has insisted we should bring Sutton and Albin tacos after Albin's surgery."

"Like you do."

"Exactly the point Harper made." Because in their little world, it was what you did.

Bryce set down his beer and turned to face Kate completely, then folded his arms. "And are you?"

"Am I what?"

"Bringing tacos?"

Oh, right. That. "I haven't decided."

"And Harper took that as an answer?" He knew his niece well.

"I told her it was complicated."

"Your preferred version of because I said so. Well played."

She wasn't sure how well played it was, or what she should do. Or, for that matter, what she should tell Harper about how close she and Sutton had been back in the day. Because knowing they were together would lead to questions about why they broke up. And while she was pretty sure she could keep the reasons general, she absolutely, positively, one hundred percent would not stand for Harper thinking her coming into the world was anything but the best thing that had ever happened in Kate's life. "Can we talk about you now?"

"Eh?" He shrugged.

"Is it work, your love life, or something else?" He wasn't one to dish on his personal woes, so she prepared to beat it out of him. Tit for tat and all.

"Elena is leaving."

Elena was both his coworker and, as of about four months ago, his girlfriend. "Leaving you or leaving LSU?"

He sighed. "Both. But only leaving me because she's leaving LSU."

Bryce still lived in Duchesne, but he commuted the forty-five minutes to Baton Rouge every day for his job as an academic adviser. It was his compromise in a way, allowing him to have a foot in two worlds. A hometown boy at heart but, at least to her knowledge, the only trans guy currently residing in their town of less than a thousand. She was glad he did it, but a little sad he needed to. "Go on."

"She got a job at UGA. Assistant director and head of pre-law advising."

"Oh." It sounded like a promotion, so Kate wouldn't begrudge her, but she'd sort of hoped this one would stick. Bryce was the sweetest guy she knew, and good-looking on top of it, but he'd been battered by dating.

"I don't think she would have broken up with me otherwise, but she clearly didn't consider our relationship worth sticking around for. Which sucks, you know?"

She did. "I'm sorry, B."

"I'll live." He picked up his beer and drained the bottle. "I also think it might be time to take a break from women without any queer sensibilities."

"What do you mean?"

He let out a sigh, then looked at her with mischief. "It's complicated."

She did her own pivot on the swing, pulling up her legs and poking his thigh with one of her feet. "I'm not ten. That doesn't work on me."

He didn't answer right away, but she got the sense it was something he'd been mulling over. "I'm not the trans guy who wants to pass and pretend I'm just like every other cis guy. Cis guys bring a lot of toxic baggage to the table."

She leaned forward and put a hand on his knee. "You're way cooler than the average cis guy."

"I don't want to be cooler, but being trans is part of my identity. I want to be with someone who values it instead of tolerates it. Or ignores it."

He didn't seem upset, but her heart broke a little anyway. "You should be with someone who values everything about you."

"Exactly. It's like…" He stared at the porch ceiling. "It's like how you'd only want to date someone who loves that you're a mom, not someone who simply doesn't mind that you are."

She wouldn't have made that connection, but now that he had, she knew exactly what he meant. "Yeah."

"Easier said than done, maybe, but we'll see."

She finished her beer and stared into the distance. A pair of hummingbirds flitted around the honeysuckle bush off the front porch. "So, where are you going to find a woman like that?"

"Beats me." He looked at her with an almost impish smile. "How about you?"

Before she could stop it, Sutton's face appeared in her mind. The way she smiled at Harper, talked to her like she was a real person. She shook her head, denying any half-baked notions her subconscious might be trying to cook up. "Same, B. Same. Beats the hell out of me."

CHAPTER FOUR

Sutton woke to the sound of a rooster. Why was a rooster crowing? Roosters weren't allowed in her neighborhood. Chickens either, despite the heavy campaign her next-door neighbor launched the previous summer.

She opened one eye, then the other. Instead of her townhouse, the cornflower blue walls of her childhood bedroom greeted her. Right.

She hadn't bothered to close the curtains and sunlight poured in, creating a patch on her quilt where Hugh lounged contentedly. She blew out a breath and sat up, rubbing her hands over her face. What time was it?

She reached for her phone, but the ancient clock radio she'd inherited when she was eight remained on the nightstand. The digital display read 7:04. Sleeping in by her standards.

At the sound of her rustling, Duke picked up his head. He gave her a look that said he'd been waiting patiently, thank you very much, but it was time for his morning loop of the back yard and breakfast. "All right, all right."

She climbed out of bed and pulled a T-shirt on over her boxers. Duke followed her to the back door. After letting him out, she turned her attention to the coffee pot. Before the first drip landed, Hugh appeared, clearly judging her priorities. She fed him, got Duke's breakfast ready, and let him in. Funny how two animals could feel like a menagerie.

She had her first cup of coffee standing at the kitchen sink. Some habits, it seemed, withstood the boundaries of time and space. She needed to be at the hospital by noon, leaving enough time to tackle a couple of chores. Cutting the grass came first, since the temp probably hadn't hit ninety yet. And she'd want to be in shouting distance for the first day or two Dad was home.

She ate a bowl of cereal and changed, put on her headphones, and headed outside. The mower—the same one she'd used before leaving for college—sat in its usual spot in the shed, the ancient metal gas can next to it. Oddly comforted by how familiar it all was, she filled the tank and fired it up. She finished the front and had just started on the back when her phone pinged.

Hey. It's Kate.

Sutton stared at the screen and racked her brain for a Kate other than the one she'd been thinking about virtually nonstop. She had one grad school friend named Kate, but she lived in Dubai now. And this Kate was texting her from a south Louisiana area code.

How did Kate get her number? And more importantly, why was she texting her?

Probably better not to lead with twenty questions. *Hey.*

Got your number from Perry. Hope that's okay.

Was it? Well, it wasn't not okay. Because it might be weird, but she was smiling at her phone like a goofy teenager. *Of course. What's up?*

Kate didn't answer right away, leaving Sutton to wonder if she was having second thoughts about whatever had inspired her to reach out in the first place. Since a watched phone never rang, she stuck it in her pocket and went back to cutting the grass.

Harper wants to bring you and Albin tacos.

Sutton stared at the words. A simple enough statement, but it threw her more than getting a text from Kate in the first place. Her mind jumped from her encounter with Harper at the store to the image of sitting around the kitchen table with her father, her high school girlfriend, and that girlfriend's daughter. A mixture of curiosity, dread, and longing followed.

You can say no.

It made her feel slightly better that Kate seemed to have mixed emotions, too. *Do you want me to say no?*

Another pause. *No. But I don't want you to feel pressured, either.*

Okay, she could work with that. *I'm sure my dad would be thrilled to have company.*

Was it a cop-out to make it about him instead of her? Maybe. But Kate had essentially done the same thing, saying the offer was Harper's idea and not hers.

Is he home yet?

Sutton moved from the middle of the yard to the shade of the oak tree. *Should be this afternoon if the surgeon gives him the all clear.*

We can do any night but Wednesday. Let me know what works for y'all.

She ran through the comments from the doctor about what to expect the first week after surgery. *Friday? I'm sure he'll want a distraction by then.*

She almost threw in a comment about not wanting to crash any hot dates but thought better of it. Because even if she told herself it would be a joke, she cared about the answer. She had no business knowing whether Kate dated and even less business caring.

Perfect. Carnitas good?

Her stomach rumbled involuntarily. *For sure.*

We'll be there at 6.

It felt disturbingly natural to iron out the details of dinner plans, a thought Sutton shoved to the back of her brain. *Let me know if I can pick up anything to have on hand.*

That's not how it works. You've been away too long. She added the eye roll emoji, followed by a laughing one.

The faces were probably meant to take any sting out of her words. Or maybe imply Kate didn't care one way or the other. But as she restarted the mower and resumed a chore she'd not done since she was eighteen, the comment stayed with her. Along with memories of all sorts of other things she did at eighteen.

❖

"Who are you texting?" Harper leaned in and tried to get a peek at the screen.

"None of your beeswax." Since Harper didn't make a habit of invading her privacy, or her phone, Kate didn't hesitate to tease instead of scold.

"Yeah, but you're grinning like I did the day you said we could get Frances."

She smiled at the memory. Harper had been begging for a dog for the better part of a year. She'd mostly kept it to logical arguments and assertions of being responsible over pure whining. So, for her eighth birthday, she'd given Harper a collar and a leash as her big gift. They went to the shelter the following weekend and it was a case of mutual love at first sight. Frances howled her beagle howl and wagged her tail like her life depended on it. And Harper was so beside herself with excitement and joy, she cried.

"Ah, ahem." Harper pretended to clear her throat and folded her arms.

Again, not exactly the behavior she wanted to reinforce, but Kate couldn't help but laugh. "I was thinking about the day we got Frances."

Harper went over to where Frances was sleeping on the sofa and gave her head a pat. "Best day ever."

"My best day was when I got you." A cheesy mom line, but she meant it.

"Wait. Are we getting another dog?" Harper's eyes got huge. "Am I getting a sister? Or a brother?"

Kate laughed. "No on all fronts. Sorry to disappoint."

Harper's shoulders slumped but she didn't seem to really mind. "So, you're not going to tell me? You're supposed to spread joy, Mama."

She'd sort of hoped the tangent would make Harper forget her initial question. No such luck. "I was offering to bring tacos over to Mr. Albin after his surgery, just like you suggested."

"Were you texting Sutton?"

For as brief as the interaction had been, Harper seemed pretty enamored with Sutton. That could prove problematic. "I was."

"Did she say yes? Are we going over?"

"Yes, but not til Friday."

Harper danced back and forth, chanting "tacos" over and over. When she stopped, she looked at Kate with all the seriousness of someone twice her age. "Does this mean you and Sutton are going to be friends again?"

The way she saw it, she had two choices. She could say yes and leave it at that, and hope Harper didn't ask any more questions. An appealing option, but not one likely to work. The second option would be to explain her history with Sutton, or rather, an age-appropriate version of it. As much as she wanted to believe Harper didn't need to know, chances were high someone, somewhere would say something that would clue her in. It wouldn't take much; very little got by her. And if Kate spent any amount of time with Sutton, people were bound to talk.

If she'd learned anything—in life or as a parent—it was to be in charge of her own story.

"I don't know if we'll be friends, but I'm going to try to be friendly."

Harper nodded, mulling over the distinction between the two.

"Remember when I said we stopped being friends because she moved away?"

More nodding. "Yeah."

"Well, it was more complicated than that."

"Oh. Do you want to talk about it?"

It was what she asked whenever Harper was upset about something. Having Harper mirror it made her proud and a little mushy. "I think I do."

Harper sat on the sofa cross-legged and turned to face her. "Okay. Lay it on me."

The line, one Harper had picked up from her grandfather, made her laugh. "You know how I like both men and women?"

Harper nodded. "You're bi."

Oh, to have had that vocabulary at her age. "Yes, exactly."

For the second time in their conversation, Harper's eyes got huge. "Did you want Sutton to be your girlfriend?"

Kate took a deep breath. No going back now. "Sutton was my girlfriend."

"Oh." Harper dragged the word out almost comically.

She laughed, at the reaction but also because Harper's understanding of what that meant was obviously not as sophisticated as she believed it to be. "Yeah."

"Did you break up with her or did she break up with you?"

"Um." She should have thought this through before launching in.

"Mama, did Sutton break your heart?" Harper put a hand on Kate's knee and her nine-year-old eyes held so much love and understanding it made Kate's heart both swell and break a little.

"I think we broke each other's hearts." Because as much as Sutton's rejection had broken hers, she could appreciate the betrayal Sutton must have felt when she came home for Christmas break and discovered the girlfriend she'd left behind had not only slept with a member of the football team but was pregnant.

Harper nodded slowly, making Kate wonder if this was the first time she considered that option. In the books she read and the movies they watched, there was almost always a good guy and a bad guy. Or girl, obviously. But either way, right and wrong remained fairly black-and-white.

"You know how sometimes you have a fight with one of your friends and you both hurt each other's feelings?"

That seemed to resonate. "Yeah."

"The same thing can happen with boyfriends or girlfriends."

"That makes sense." She made a face. "Is your heart still broken?"

The sharp pangs of sadness had faded a long time ago. She wouldn't pretend she never had moments of longing—fueled by memories or daydreams or one too many glasses of wine—but she no longer classified it as heartbreak. Realizing that, putting it in concrete terms, made her heart feel light. "No, honey. Not anymore."

"That's good." Relief shone on Harper's face. "Do you think Sutton's is?"

She'd not given much thought to Sutton's heart for years. This conversation, on top of seeing her, made Kate wonder. "I don't think so."

"Then it sounds like you're ready to forgive and forget."

This was how she'd taught Harper to move past hurt feelings and arguments with people she cared about. Not being a doormat, of course, but not holding grudges, either. It was more than a little disarming to have the advice turned back on her in such an obvious way. "Maybe you're right."

"I usually am." There was no irony in Harper's voice, which made Kate smile.

"Well, we're going over for tacos, so that's a pretty good start, right?"

"Tacos make everything better." Again, no irony.

"They do. So, do you want to go to Mawmaw and Pawpaw's today or come to the store?"

Harper narrowed her eyes. "Are you trying to change the subject?"

"Yes." They'd also discussed how honesty is the best policy.

The answer made Harper giggle. "I want to go to Mawmaw and Pawpaw's. Mawmaw said we could make lemon icebox pie."

Mmm. She hadn't had that in ages. "Will there be sharing?"

Harper hopped off the couch and danced around. "If you play your cards right."

Kate laughed. Her daughter's ability to retain sayings and phrases started about as soon as she learned to talk. But as she got older, her use of them was improving. She had no doubt she'd rue this fact during Harper's teenage years, but for now, it remained both entertaining and impressive. "I guess I better go get ready and I'll make us lunch before we go."

"Okay."

Harper danced in the direction of her room, leaving Kate alone with her thoughts. That had gone well, right? She'd been honest but kept things age appropriate. And like Harper said, maybe it was time to forgive and forget.

She headed to the kitchen and pulled out the fixings for sandwiches. Offering to bring a meal to Albin and Sutton had been about proving a point. Well, that and it's what you did when someone was sick or laid up, died or had a baby. It's what she was raised to do and one of the reasons she never planned to leave Duchesne. But as she layered turkey on top of Swiss, slathered mayo, and sliced a tomato, she couldn't help but wonder if it was their chance to let bygones be bygones.

It wasn't like they needed to be friends or anything. But three months was a long time to avoid someone in a town this size. Trying would be exhausting. It also wouldn't set a very good example for Harper.

Forgive and forget. She could do it. Could Sutton?

Chapter Five

Sutton heard a car in the driveway and looked up from her book. It had been years since she'd lived somewhere quiet enough for that to be a thing, but it seemed like some habits died hard. And kind of nice, in a way. A bright red hatchback sat in the driveway. Kate and Harper piled out and the back hatch popped up.

"I'm going to see if they need any help."

"Huh? What?" Dad sat up in his recliner, clearly caught dozing.

"Kate and Harper are here. I'm going to help them bring stuff in."

"Right, right. Of course." He patted the top of his head, then the front of his shirt. He found his glasses tucked in the front pocket and slipped them on. "Of course."

By the time she made it off the front porch, Harper was ambling in her direction with a canvas grocery bag clutched in front of her with both hands. Kate followed a few steps behind with a slow cooker. "Can I give you a hand with that?"

Harper beamed at her, all confidence. "I got it."

Not sure which she found more charming—the smile or the self-assurance—she turned her attention to Kate. "How about you?"

Kate's smile was more reserved, but it was a smile, so there was that. "Just the door."

"That I can do." She took the steps two at a time and held the door wide. "Kitchen is back and to the left."

Harper smiled, but Kate's expression turned incredulous. She didn't say a word, but her eyes made it clear that, while maybe ten years had passed, she knew where the damn kitchen was. Unsure whether to be amused or cowed, Sutton coughed.

Kate walked past with a smirk. "Thanks."

She followed Kate and Harper to the kitchen, Dad behind her with his cane. Kate set the slow cooker on the counter and Harper hefted her bag onto the kitchen table. Duke roused himself from his bed to see what all the fuss was about. Kate gave him a smile that seemed to hold nostalgia and ruffled his ears, introducing him to Harper before Sutton had the chance. He accepted another round of pets before shuffling back to his bed.

She eyed the bags and containers Kate pulled from the bag, suddenly starving. "I don't even know what all of this is, but I'm excited."

Kate offered her another smirk before shifting her focus. "Mr. Albin, you didn't need to get up."

He waved a hand. "I'm supposed to walk around every hour or two. Therapeutic torture is what they call it."

"It is?" Harper looked horrified.

Sutton chuckled. "It's actually called physical therapy, but someone likes to be dramatic."

Harper nodded. "Mama says I'm dramatic sometimes, too."

"And there's nothing wrong with that, when the situation is dire." He wagged a finger at Harper.

Harper wrinkled her nose. "What's dire?"

"Hmm." Kate looked at the ceiling. "Very serious and urgent." She nodded slowly. "My need for tacos is dire."

Sutton couldn't help but grin, both at the interaction and the nerdy streak Harper seemed to have inherited from her mother. It made her wonder if Harper had many traits from her father. She certainly couldn't detect any, but she'd hardly known Randy. Was that something Kate thought much about? Did it make her happy? Or sad?

"Sutton." Dad practically screamed her name.

"Christ, why are you yelling? What?"

Kate regarded her with amusement and Harper giggled. "He said your name, like, five times," Harper said.

"Oh. Sorry." Nothing better than looking like a space cadet to pump up the old ego. "What?"

Dad gave her a look that said he knew exactly where her mind had wandered. "I thought you could get everybody drinks before we set the table."

"Yeah. Sure. Absolutely." Was she fated to be a bumbling idiot every time she came within twenty feet of Kate? She sure as hell hoped not. "We've got sweet tea, Coke, Diet Coke, and beer."

"Mama, can I have a Coke?" Harper asked.

"You may." Kate turned to Sutton. "You know, I'll have one too."

Sutton got down glasses, filled them with ice, and started pouring. "What about you, old man? No beer til you're off the pain meds."

He grumbled, but there was no heat behind it. "I guess I'll have a Coke, too, then."

She poured a third, then fixed a Diet Coke for herself. Kate brought two glasses to the table, then came back behind her. "I can't believe you still drink that stuff."

It had been a thing between them in high school. Sutton, who hadn't yet developed a taste for coffee, drank it almost constantly. "I drink coffee now. Seltzer, too. But nothing hits the spot quite the same."

Kate shook her head, but smiled. "Some habits don't ever break."

She got the impression Kate was talking about more than her beverage choices, but couldn't put her finger on exactly what. And with Dad and Harper standing right there, this wasn't her chance to find out. So she settled on, "I've learned to pick my battles."

That could have any number of meanings, too. She wondered if Kate picked up on that. Or if she cared. Kate's eyes seemed playful almost, the teasing gleam so familiar and so full of memories it made Sutton's heart thud. She didn't know what she wanted her gaze to convey in return, but she couldn't tear her eyes away.

"Are we ready to eat?" Dad asked.

The spell between them, real or imagined, was broken. Sutton looked away and told herself to pull it the fuck together.

"Tacos! Tacos!" Harper pumped her hands in the air with each exclamation.

Sutton cleared her throat. "What else needs to be done? How can I help?"

Kate took over, giving directions and running the kitchen like it was her own. Her weird, tangled up feelings notwithstanding, it was fun to watch. In a matter of minutes, the four of them sat around the kitchen table, piling pork and cheese and all manner of toppings into tortillas. Harper pretty much carried the conversation, asking questions and talking about swimming lessons, *Charlotte's Web*, and the Girl Scout camping trip she absolutely, positively couldn't wait for.

Dad seemed to bask in having a full table and endless chatter. It made her wonder if he ever regretted the way things between Kate and her ended. He'd been quiet about it at the time—stoic, even—encouraging her to get back to school and focus on work. But it didn't take her imagination long to concoct a different version of the story. One where she and Kate got married and had kids and lived a few streets over.

"Sutton." Her father's voice had, once again, risen to a near yell.

Knowing she'd been caught daydreaming this time, she cleared her throat. "Sorry. What?"

Kate shook her head and Harper giggled. Harper said, "He asked if you'd get his pills."

"Oh. Right." He was supposed to take them with food.

She brought the bottle to the table, then tried to cover her second bout of daydreaming by being overly attentive. She asked Kate about her family. She'd heard about Bryce's transition but had not seen him since. Kate talked about him with more fondness than irritation—a shift from their teenage years. She seemed so completely at ease, it made Sutton feel like her own worries and hesitations bordered on irrational. Of course, Kate's ability to put her chin up and pretend things were okay when they weren't was one of her many talents. Or, if not talents, habits.

After dinner, Harper offered to help clear the table. Kate kept an eye on Harper, but let the two of them handle the task. Sutton scooped leftovers into containers while Harper loaded the dishwasher. She washed the slow cooker while Harper wiped down the table like she spent her days working the lunch counter at a diner.

The whole thing made her realize she didn't have a good handle on what kids could or should be expected to do at different ages. Which made her wonder how Kate had figured it out. Did it come naturally or was it something that kept her up at night? She'd be the latter, reading books and blogs and worrying constantly about whether she was doing it right.

With everything cleaned and put away, Sutton considered asking if everyone wanted to move to the living room. Dad would be more comfortable in his recliner. And while she didn't want to seem clingy, she wasn't quite ready for Kate and Harper to go. But before she could say anything, Kate and Harper exchanged looks. Kate nodded and Harper tore down the hall and out the front door.

"Everything okay?" she asked.

Kate grinned. "She's getting dessert."

"Ah." Sutton returned the smile, more excited by the prospect of them staying a bit longer than having dessert. Not that she'd pass on dessert.

"How about we go sit in the living room where it's more comfortable?" Dad said.

"Great idea." She looked to Kate. "Is that okay?"

"Of course. We just need—"

Harper came running back into the house, clutching a large Tupperware container. "Mama and I made snickerdoodles."

Kate lifted a shoulder and angled her head. "Napkins."

Sutton grabbed a stack from the holder on the table and they filed into the living room. Dad settled into his chair and Kate took one end of the sofa. Sutton debated between joining her and taking the rocking chair, but no one ever sat in the rocking chair and Kate knew it. She joined her on the sofa, leaving the middle cushion as a buffer.

Harper made her way around the room, holding out the container for each person. When everyone had a cookie, she helped herself to one and took the seat between them without a second of hesitation. She lifted her cookie in the air. "Bon appétit."

Sutton took a bite of her cookie. If she were the type of person to fall for kids, she'd be pretty far gone over Harper already. That wasn't fair. She was the type of person to fall for kids. She just didn't spend much time around them. Without siblings to give her nieces and nephews, and with living so far from her cousins, the only time she really interacted with kids was when her coworkers invited her to barbecues and stuff. And then, she spent most of her time interacting with the other adults. Being around Harper reminded her how much she enjoyed kids, and maybe, a little, reminded her how much she wanted a couple of her own.

She shook off the direction of her thoughts. Getting caught zoning out a third time would be beyond pathetic. Besides, the cookies were to die for. She made a point of turning her attention to Harper. "These are delicious. I love snickerdoodles."

"Mama said you liked them."

It was hard to say what surprised her more: Kate remembering in the first place, Kate remembering and deciding to make them, or all that and sharing that sort of detail with Harper. Sutton stole a glance at Kate, who regarded her with a raised shoulder and a half smile. "And cinnamon goes well with Mexican."

"Of course." She polished off the cookie and reached for another. "Well, thank you either way."

"Do you like to bake?" Harper asked.

"Sometimes. But I was never as good at it as your mom."

Harper nodded. "She's the best baker. Well, her and Mawmaw. I'm learning from both of them."

Sutton nodded. "Hands-on experience is the best way to learn."

"You could come over and we could bake together. I'm pretty good at snickerdoodles and chocolate chip cookies, but I want to make fancy cupcakes. Mama says that requires a lot of equipment, so I asked for some stuff for my birthday. If I get it, we could do that together, too."

She blinked, not confused by the rapid-fire train of thought but maybe a little overwhelmed. "Sure."

She braved another look at Kate, who offered both a full shrug and a full smile. "Welcome to my world."

"And you could meet Frances. That's our dog. She's a beagle."

"She sounds great." She had no idea if she was supposed to accept the invitation or cross her fingers and hope Harper moved on to something else. Not that a little part of her didn't want to spend a day with the two of them.

"Is Duke your dog or Mr. Albin's?"

"Oh, he's my dad's, through and through." Duke had come to her place once for Thanksgiving. He'd been less than impressed with her excuse for a yard, made his feelings known, and had stayed home after that.

"Do you not have a dog?" Harper seemed equal parts confused and sad that an adult, who ostensibly had the power to do whatever they wanted, would choose not to have a dog.

"Well, I work a lot and I don't have a big yard, so I have a cat instead."

"Oh." Harper nodded, appeased. "Cats are cool, too."

As if on cue, Hugh sauntered into the room. He headed straight for Kate and rubbed himself against her ankles. Sutton gestured, doing her best not to stare at Kate's legs. Her toenails were painted a deep purple and the strappy sandals invited Sutton's eyes to take in her perfect calves. Did every inch of her have to be so perfect? "This is him. His name is Hugh."

"He's cute." Harper bent down to pet him and he responded by jumping into her lap.

"He also loves attention."

"Grant or Heffner?" Kate regarded her, humor dancing in her eyes.

God, she'd missed that look. "What?"

"I'm curious how Hugh got his name."

Oh, they were going to be playful. She could do playful. "Langston."

Kate tipped her head slightly, as though conceding the point. "Better."

Sutton felt herself smile. "Give me a little credit, at least."

"Who's Langston?"

It had felt, for a second, like they were having a moment. Maybe it was just her. "His name is Langston Hughes and he's a poet."

"Oh." Harper seemed let down by the explanation.

"He was one of my favorite poets when I was in school," Kate added.

She didn't expect Kate to own up to that in this setting and she had a flash of self-consciousness over the possible implications of her explanation. "He was one of mine, too. Though your mama was always better at poetry than me."

They fell into a moment of silence—perhaps the first since their arrival. It was somehow both calming and unnerving and she sort of hoped Harper took off on another tangent of twenty questions. Instead, Dad started to snore.

Harper giggled and Kate offered a soft smile. "I think that's our cue."

They'd stayed longer than Sutton thought they might, but she was still a little sad to see the evening end. "Thank you so much for dinner. And for coming over. The company did us both good."

"It's what we do, right?" Kate winked.

She couldn't tell if the compliment made Kate uncomfortable or she meant to drive home that there was nothing special about the gesture, or perhaps, the recipients of the gesture. "It still means a lot."

Kate slapped her hands on her thighs and stood. "You ready to go, H?"

Harper, who'd yet to stop petting Hugh, looked at her with pleading eyes. "Can we get a cat?"

"Not a conversation for when we're guests in someone else's house."

Harper's shoulders slumped, but she didn't argue. "Yes, ma'am."

Between the show of manners and the obvious affection for her cat, Sutton's heart definitely melted a little. "You can come over and snuggle Hugh anytime."

Kate shot her an exasperated look.

"Anytime your mama says it's okay, of course."

Kate shook her head then, but smiled. "Amateur."

"Yup." She wasn't going to pretend otherwise.

She and Kate went to the kitchen to gather her things while Harper said her good-byes to Hugh. Sutton grabbed the slow cooker to have an excuse to walk them out. Harper, without hesitating, gave her a hug before getting in the car. Kate did hesitate, though Sutton was pretty sure it wasn't about whether to give her a hug. "Thank you for talking to her like a person. So many people treat her like a baby still and it drives both of us nuts."

"She's a great kid. Like, a really great kid." Sutton looked at her feet. "Sorry about telling her she could come over. That was an overstep."

Kate seemed more amused that irritated. "You're the one who might be stuck with her for hours on end."

She shrugged. "That wouldn't be so bad."

"Well, we'll see. In the meantime, I'm sure I'll see you around."

"Yeah. For sure. Thanks again for dinner. And for leaving the leftovers. You didn't have to, but I'm glad you did."

"Enjoy." Kate opened her car door. "See ya, Sutton."

She wanted to say something more than "bye," but the way Kate said her name made her breath catch and before she could, Kate got in and shut the door. She settled for a wave and watched them pull away. Inside, Dad continued to snore. She let him be for now and went to the kitchen to finish cleaning up. Only there was no cleaning up left to do. Kate was clearly a pro at delivering dinner and it made Sutton wonder how often she did it. And for whom.

CHAPTER SIX

K ate toggled between the spreadsheet and the graph, trying to decide which better represented the shifts in buying trends season to season. She liked the specificity of the spreadsheet but had a feeling her father would prefer the graph. He was more of a big picture guy. Her mother would want to see both, but more because she cared about what Kate cared about than she wanted to get involved in the nitty-gritty of inventory.

When the bell over the front door jingled, she looked up. With Harper at her grandparents', she was filling the role of manager and greeter. Which was fine by her. But when Sutton strode in, wearing a dark gray tank top and a pair of carpenter pants, a part of her longed to have Harper there as a buffer.

Not buffer. She didn't need a buffer with Sutton. It was just that Sutton had been invading her thoughts more and more over the last few days and she was pretty sure one-on-one time wasn't going to help that fact.

Sutton caught her eye and smiled. "Hey."

"Hey." She would have attempted small talk, but her throat had gone dry.

"Where's your customer service queen?"

"With Mawmaw and Pawpaw today. They're making pickles, apparently."

"Yum." Sutton's eyebrows went up and her face took on an air of mischief. "But, if she's not here, who's in charge?"

"Funny. You're funny."

She lifted a shoulder and, if Kate didn't know better, she'd almost think Sutton was flirting with her. "I guess you'll do."

Kate bit her lip and told herself not to smile back. Not because she wanted to be unfriendly, but because if she wasn't careful, it wouldn't be hard to cross the line into way too friendly. And she definitely didn't want to go there. "I do know my way around the store."

"From what I hear, you're running the place these days."

Based on her tone, Sutton meant it as a compliment. It unnerved Kate, more than teasing would have and almost as much as Sutton's muscular arms on complete and perfect display. How did a tech geek get arms like that, anyway? "Eh." She flipped her hand back and forth. "I manage the day-to-day, but it's still my parents' store."

"Chief operations officer. Very important role." Sutton looked at her with a smile that had the potential to be downright dangerous.

"We don't bother with fancy titles like that around here, but sure." She stuck her hands in her pockets. "So what are you looking for today?"

"Oh, right," Sutton said, as though remembering why she'd come into the store in the first place. "Outlets."

"Outlets?" The idea of Sutton doing electrical work caught her off guard. Even if Sutton nailed the sexy handybutch aesthetic.

"Yeah, there are still a few of the old two-prong outlets in some of the bedrooms. I made a list of projects to keep me busy and switching them out is first up."

She wanted to ask if Sutton knew how to do that, but resisted. It wasn't any of her business. "Right this way."

She headed down the electrical aisle, stopping in front of the outlets, junction boxes, and other home electric supplies. "Do you know what you need?"

"You seem surprised that I might." Sutton smiled again. A slow and confident sort of smile, the kind her body couldn't help but respond to.

"I mean." Great, now she was stuttering. "It's not that. I just…" She trailed off because continuing to try would only make it worse.

Sutton folded her arms and shifted her weight, sending her left hip out ever so slightly. A subtle display of confidence, to be sure, the effect was anything but. "It's an outlet. I'm not rewiring the house."

And then Sutton winked. An honest to God, I could so be flirting with you right now, wink. What was she supposed to do with that? Not blush, obviously. Even though she could feel the heat rise in her cheeks. "I'm sure you know what you're doing."

Sutton laughed. "I have my moments."

The front bell jingled and she'd never been so grateful for the arrival of a customer. "I should go see to that. You're all set here?"

"I am. Thanks for the help."

She fled to the front of the store, flustered and, worse, feeling foolish for being flustered. At the sight of one of her regulars striding toward her with purpose, relief washed through her. "Well, hello, stranger. I haven't seen you in like two whole days."

Jim laughed. "Can't go too long without seeing your pretty face now, can I?"

"Can I help you find what you need today?" Please let him need all her attention.

He waved her off. "If I can't find the screws and drill bits by now, you should revoke my discount."

"You don't get a discount."

"But I'm going to keep trying."

"Well, it's good to have dreams. Holler if you need me." See? That was better. She could banter with customers in her sleep. Not whatever she'd just fumbled through with Sutton.

"Will do." He winked at her and headed down one of the aisles.

Unlike Sutton's wink, this one had absolutely no effect. What had gotten into her?

Before she could come up with a convincing answer, Sutton emerged from the electric aisle, several outlets and a roll of electrical tape in hand. "You don't have any of the ones with USBs built in, do you?"

"We carry them, but they're on backorder at the moment. There was a writeup in the paper on how easy they are to install and we had a run on them." Which irritated her to no end. Not the run, but the being out of stock. "I could give you a call when they come in."

Sutton smiled that same easy, way sexier than it had any right to be, smile. "That would be great. I figure if I make it easy enough, Dad might actually keep his phone charged."

Kate laughed. "I'm glad my parents aren't the only ones who struggle with that."

"Oh, no. The main reason I haven't encouraged him to ditch his landline is I don't want to have a panic attack every time he doesn't call me back because he hasn't looked at his cell for three days." Sutton rolled her eyes, but they sparkled with humor.

"When did we become the ones who had to worry about them?" There, this was nice, normal conversation.

"I don't know but I wish someone had warned me it was coming." Sutton placed her items on the counter. "I think this will do me for today."

She started ringing up the sale. "I'm sorry we didn't have everything you wanted."

Sutton waved her off. "No worries. I'll be back soon enough. It's a long list."

"If you want to create a bigger list of everything you need, we can pull it all together for you." They mostly did that with contractors, but not exclusively.

Sutton angled her head. "Is that your polite way of saying you don't want me poking around your store day in and day out?"

"Oh, my God. Of course not. I didn't mean it that way at all. I just—"

"Kidding." Sutton lifted both hands. "Sorry."

She pinched the bridge of her nose and shook her head. "No, I am. I didn't mean to overreact. I don't want you to think you aren't welcome here." Why couldn't she get out of her own way?

"Well, as long as it's not that." Sutton passed over her credit card with something resembling a smirk.

"We try to be full service is all. You know, not like the big box stores." She needed to stop talking. She was making things worse.

"Oh, I'm a big proponent of supporting local business. Don't you worry about that."

She passed the credit card slip and a pen to Sutton, causing their hands to brush ever so slightly. Less than a second, for sure, but it sent a jolt of electricity through her. It was all she could do not to jerk her hand away. From the look on Sutton's face, and her attention to signing the receipt, the spark hadn't been mutual. It shouldn't have disappointed her, but it did. "Glad to hear it."

Sutton handed her the paper back. "Besides, I definitely want to shop where the COO knows my name."

The comment—maybe teasing but definitely harmless—broke the tension. Though, did it count as tension if she was the only one who felt it? "I'm going to try to convince my parents to give me that title."

"I'm sure you deserve it. Raise, too."

The banter helped her relax, but her skin still buzzed from the brief contact. "I'll be sure to pass that along."

It looked like Sutton might be on the verge of saying something else, but Jim appeared. Kate had almost forgotten he'd come in. "For all my talk, I can't find the three-inch hex screws."

She glanced his way. "Coming."

"I'll see you soon, I'm sure," Sutton said.

She nodded, wishing for something clever to say. "We'll be here."

Not what she was hoping for but, at the end of the day, it didn't really matter.

❖

Sutton turned left outside of the parking lot instead of right, taking the long way home. Well, longer. It made the drive about five minutes instead of two. When she pulled in the driveway, she left the engine running to give herself another minute before she started roasting.

What had that been about?

She'd spent the better part of the morning psyching herself up to walk into the store and play it cool. The way Kate had played it cool the last time, and when she brought over dinner. And she was managing it just fine.

But then Kate had to get shy and awkward. And Sutton was pretty sure she blushed at one point. What was she supposed to do with that?

The whole thing left her confused and unsteady. And more attracted to Kate than ever. Which she knew was a bad idea. But knowing something and making it so weren't the same thing. That was a lesson she'd learned the hard way.

Shaking her head, she gathered her purchases and went inside. She found Dad in the kitchen, making sandwiches. "I've been gone twenty minutes. You can't sit still for twenty minutes?"

He pointed at her with a butter knife covered in mayo. "I'm supposed to get up and move around. I'm moving around."

He was. But she worried about him overdoing. Or getting caught up in some activity and moving the wrong way. "Slow and careful walking, with your cane. Puttering around the kitchen and making lunch is not that."

He rolled his eyes and went back to what he was doing. "You going to cluck and fret over me like a mother hen for the next three months?"

Now that they were both adults, she didn't hesitate to give it back to him. "Depends. You going to act like an obstinate child for the next three months?"

"You're fussing."

"You're a bachelor unused to answering to anyone but yourself."

He cut the sandwiches in half and dropped the knife in the sink before gesturing to them. "How about you bring them to the table then? And grab me a beer while you're at it."

In an argument like this one, she took the gesture as a concession. She carried the plates to the table and grabbed a bag of Zapp's from the pantry. And since he wasn't arguing too much, she got him a beer from the fridge when she pulled out a Diet Coke for herself. "Was that so hard?"

He scowled, but without malice. "Yes."

"It's a good thing I love you."

He lifted his chin, but his eyes were playful. "Ditto."

She took a bite of her sandwich—sliced cold pork roast with mayo and a hint of spicy mustard—and hummed her approval.

Damned if he didn't make a fantastic sandwich. "I'm still mad at you, but thank you."

"No, you're not," he said without hesitation. "Did you get the fancy plugs you wanted?"

"Yes and no. The charger ones I was telling you about are on backorder, so I'll have to go back."

He nodded. "Did you give Harper a hard time about it?"

The question made her wonder if Kate would have behaved so strangely if Harper had been there. "She was off today."

He tutted. "Hard to get good help these days."

She chuckled at the idea of Harper calling in sick, playing hooky. "Kate was there, though. She took care of me."

"You feeling okay about seeing her so much? You seemed a little spooked the first time. And I'm not going to lie, I was surprised as all get-out when she brought dinner over." The teasing tone had vanished. In its place, genuine concern.

"I thought so, but she had this vibe today and I don't know what to make of it."

He polished off his lunch and leaned back in the chair, clearly expecting her to elaborate.

"I went out of my way to be laid-back and friendly. And she clammed up like she didn't know what to do with me. Like when you're flirting with someone and it goes sideways."

He scowled and she instantly regretted saying anything. "What do you mean, flirting?"

She waved a hand. "Nothing. It wasn't flirting. Just kind of weird. I'm probably imagining it."

He frowned but didn't say anything else. They finished eating in silence and he didn't argue with her about taking care of the dishes. She managed to get a couple of the outlets replaced before needing to shower and get ready to take him to his PT appointment. She settled on shorts and a T-shirt since it was hotter than Hades out and grabbed a book to keep her occupied while he had his session.

She found him in the living room, tapping the foot of his good leg. It hadn't occurred to her he'd be nervous, but he clearly was. It made her feel bad about giving him a hard time earlier. "Ready?"

"Ready to get it over with, that's for sure."

She helped him into the car, trying to make it seem like she wasn't, then rounded the hood and climbed in. She was glad he had the option of doing his PT in Thibodaux. Doing a twenty-minute drive three days a week would wear on both of them a lot less than an hour there and back to New Orleans.

They walked into the clinic, a bright if slightly generic space that looked like it might have started out as a store of some kind. An older woman sat at the reception desk, talking to a guy with his nose buried in a chart. They looked up at the same time and Sutton realized she knew them both. "Josh?"

He studied her for a moment before recognition dawned. "Sutton."

His mom recognized her a second later and they both came around the front counter to pull her into hugs. Josh stuck out his hand to Dad. "Mr. Guidry, how have you been?"

Dad shook it with enthusiasm. "Crap knees, but otherwise good."

"Albin, it's been too long." Miss Yvette didn't bother with formality and pulled him into a hug as well.

"I knew you'd gone into a PT program, but I didn't realize you'd come back here," Sutton said. It gave her a pang of guilt to realize she'd lost touch with one of her closest friends from high school.

Josh shrugged. "Never left, really. I did my field placement here, started full time right after school, and took over the place last year."

"Wow. That's awesome." She'd thought maybe he would leave. Not easy to be one of only a handful of African-American students in a graduating class.

"I like being so close to home. I got to hire my own receptionist." He angled his head toward Yvette, now engrossed in conversation with her dad. "And we both know I'm a mama's boy."

She grinned at the assessment. She wouldn't have said it, but she wouldn't disagree with it, either. She gave Dad's shoulder a squeeze. "Don't be afraid to put this guy through the paces, okay?"

Josh grinned. "Don't worry, Mr. Guidry. I'll take good care of you."

They headed back and Sutton took a seat in the waiting area, checking her email and reading the news while watching patients come and go. In a little under an hour, Dad emerged, looking none the worse for wear. Since Josh was with him, she got up to join them at the reception desk.

Yvette clicked her mouse a few times. "It looks like we'll be seeing you back here quite a bit."

"Can we get those scheduled out for a couple of weeks?" Dad asked.

"Some of us like having a routine," Sutton said.

"Who doesn't?" Josh clearly hadn't lost his knack for putting people at ease.

"Sure, sure. Take his side." She chuckled, then added under her breath, "With you and your mom as part of the deal, it might not feel like pulling teeth to get him here three times a week."

"We'll get you back to rights in no time, Mr. A. Elevation and ice when y'all get home and I'll see you in a couple of days." Josh clapped Albin on the shoulder but made eye contact with Sutton. "How long are you in town?"

"Three months or so." She angled her head. "Gotta get this guy through the second knee."

"We should get together."

"That would be great." She had hopes of reconnecting with old friends, but hadn't yet figured out where to start.

He grabbed a card and scribbled on the back of it. "That's my cell. I'm still living in Duchesne, so we can grab a drink or something whenever. Just text me."

"I definitely will. It'll be good to catch up." Often, she said that sort of thing because it was the thing to say. It was nice to mean it.

CHAPTER SEVEN

Kate checked her lipstick in the rearview mirror before cutting the engine. She really should go out more. Between how single she'd been the last couple of years and having more babysitters than she knew what to do with, she had no excuse. She made a promise to herself to do just that as she headed inside.

Clotille's was bumping, as it always was on Friday nights. Folks got paid and had an itch to let off a little steam. Tonkie Honk was already into their first set, covering old country songs as much as new and throwing in a few originals. Older couples two-stepped around the dance floor and a handful of kids ran around. Both pool tables and all three dartboards were in use, and every barstool had a butt in it. Cliché? Yes. But it made her smile.

"Kate. Over here." Delia's voice carried over the music and low din of several dozen conversations going at once.

She turned, finding her friends crammed into the corner table, filling the chairs and the L-shaped bench. Delia waved, then sat back down next to her girlfriend, Greta. Next to them were Jody and her husband, Josh. Two of Josh's cousins took up the rest of the booth and Bryce sat in one of the chairs next to a woman she didn't recognize. New love interest, maybe? But before she had a chance to consider that possibility, the person next to the mystery woman turned around and looked her right in the eye. Sutton.

She repressed a groan as Sutton's hand went up in a tentative wave. Did she have to look so apologetic about it? Well, apologetic and gorgeous, of course. Because Sutton couldn't manage to look anything but gorgeous.

Kate returned the wave, then made a point of making eye contact and waving at the rest of her friends. It was fine. Just because she'd acted like an idiot last time Sutton came in the store didn't mean she would again. No one had to know that she hadn't been able to block the image of Sutton's torso in that form-fitting tank top. She repressed another groan and headed for the bar.

She nodded at a few people she knew from the store while she waited for Lionel to make his way down the bar to her. Delia sidled up next to her. "I didn't know she was coming."

She could have asked who Delia was talking about, but it seemed like an unnecessary charade. "It's fine. We're fine."

"Are you sure? She came with Josh. They were math nerds together, if you recall. And her dad is getting PT at his clinic."

"I brought her and her dad tacos last week. We really are fine." She didn't love the idea of bumping into each other literally everywhere she went, but she meant it. The ogling and stuttering were a one-time thing. They had to be.

"Okay. If you're sure."

Lionel finally made his way to her, greeting her with a lift of his chin. "What'll it be, gorgeous?"

He was older, but not a bad looking guy. He'd been the bartender at Clotille's for as long as she could remember, including that one time she tried to buy beer with a fake ID and he'd cut it in half but promised not to tell her parents. She really did need to come out more. "Crown and Sprite."

She'd planned a beer because they were so filling and she could pace herself better, but whatever.

He looked at Delia. "You need another, beautiful?"

"Not yet." Delia lifted a hand. "You know what? I'll have what she's having. Save me a trip."

He fixed their drinks and Delia insisted they both go on her tab. She lifted her cup, so Kate did the same. "Cheers."

They made their way back to the table. Of course the only open seat was next to Sutton. Delia shot her a questioning look, which she returned with one that she hoped conveyed a slightly exasperated I'm fine, before sitting down.

"Hey." Sutton's smile held the same tentativeness as her wave, like she half-expected Kate to shoo her away. They were going to have to work on that.

"Hey." She tried to make her smile encouraging. "Your patient give you a night off?"

"He said if I didn't give him a few hours to himself he might kill me in my sleep."

Kate bit her lip and snickered.

"He said it jokingly, of course, but I figured it best not to take chances with that sort of thing." She angled her head toward Josh. "And he and I bumped into each other and agreed we should catch up."

"I'm glad you listened." She nodded, perhaps a bit more earnestly than necessary.

"I hope you don't feel like I'm trying to invade your life."

It felt a little like that, but she didn't want to give Sutton the impression she was bothered by it. "It's a small town. We're going to bump into each other."

"Yeah." Sutton's voice held a wistfulness she couldn't decipher. "I'm cool if you are."

It was Sutton's turn to nod vigorously. "Totally cool."

"Here's to Fridays." She lifted her drink.

Sutton's smile wasn't timid this time. "To Fridays."

They tapped their cups together, inspiring the rest of the table to join in. Bryce, who'd been all wrapped up in his date, noticed her and got up to give her a hug. Conversations resumed, the band started a new song, and she let herself settle into a night of sharing the company of other adults.

❖

Sutton wasn't sure what she expected when Josh invited her to "a casual thing" at Clotille's, but it wasn't this. She knew about half the group crowded around their table, even if she hadn't seen them in years. The new additions—girlfriends and spouses and such—made it feel not quite like a reunion, which she appreciated. Everyone seemed happy to have her there. Even Bryce, who she expected to give her the cold shoulder, acted like she was one of the gang.

And Kate.

Well, Kate remained a bit of a mystery. Looking utterly stunning, of course, in a white sun dress with bright red poppies splashed over it and her hair up in some sort of twist that left little blond pieces to curl around her face. Friendly, but definitely with her guard up. Chatty, but never with her one-on-one.

It probably wasn't good to over analyze it, but over analyzing was her style. So that's what she did while catching up with Josh and getting to know his wife. While wondering if Bryce was no longer mad at her or merely reserving judgment. And while thinking, at least a little, of how much she'd love to have Kate in her arms on the dance floor.

At some point, a second drink appeared in front of her. Unable to figure out who bought it for her, she shrugged and decided to come out more while she was home to return the favor, at least in the karmic sense. Kate, on her second drink as well, offered her an unguarded smile. "You look like you can't decide if you're having fun."

"Oh, no, I'm definitely having fun." She took a sip from her drink, as though that might prove the point.

"Just lost in your thoughts."

It was a trait she'd had most of her life and one Kate had teased her about when they were together. "Some things never change."

Kate nodded like she might be debating how to respond. But before she could, the party seemed to break up all at once. Josh and Jody cited needing to get home to relieve the babysitter. Delia and Greta were leaving early the next day for a camping trip. Even Bryce and his date couldn't get out of there fast enough. Everyone needed to go, except Kate.

When Sutton looked at her expectantly, she lifted a shoulder. "I was going to finish this drink at least. You?"

Even if the prospect of being alone with Kate—at a bar, no less—set off warning bells in her mind, she couldn't leave. Or didn't want to. One of those things. "I'm good to stay for a bit."

Rounds of hugs were exchanged between old friends and new. It occurred to Sutton she'd been hugged more in the last few hours than probably the last month she was in Atlanta. Not that she didn't have friends or never hugged those friends. But there was something different about this, about being home.

When everyone had gone, and it was just the two of them sitting at the big table, Kate leaned forward and propped her chin on her fist. "You've got that look again."

"What look?"

"A million miles away."

Sutton shook her head. "No, I'm very much here. Just processing how it feels to be home. What's different, what's still the same."

"Like what?" Kate regarded her with what appeared to be genuine curiosity.

There were so many ways she could answer that question, the changes in Kate's life front and center. But she didn't want to make it all about that. "We're all adults, you know? Like, I knew it intellectually, but it's strange to see it. The way it's played out differently for each of us."

"I guess it's different when you're not here to see it unfold."

"Exactly. And yet, people are still the same deep down. Even Bryce, for as dramatically as he's changed, is the same person. Like his essence is what it always was." She wanted to smack herself for such a hokey line, but Kate nodded slowly.

"And you? Has your essence changed?" Kate asked.

"You know, I don't think I'd given it much thought."

Kate leaned back and folded her arms. "Wait, there's something you haven't thought to death?"

"Ha ha. I guess I think about the ways I have changed more than the ways I haven't. But being home has that flipped."

Kate looked down at her drink for a moment before making eye contact. "Does that have you itching to run back to Atlanta?"

There was a time when that would have absolutely been the case. When she wanted to forget as much of her life here as possible. Yet, in this moment, all she could think about was what she'd missed. Like friends who welcomed you back into the fold without batting an eye. Like bars older than she was that served cheap drinks and decent music without pretense. Like the fact that she still got a ripple of pleasure from the way Kate looked at her, the way she teased her. "No."

Kate grinned. "Well, I think that's progress."

The choice of words struck her. The idea that Kate would be thinking about her relationship to this place, her feelings about being home. It left her more confused than the awkward and shy bit at the store and more unsettled than her initial belief that Kate would want nothing to do with her. But in spite of that, she couldn't stop the warm feeling that started in her chest and radiated through her. "Thanks."

They finished their drinks in comfortable silence. Sutton continued to mull over the conversation, all while debating the relative pros and cons of asking Kate to dance. Before she'd landed on one side of the fence or the other, Kate said, "I should probably head home, too."

"Yeah." It wasn't that late, but later than she'd stayed out in as long as she could remember.

They got up and headed outside, past the smokers and a couple making out in the glow of a neon Abita sign, toward the small parking lot. Away from the music and the crowd, the questions and the restless energy that had been chasing her for days resurfaced. When they got to her car, she realized Kate had parked in the next spot over. A sign, maybe? Or maybe having a couple of drinks in her gave her courage.

"So, like, are we friends now?" Sutton looked at her hands before braving a look into Kate's eyes.

Kate shrugged. "I don't see why not. Life's too short to hold grudges, right?"

"Is that what you think I've been doing?" Sutton leaned against the hood of her car. It wasn't how she'd classify her attempts to move on.

"Isn't it?"

"You broke my heart, Kate." For all the fights they'd had when she learned Kate was pregnant, she'd never uttered those words. The angry and broken eighteen-year-old version of herself couldn't bring herself to.

Kate folded her arms. "And you don't think you broke mine?"

"I couldn't not go to college. It would have killed my dad. You know that. You knew it then, too. Or at least you said you did."

"I did. I do." Kate dropped her arms and shook her head. "I was ready to wait for you."

It shouldn't still feel like a knife to the heart, but it did. "But you didn't."

Something passed through Kate's eyes that she couldn't decipher. "I made a stupid, impulsive mistake. I'm pretty sure that comes with the territory of being seventeen."

If only it had been just that. Something she could forgive and try to forget. But it couldn't be that easy. Kate's mistake had resulted in a baby that, at the time, felt like so much more than she could handle. Not to mention a massive, constant, and insurmountable reminder of the fact that Kate had cheated on her. "But it changed everything."

"It did. I was sorry then and I'm sorry for that still."

At the time Sutton refused to let the apologies sink in. But the magic of time and space worked wonders and she felt Kate's words seep in, take root. "I know. And I'm sorry I ran."

Kate nodded. "You did what you had to do. So did I. I'll never regret Harper's existence. And I'm sorry I hurt you, but I won't be sorry for the fact that she was born."

The ferocity in Kate's voice, the unflinching certainty of her words, hit Sutton hard. It was that ferocity, at least in part, that made her fall in love with Kate in the first place. It looked as good on her now as it did then. "Harper is amazing, and you've done an amazing job raising her. I'm only just getting to know her, but that much is clear."

Kate's features softened. That was a good look on her, too. "Thank you."

"I mean it. It sort of filled me with dread knowing I'd wind up meeting her, but she's absolutely impossible not to like."

Kate angled her head and a hint of a smirk played at the corner of her mouth. "Dread seems a bit much, doesn't it?"

"I thought seeing her would remind me over and over of why we broke up." It felt pathetic to say that out loud, but if they were going to have this conversation, they might as well have all of it.

Kate let out a sigh. "I don't see that at all."

Sutton shook her head. "I don't either. She's so her own person, but also like a mini version of you at the same time. The you I met in fourth grade and wanted desperately to like me."

"I'm not sure if I'm supposed to take that as a compliment."

"You are. It is." Sutton chuckled. "I've been wanting to tell you that but I haven't been sure how."

Kate regarded her with something just shy of suspicion. "Okay."

Sutton blew out a breath. "I haven't been holding a grudge."

That only seemed to confuse her more. "Then what have you been doing?"

Holding on to that broken heart? Focusing on work and living in a city she was growing to hate because she wasn't willing to take a chance on anything else? "I'm not sure."

"Well, I've been living my life and trying not to hold on to regrets or hard feelings."

She felt her shoulders slump, unsure she could say the same.

"What do you want, Sutton?"

Kate's tone was gentle but it was a loaded question if she ever heard one. Kate stood across from her, arms folded and her hip cocked slightly. And the only thing coming through loud and clear in Sutton's mind was longing. "I'm not sure of that, either."

"Well, if you don't know, I can't help you." There wasn't anger in Kate's voice, or even impatience. Just a simple statement of fact.

"Friends would be nice, though, and more than I expected." In this moment, she couldn't remember why that felt so impossible.

Kate dropped her arms and tilted her head to one side. Kind of a what am I going to do with you look, but with affection. She came and leaned on the hood beside her. After a long moment, she gently bumped her shoulder to Sutton's. "Seems like a good start."

Could it be as simple as that? Kate made it seem so. One more thing Sutton loved about her. She could make anything seem, not just possible, but eminently doable. "Agreed."

They stayed like that for a while, shoulders touching. She didn't want to keep Kate, but she also didn't want to lose this moment, this feeling. Not that she feared it would undo the peace they'd just made. More, she hadn't realized how much guilt and sadness and even anger she'd still been carrying around. Shedding it left her feeling so light, she wanted to sit and enjoy it. Whether Kate sensed that, or was having a moment of her own, she couldn't be sure. All she knew was that sitting together, like this, on a sultry June night reminded her of so many nights spent just like that. And it was the closest she'd been to perfection in a long time.

Chapter Eight

Kate pulled into her parents' driveway and hadn't even cut the engine before Harper was climbing out of the passenger seat. "Uncle Bryce! Uncle Bryce!"

He must have beat them there by barely a minute because he hadn't even made his way inside. "Hey, gorgeous girl."

They hugged and Bryce lifted her off her feet, spinning her around a couple of times before returning her to the ground. She giggled with delight, making Kate's heart melt a little. She loved how close they were, even as seeing them together gave her a pang of worry about him finding someone and starting a family of his own.

Kate caught up to Harper and she and Bryce exchanged a hug as well, though he left her on the ground. "Hey, you."

"Hey." He grinned at her then poked her in the ribs. "We need to talk about Friday night."

Before she could ask whether he meant his exploits or her own, Harper opened the back door and announced their arrival. They all saw each other more days than not, but it didn't stop the robust round of hugs and kisses and hellos. Mama recruited Harper to make fruit salad and Daddy asked Bryce if he would take a look at the television, which had, of its own volition apparently, turned on Spanish subtitles for every program.

Kate debated her options for only a second before following Bryce. She wanted to hear if the girl he'd been with had any promise. They headed to the den and Bryce picked up the remote. He turned it on and started poking buttons, navigating through the various menus. It didn't take long for him to scowl in frustration.

"Give it." She took it from him and found the right combination of enters and arrows to turn the feature off.

"How'd you do that so fast?"

She rolled her eyes, but smiled. "My child's been poking buttons she shouldn't for years. I've had practice."

"Of course. What was I thinking?"

"Well, maybe you were thinking I was smarter than you because that's true, too." She stuck out her tongue at him.

"Ha ha. So, Miss Smarty Pants, you and Sutton looked pretty chummy at Clotille's Friday night." He clearly meant to get a rise out of her, but at least he had the decency to do it under his breath and out of earshot of their parents.

"We did not look chummy." At least not before he and—oh, what was her name?—Jasmine took off.

"You're right. You looked like awkward teenagers who are super into each other but who don't have the nerve to just talk to each other already."

If he'd only seen them at the store last week. "It's not like that."

"No?"

She'd planned to tell him, just not with Mama and Daddy and Harper lurking in the other room. "If you must know, we left at the same time and ended up talking in the parking lot. We cleared the air."

"Uh, is that the new code word for Netflix and chill?"

"You're so obnoxious."

"Okay, so what does it mean?"

She'd replayed the conversation in her mind more times than she cared to admit—the flash of pain in Sutton's eyes when she said Kate had broken her heart, the genuine enthusiasm in her voice when she talked about Harper. "I think it means we're friends."

He looked incredulous. "Friends."

"We're adults, Bryce. We don't have to hold on to stuff that happened a decade ago." Which was what she'd been saying all week—to Mama, to Delia, to Harper.

He shook his head. "That's not what I meant. I know you've moved on and if Sutton is in the same place, then that's great."

"Then why do you look so suspicious?"

He glanced toward the kitchen, where their parents continued to congratulate each other on their mastery of their new backyard smoker. "Because I saw the looks you were giving each other when you thought the other wasn't looking. It makes me wonder if you're going to be those friends with unresolved sexual tension or the ones who fuck."

"Fuck? Are you kidding me?"

"Katherine Elizabeth. Language." Mama's voice carried from the other room.

She closed her eyes and shook her head. "How is it you always start it and I'm always the one who gets caught?"

"Because I'm smarter than you."

She punched him in the arm as Harper walked in. She made an exaggerated eye roll. "Language, Mama. And no hitting."

Kate laughed in spite of herself. She was mostly good at not cussing in front of Harper, but she definitely had her slips. Which was why they'd had the conversation about words you use in public versus ones you don't. "Sorry."

Harper shook her head as though she was the long-suffering parent in the equation. "Supper's ready."

She switched the television off and headed to the kitchen. The spread was typical for Sunday supper—three times more food than the five of them would be able to eat. But since Mama would send them home with leftovers, she'd neither complain nor critique. Dishes made their way around the table and, after Daddy said grace, they all tucked in.

"So, Mavis tells me Albin is doing his physical therapy at Josh's place in Thibodaux. She saw him when she was there for an appointment for her shoulder. Sutton, too, she said, looking all grown up."

She'd told her mother about bringing dinner over to Albin and Sutton, mostly so Harper wouldn't accidentally out her. Apparently, Mama took that to mean curiosity about all things Sutton. "Yeah, I think Sutton and Josh reconnected because he talked her into coming out to Clotille's last night."

Again, better to put it out there than look like she had something to hide.

"You went out last night?" Mama looked offended. Not because her daughter had gone out, of course, but because she'd not been called upon to babysit.

"Harper had a sleepover at Macy's for Macy's birthday."

"Okay, then."

"I wanna have a slumber party for my birthday," Harper said.

It was the first Kate was hearing of it, but it didn't surprise her, given how many stories she'd heard in the last two days. "I think that could probably be arranged."

Mama pointed her fork at Kate. "It's good for you to get out. You should do it more often."

She thought about catching up with her friends, having adult conversation. It was nice to wear something other than jeans, too, since that's all she wore at work. "I think you might be right."

"It was cool to have Sutton stop by," Bryce said with a wink in Kate's direction. "I hadn't seen her since she got back. I don't think anyone else has, either. A little reunion of sorts."

"Sounds like old times." Daddy's voice had a trace of edge to it. He'd never quite forgiven Sutton for bailing on her, regardless of the circumstances. Daddy prerogative, she supposed.

"It was nice to hang out and catch up, but I wouldn't go that far." She looked to Bryce for backup.

He gave her a you wish look. "Yeah, we're old and crusty and most of us headed home by ten, but Kate and Sutton were still going strong."

Kate took a sip of sweet tea and cleared her throat. Two could play at that game. "You and Jasmine cleared out even before that. You two hitting it off?"

"Who's Jasmine?" Mama asked, a mixture of curiosity and disappointment in her voice. "What happened to Elena?"

Bryce glared at her and she offered him an apologetic wince. She'd wanted to divert attention, not throw him to the wolves.

Mama had high hopes for Bryce's relationship with Elena, up to and including more grandbabies. "She's moving for a job."

"Oh, honey." Mama reached across the table and grabbed his hand.

"It's fine, Mama. It's a really good job. I would have taken it if I was her."

Little made Bryce more uncomfortable than his parents taking an interest in his love life. Kate couldn't blame him. While they'd been supportive of her sexuality, his gender identity and transition triggered every protective parental instinct they had. In addition to taking it upon themselves to educate the entire town on trans issues, they'd become deeply invested in his finding a partner who accepted and appreciated and loved him. Well, their mother more than their father on that last score. Daddy mostly preferred to keep his nose out of people's relationships.

Mama sniffed her disapproval. "Well, I just don't understand women these days, always putting their careers in front of family."

Kate coughed loudly and angled her head toward Harper, who seemed to be watching the conversation unfold with fascination.

Mama cringed. "I mean—"

Harper didn't let her finish. "Women should be able to pursue whatever career they want. Or stay home and take care of the kids. Or both. It should be their choice."

Kate smiled. Harper had been quoting feminist talking points since she was old enough to talk. While it had been adorable, she appreciated that Harper was getting to the age of understanding what most of it meant. "What she said."

Mama straightened her shoulders. "Of course. I just don't think women should feel pressured to pursue high-powered careers because they're smart."

She shot Kate a pointed look, to which Kate offered a nod of concession. "Nice recovery."

"I'm going to be a marine biologist or a firefighter or jewelry maker. Or I'm going to open a bakery." Harper counted off the options on her fingers as she spoke.

"Marine biologist, huh?" Bryce looked at her with curiosity.

A recent addition to the list, bumping teacher. Just as firefighter had bumped doctor when her school's fire safety day included a visit to the local fire station. Harper nodded decisively. "They get to work with manatees and dolphins."

"Ah." He nodded as though that was the most obvious explanation.

A curious look passed over Harper's face. "Mama, what's Sutton's career?"

The abrupt shift in the conversation—to Sutton, of all people—got her attention. "You know, I'm not a hundred percent sure. Something with computers."

"We should ask her next time we see her."

"I'm sure she'll come in the store again sooner or later." She hoped she sounded more casual than dismissive.

"I'm going to bring my notebook and that way I can ask her questions and take notes."

The answer was classic Harper, but it gave her pause. It gave Daddy pause, too, if the look on his face was anything to go on. She made a mental note to reinforce the fact that Sutton was only in town temporarily. Because even if she and Sutton had agreed to be friends, it was more about making peace than getting close again. She might know better than to get attached, but it was a skill Harper had yet to master.

"I'm sure she'd be happy to answer your questions," Mama said, when it became clear no one else was going to respond.

Harper seemed satisfied and resumed eating. Around a mouthful of potato salad, she said, "I'll come to work with you tomorrow, in case she comes in."

Since Harper would have likely opted to come to the store anyway, she didn't read too much into it. Or at least she tried not to.

❖

Sutton moved down the row of tomato plants on her hands and knees, yanking weed after endless weed. It wasn't a huge garden by any means, but she'd been at it for close to an hour and was barely half done. How had Dad maintained this before his surgery? Her knees were killing her. Her back and hamstrings weren't too thrilled, either.

She shuffled another few feet, dragging her weed bucket with her, when her ringtone cut into the chorus of John Cougar's "Ain't Even Done with the Night." She fished her phone from the pocket of her shorts and swiped a finger across the screen. "Hey, Boss."

"Hey, hey. How's my favorite project manager doing?" Jay's voice, with its chipper Indian-slash-British accent, came blasting through her headphones.

She quickly adjusted the volume. Then she rolled her eyes, but smiled. "You call all your project managers your favorite."

"But I mean it when I'm talking to you," he said without missing a beat.

She gave him a hard time, but she knew he did mean it. Her implementations went smoothly and rarely did her clients escalate any issues to his desk. She saved him work and he loved her for it. "Are you buttering me up because you love me or because you want something?"

"My dear, you say that like those things are mutually exclusive."

He'd not called her for the better part of three weeks—a good week and a half longer than she expected to go without hearing from him. "Mm-hmm. What do you want?"

"You'll never guess who I just got off the phone with."

Sensing this wasn't going to be a quick check-in, she hauled herself to her feet, barely suppressing a groan. She straightened and stretched before heading to sit on the porch steps. "Who's that?"

"The dean of Tulane Law and her chief technology officer."

Since she didn't know either of those people personally, it had to have something to do with a potential contract. "And?"

"And they implemented a new CRM but it doesn't talk to half the homegrown systems they've been using for the last five years."

It was the bread and butter of their business—stitching together platforms and systems colleges and universities bought and implemented, but that were never designed for integration. But it didn't seem like a particularly large project, or a complicated one. Nothing that would require her particular expertise or political savvy. "Does that mean you're coming for a visit? I'd be happy to show you around the French Quarter or the spectacular sights of Duchesne."

"She wants you."

Sutton wiped her forehead with the back of her hand. God, it was hot. "Me? How does she even know who I am?"

"Her partner is the former liberal arts dean at Clemson. She's now the provost at Loyola, in case you were wondering."

Clara Jackson. Sutton smiled at the memory. The woman had been an absolute spitfire, not to mention the only woman of color in the senior leadership at Clemson at the time. They'd hit it off immediately, despite the fact that Clara was an English professor by training and not keen on spending half a million dollars on data management. In the end, it was one of her favorite projects, and not just because she got to team up with a fellow lesbian. She'd even met Clara's partner once, but was blanking on the name.

"Your silence tells me you're looking at your calendar for weeks you might be able to fit this in."

It irritated her that he assumed she'd agree. She probably would, but it irritated her nonetheless. "What makes you think I'll say yes?"

"Because you're a worker bee by nature and probably bored out of your mind already." He waited a beat. "And because you love working with powerful lesbians."

She laughed because of how right he was. Generally, at least. She'd worried about being bored, but between the PT appointments and catching up with people she hadn't seen in years, she hadn't yet felt the itch to get back to work. Plus the time she found herself spending with Kate—not much yet, but she liked where it was going. "Can I call you back?"

"Seriously?" He sounded more surprised than upset.

"I'm not turning you down, but I'm not quite ready to say yes. And in either case, I'm weeding the tomatoes and can't really get to my calendar." She stood and rolled her shoulders.

He laughed. "Weeding. Sure. You're a six-figure systems implementation consultant, but by all means, get those weeds taken care of."

"You're a jerk."

"Call me later, Farmer Brown."

The line went quiet for a second before her music kicked back on. She rocked back on her heels and mulled over the conversation. But not the project, strangely enough. She kept going back to his comment about her being bored, and how not bored she was. Maybe she needed a break more than she'd realized. Or maybe, she'd allowed her life to get way too one-dimensional.

She returned to the garden and surveyed half-weeded rows of tomato plants. She'd definitely not missed her calling on the gardening front, but maybe there was more to make of her time off than puttering and doing chores around the house. What that might be, she had no idea. Still, realizing it had to count for something, right?

Without meaning to, she thought about Kate. Her college plans were derailed when she got pregnant, but Sutton didn't know much beyond that. Did she like working at the hardware store or did it just pay the bills? Did she want to take over someday or did she dream of doing something else?

She returned to the weeds and powered her way through the last rows, mulling. She wasn't bored, nor did she want to give Jay the satisfaction of an immediate reply. But, like he said, she was a worker bee by nature. And she liked the idea of a job so close, working with Clara's partner. Maybe she'd get to connect with Clara, too.

She'd look at her calendar to see if she might have a week or so before Dad's second surgery where she could commute in to New Orleans for at least half days. As for the rest of it, she'd figure it out. Somehow.

CHAPTER NINE

As promised, Harper accompanied Kate to the store the next day, and the day after that. She brought her notebook, but didn't seem overly obsessed with when she might see Sutton again, which was a relief. In addition to her role as greeter, she helped Kate tidy the gardening department and took it upon herself to arrange the seeds in the new display rack that had come in. She'd decided to organize the packets alphabetically and was currently debating whether zucchini should go under Z or S.

"I wish you had this level of interest in organizing your room," Kate said.

She was rewarded with a look of complete exasperation. "Well, if I had a cool display rack for my stuff, maybe it would be easier to be organized."

Her delivery had more sass than Kate would have liked, but the point was valid. "So, if I buy you a cool rack, you'll keep your room clean?"

"Maybe." Harper elongated the word and batted her eyelashes.

Other than new bedding, she hadn't bought much for Harper's room lately. And good storage did make it easier to stay organized. Her studio provided proof of that daily. "Okay."

Harper's eyes lit up. "Like what?"

She imagined a new set of shelves, perhaps with those little square totes that kept everything neatly tucked away. But even as she envisioned it, she knew it would work better if Harper took ownership. "How about we brainstorm when we get home tonight and then we can go shopping this weekend?"

"To Target?"

She said it with a hint of wonder in her voice and Kate couldn't help but laugh. It wasn't like they never went, but it was a bit of a drive so it tended to be for things like school supplies or holiday shopping. "To Target."

Harper dropped the zucchini seeds and started a hips jutting, arms flailing happy dance. It made her realize they didn't do silly, indulgent things often enough. "We could go out to lunch, too. Maybe even get pedicures."

The dancing intensified and several of the neat stacks scattered.

"We have to earn our fun, though. You finish this and I'm going to go order paint."

Harper let out a huffy sigh, but didn't complain. She got back to work and Kate left her to it, confident it would be done to perfection. She grabbed the iPad and headed to the front of the store, thinking she could give Owen his break and get her order placed at the same time. Of course, she'd no sooner pulled up the wholesaler's website when the door jingled.

She set the tablet down and looked up, only to find herself face-to-face with a tall drink of Sutton. She wasn't in work pants this time, or a tank top, but her shoulders filled out the faded gray tee almost as nicely. Not that she noticed that sort of thing, or thought about how different it was from Sutton's lankier teenage body.

"Hey, Kate." Sutton's hundred-watt smile only added to the overall appeal of the package. Again, not that she was noticing. Not that and not how much she liked Sutton's voice or the way Sutton said her name.

"Hey. How are you this gloriously cool June morning?" A front had passed through and temps had dipped below sixty overnight.

"Equally glorious, thank you. I slept with my windows open and woke up almost chilly."

Things not to be taken for granted during a south Louisiana summer. "I wish I'd thought to do the same."

"Should be decent enough tonight, too. Not quite as cool, but still not humid."

Talking about the weather could have—should have—been the most boring and banal thing possible. But she couldn't stop herself from wondering if Sutton still wore boxers to sleep or if she still had a tendency to sprawl across the bed. Not boring or banal. In fact, it had her a little hot and bothered.

"You okay?" Sutton regarded her with concern.

She shook her head, feeling like an idiot. "Sorry. Daydreaming about sleeping with the windows open."

Sutton's smile softened. "That's nothing to apologize for."

Okay, was she imagining it or was Sutton flirting with her? It sure felt like flirting. More, she kind of liked it. What had gotten into her? She cleared her throat. "Anyway. What can I do for you today?"

Sutton continued to smile as she pulled a folded piece of paper from her pocket. "I need a few things, but I can probably manage to find them on my own."

"Oh. Okay." Why did that leave her disappointed?

"But I was hoping to talk to you, too."

"You were?" Or was she saying that to be nice?

"Yes, I was wondering if I might pick your brain."

She imagined Sutton elbow-deep in a project and hitting a wall. That was much safer than picturing her in bed. "Sure. Though I should confess I know more about DIY in theory than from personal experience."

Sutton laughed and she tried not to notice how sexy the sound was. "No, no. This is a personal question."

She raised a brow, curious but a little suspicious, too. "Personal?"

Sutton waved a hand back and forth. "No, no. Not personal like that."

Since she hadn't indicated what kind of personal she meant, Sutton's answer offered little in the way of clarity. "All right. What can I do for you?"

Despite the invitation, Sutton hesitated. Eventually, she said, "I guess I wanted to ask you about—"

The bell jingled again and Sutton paused. Kate glanced toward the door instinctively, hoping it was a regular she could smile a hello to and leave it at that. No such luck. It was one of Daddy's friends, one of the chatty ones. And since Daddy wouldn't be in until afternoon, it left her to listen to the trials and tribulations of his latest project. "Hey, Mr. Bruce."

"Hey there, pretty lady. What's the good word?" He strolled over and rested his elbow on the counter, then gave Sutton the once-over. "You Albin's girl?"

Sutton offered a polite smile but was clearly uncomfortable. "I am."

"Haven't seen you since you were yea high." He held up his hand to his midsection. "Where you been hiding?"

"I live in Atlanta now."

"Oh, big city girl. You got a fancy job or a fancy husband?"

Sutton's mouth opened, then closed. It was all Kate could do not to laugh. "Um, fancy job, I guess. I'm not really the husband sort."

He lifted both hands, with a bit more vigor than was necessary. "Sorry, sorry. You could have a fancy wife, too. That's fine."

Now Sutton seemed to be suppressing a laugh, so that was a good sign. "Thank you, but neither. Just me."

"Well, good for you. Don't see your Daddy much now that he's retired. You tell him Bruce Babin asked him how life on the pension is treating him."

"I'll do that." Sutton glanced at Kate, her helpless expression cuter than it had any right to be.

"What can I do for you today, Mr. Bruce?" Kate asked.

"Need my propane refilled."

"I'll be right out," Kate said. Bruce went out the way he came in and she offered Sutton an apologetic look. "I need to take care of that."

Sutton waved her off. "Go, go. I'm the one disturbing you at work."

"Thanks. Cliff is stocking shelves somewhere if you need anything. I'll be back in a minute."

"Sounds good."

Sutton wandered down one of the aisles and Kate went out to the propane station. She'd filled enough tanks that she could do it in her sleep. Likewise, she'd mastered the art of half-listening to chatty customers, throwing in mm-hmms and oh dears as needed. She did just that as Mr. Bruce launched into a tale of bunnies who'd raided his garden patch, eating the lettuce clear down to the ground. She tutted and agreed that netting was an eyesore but sometimes necessary. All the while, thinking about Sutton. Her mystery question, of course. Not all the other stuff that had flitted through her brain while Sutton talked about sleeping naked with the window open.

Wait. Sutton hadn't mentioned anything about sleeping naked. That was all her own imagination. Oh, that wasn't good.

She forced herself to turn more of her attention to Mr. Bruce, asking questions as he followed her inside to pay. No sign of Sutton, so she rang him out then busied herself with replacing the receipt tape. Owen strolled up from the back, grooving to whatever must have been playing on his headphones and drinking a Dr Pepper.

When he got to the register, he pulled out the ear buds and tapped at the screen of his phone. "Did I miss anything good?"

"Just Bruce's weekly visit."

Owen rolled his eyes but smiled. "Oh, damn. That's too bad."

She snagged the iPad she'd not gotten back to. "I'm going to check on Harper, then hopefully get paint ordered. You need anything?"

He made a motion with his hands to indicate his surroundings. "Under control."

With Owen back covering the front, she headed to the gardening department, wondering if Sutton was still shopping or if she'd stumbled upon—and been ensnared by—Harper. What she found made her stop in her tracks. Sutton sat on the floor, cross-legged. She handed stacks of seed packets to Harper, who situated them in the display and checked them off a list.

"Watermelon," Harper said.

"Watermelon." Sutton held up a stack. "But not watermelon radishes."

Harper pointed her pencil at Sutton with all the confidence of a seasoned manager. "No, those are under R because they're not really watermelon."

Kate took a step back to avoid being seen. She folded her arms and listened, taking surreptitious peeks around a stack of potting soil.

"I think that just leaves zucchini." Sutton handed her the last stack.

Harper took them, tucked them into the slot. "Done."

Sutton got to her feet and gave the rack a spin. "A job well done."

They exchanged high fives, then Harper said, "Thank you for your help. I should compensate you for your time."

Sutton laughed, making Kate wonder if it was the offer or Harper's use of the word compensate. "No compensation required."

"What if you let me do something nice for you?"

She expected Sutton to refuse, which would be her cue to cut in and move them both along to other things.

"Like what?"

The question gave her pause. What could Sutton have in mind? Or maybe the better question was, what would Harper offer? She took another step back to ensure there was no chance she could interrupt them.

"I could make you supper."

"Hmm. That seems like an awfully big thank you for a few minutes of help."

"Well." Harper let the word drag. The girl sure had her delivery nailed. "I have an ulterior motive."

Sutton laughed and Kate bit her lip to keep from doing so, too. "That sounds dangerous. What is this ulterior motive?"

Kate wanted to know, too.

"I want to learn about your career."

Oh, right. That.

"You do?" The genuine surprise in Sutton's voice was kind of adorable.

"Mama said it had something to do with computers, but she didn't know what else."

Kate inched forward enough to see Sutton nod. "She's right. I do work with computers."

"But I want to know what you do with them. I'm very interested in learning about careers."

Sutton hesitated, making Kate wonder if she was looking for a polite way to decline. Eventually, she said, "I'm happy to tell you whatever you want to know. It's not very glamorous, though."

"You mean like being a movie star?"

She snickered under her breath at Harper's context for glamor. "Definitely less glamorous than that."

"Do you not like your job?" Based on the tone of her voice, the idea didn't sit well with Harper.

"No, it's not that. I do like it. I get to help people, mostly by making it easier for them to do their jobs. It's just not always the most exciting."

"Huh. I think helping people is exciting. I definitely want to help people in my career. Or make them happy. Like Mama."

"I think those are very good goals to have."

"So, you'll come over for supper?"

Another hesitation. Maybe she didn't want to, but maybe she wasn't sure she should say yes without talking to Kate first. Deciding she'd pushed the boundaries of reasonable eavesdropping, she rounded the corner. "Hey, you two."

Sutton jumped at the sound of Kate's voice. Then she smiled and fought the urge to take a step back from Harper. Kate looked more amused than upset, but she couldn't shake the flash of guilt that she'd been caught doing something she shouldn't. "Hey."

"It's all done, Mama. What do you think?" Harper shifted her legs to a wide stance and opened her arms like an alligator, showing off the finished display.

"It looks wonderful. And it sounds like you had some help."

Harper grinned. "Sutton helped me strategize and then she helped me implement."

"Strategize and implement, huh?"

"I may have slipped into project manager speak." She shrugged, feeling sheepish now. An improvement over guilt, though, so there was that.

Kate cracked a smile, which did more to make her feel better than any words of reassurance could have. "I see."

"I invited Sutton over for supper to thank her." Harper beamed, clearly proud of her display of good manners.

Sutton lifted a hand. Even if she appreciated the invitation, she didn't want Kate feeling backed into a corner. And she could answer Harper's questions about her work here as easily as anywhere. "Please don't feel like you have to—"

"I think that's a great idea." Kate made a deferring sweep of her hand. "Assuming you're available, of course. And interested."

Oh, she wanted to, all right. She was trying not to overthink how much she wanted to spend more time with both Kate and Harper. "I'd love to."

"We have plans this weekend, but pretty much any night next week is open. Name the day."

Well, that was convenient. "My dad has a poker game at his house Tuesday and I'm pretty sure I'm banished for the night."

"Perfect." Kate smiled and again Sutton wondered at the underlying cause. She hoped it was the idea of having her over more than the idea of her being displaced by a bunch of old men.

"I think we should make pizza," Harper said, then seemed to remember Sutton was her guest. "Do you like pizza?"

She stuck both hands out. "Who doesn't like pizza?"

Harper shrugged. "Some people."

"I love pizza." She looked to Kate. "Let me know what I can bring."

Kate shook her head. "This is a thank you dinner. You only need to bring yourself."

She barely stopped herself from offering to bring wine. Wine made it sound like a date. And even if a tiny part of her wished it might be that, it so very much wasn't. And not just because Harper would be there. "Dessert or something to drink at least?"

"How about a bottle of wine?"

"That I can do." She turned to Harper. "I'm guessing you don't like wine. Is there something you like to drink with pizza?"

Harper didn't hesitate. "Coke."

"Which we have," Kate said.

"I'll bring some anyway, since you're going to the trouble of making supper." She winked at Harper. "In the meantime, I'll get out of your hair."

Kate looked at her with confusion. "Did you not find what you were looking for?"

She resisted a face palm, but barely. Even if the truth of the matter was she'd found exactly what she was looking for. She fished the list back out of her pocket. "Just easily distracted it seems."

"Happens to the best of us."

Chapter Ten

A re you sure there's nothing else you need?" Sutton asked. Dad regarded her with exasperation. "Not a thing. Why are you being such an old hen tonight?"

It was a fair question. He'd been managing pretty well getting around the house and was doing well with physical therapy. Something about leaving half a dozen old men to their own devices made her nervous. Which was silly, really, since this particular group of old men had been getting together for poker every month for almost as long as she could remember. "I'm sorry. I don't know."

"Benny is bringing po-boys. Francois has the beer covered. We know what we're doing."

Sutton waved a hand. "All right, all right. I know. I'll get out of your hair as soon as I say hello."

As if on cue, a knock sounded at the back door. Before she could take two steps toward it, the door swung open. Perry and Jim walked in, carrying a bakery box and two bags of chips. "Hey, hey," Jim said.

"Hey, Jim." Sutton hugged him, then Perry. They'd worked with her dad for probably three decades and had been part of her life since she was born. She considered them honorary uncles.

"Aren't you looking all grown up? The city been treating you good?" Perry clapped her on the back the way he would a nephew perhaps more than a niece. She loved that her father's friends never seemed to question her lack of girlishness.

"Pays the bills and keeps me busy. Can't complain."

Jim lifted a chin at her. "That's not how Albin tells it. According to him, you're pretty much running the place."

Sutton grinned. "He exaggerates."

The door swung open again, this time without even the pretense of a knock. Benny, another honorary uncle, came in with a large paper bag. "Well, if it isn't the prodigal daughter, in the flesh."

"It's good to see you, too, Benny."

Francois arrived next, followed by Phil, the only one of the group she didn't know. He hugged her anyway, saying he felt like he did. She was offered a beer and invited to stay and play, with a promise they wouldn't rob her blind. She begged off, citing the sanctity of poker night and claiming hot plans of her own.

Which wasn't untrue. Well, plans at least. Not hot unless she counted the temperature outside. After six and still above ninety. But that was okay. She'd scored an invitation to Kate's and the promise of pizza with her and Harper.

She got into her car and headed to the address Kate had texted her. It was close enough that, had it not been so freaking hot, she'd have walked. Closer, even, than Kate's house when they were kids.

Not surprising, really. There were only a few square miles of Duchesne to begin with, if you didn't count the sugarcane and soybean fields that sprawled in every direction. But it made her think of all the days—or in high school, nights—they'd walk to each other's houses. Homework and hanging out had given way to homework and making out. And on those occasions where Dad had pulled a double at the plant and worked the night shift, making out had given way to more.

It didn't matter how much time had passed. She could close her eyes and still conjure those first touches. The timid exploration that took on an urgency that neither of them understood. The giggles mixed with moments of breathless wonder. The sheer magic of coming at someone else's touch for the first time.

The quick honk of a car horn yanked her back to reality. She'd stopped at a red light—correction, the red light—and gotten lost in her memories. Before she could move her foot from the brake to the gas, it turned from green back to red. Clearly, the person behind her had given her every opportunity before sounding the alert. She offered a wave of apology and kept her gaze firmly on the light until it turned green again.

She pulled into the driveway behind the red hatchback she recognized as Kate's and took a second to study the house. It was a tidy little thing, done in the traditional Acadian style. The porch spanned the whole front of the house, and both it and the house sat about two feet off the ground on brick pilings. A pair of massive live oaks shaded the yard.

Before she could get out of her car, the front door opened and Harper bounded out. "Hey, Sutton!"

God, the kid's energy was infectious. "Hey, Harper."

"I'm so excited you're here. I cleaned my room so you could see it, and Mama and I have been setting up games and getting the pizza stuff ready and I helped her make cookies, too."

Infectious and maybe a little hard to keep up with. "That's awesome. What kind of cookies?"

Harper's smile morphed into a sly grin. "Oatmeal chocolate chip. Mama said that was your favorite."

They were, and had been since Kate first made them for her in tenth grade. Since Dad didn't bake, she'd grown up on Moon Pies and Little Debbie Cakes. If she hadn't harbored a major crush on Kate already, those cookies would have done her in. What did it mean that Kate made them for her now? "They are absolutely my favorite."

"Good. Mama called them a goodwill gesture. She said that was something nice you did for someone else and she wanted to do something nice for you since y'all are friends again."

Well, that answered that. It also made her realize that, aside from the wine and two-liter of Coke, she'd shown up empty-handed. She'd been so focused on not looking too eager, she now looked like an inconsiderate ass.

Could she leave before Kate saw her? Tell Harper she'd forgotten something and run to the flower shop or something? What kind of flowers said "I'm glad we're friends again" and not "I'm still hopelessly in love with you" anyway?

"You don't have to stand in the driveway waiting to be invited in, you know."

She hadn't even seen Kate step onto the front porch. But now that Kate had spoken, Sutton had eyes for nothing else. Her hair was pulled back into a casual ponytail, showing off her perfect neck and these dangly earrings that looked like glass. She wore a paisley sun dress that fell to her knees, but showed off the tiniest hint of cleavage. Her feet were bare. Sutton's mouth went dry, along with her vocabulary. What was that about not being hopelessly in love?

"But, just in case, come on in." Kate's eyes danced with humor and a smirk played at the corners of her mouth.

"Come on, Sutton." Harper grabbed her hand and gave it a gentle tug.

She laughed, hoping she didn't look as ridiculous as she felt. "I'm coming, I'm coming."

Inside, the living room opened to the left. Through a wide opening she guessed wasn't original to the house sat a dining area and, beyond that, the kitchen at the back of the house. A hallway sat to the right, ostensibly leading to the bedrooms. The space had an airy feel, thanks to the high ceilings and open floorplan. Modern, yet classic. Was that a thing? And definitely feminine. She wouldn't have been able to describe a space suiting Kate's personality, but this was absolutely it.

"Thank you for bringing wine." Kate regarded her with a casual smile that was enough to make her forget she was clutching a bottle.

"It's the least I can do for pizza. And, I hear, oatmeal chocolate chip cookies." She hoped the comment came off as playful and not reading too much into the situation.

Before Kate could say anything in return, Harper grabbed Sutton's hand again. "Come see my room."

Harper's room was done in purples and blues and she had more books than stuffed animals crowding her shelves. Along with posters of marine life and a desk full of art supplies. "Very nice."

Harper beamed at the compliment.

"Would you like the rest of the tour?" Kate asked.

She hadn't wanted to ask, but if Kate offered, it was okay, right? Rude, even, to decline. "Absolutely."

Kate gestured to the doorway at the end of the hall. "My room is down there."

Sutton wanted to see it, but didn't want to be creepy about it. "Mm-hmm."

"Bathroom here." Kate gestured to another door, then moved to the space in front of Harper's room and flipped a switch. "And here's my studio."

Kate stepped back and made a motion that Sutton could go inside. Sutton stepped forward, thoughts torn between wondering what kind of studio Kate had and what it said that she was more inclined to show it off than her bedroom. The space was small, considerably smaller than Harper's room. Shelves lined two of the walls, most crammed with little stacking bins and drawers. A worktable sat under the sole window, next to a filing cabinet that seemed to hold a glorified toaster oven.

Paintings and prints gave the walls personality, but no indication of what Kate did in the space. "What exactly—"

"I make jewelry. Earrings mostly, but bracelets and necklaces, too. A couple of years ago, I made the leap and bought a kiln so I can make my own glass beads, too."

"You do?" She didn't mean to sound incredulous, but this setup made it seem like way more than a hobby. "I mean, you clearly do. But this is a lot. Do you sell things?"

Kate smiled, pride evident on her face. "I do. Some festivals and craft shows. And I have an online shop."

She worked at the hardware store, raised a daughter on her own, and did this. It boggled Sutton's mind and yet somehow didn't surprise her at all. "That's awesome."

"Can we make pizza now? I'm starving." Harper shifted from one foot to the other.

Sutton chuckled but Kate rolled her eyes. "Starving or bored?"

Harper shrugged. "Both?"

"Come on, then." Kate led the way to the kitchen and pulled ingredients from the fridge to finish the prep station she'd set up on the table. She offered basic instructions, since Sutton seemed oddly intimidated by the whole thing, then watched Sutton and Harper attempt to stretch out their respective balls of dough. Both had their brows furrowed with concentration, although only Harper had her tongue out.

Before she could stop it, a moment of what-if flitted through her mind. She shook it off. She'd wasted way too much time with thoughts like that when Sutton first left. They hadn't plagued her in years. Sutton's return was no reason for them to start now.

Still. It was impossible to deny how well they got along or how taken Harper was with Sutton. It wasn't hard to see why. Sutton talked to Harper like a person, not a little kid. And she was either good at faking it or genuinely interested in what Harper had to say.

Was she simply good with kids? Did the fact that Harper was her daughter make Sutton more or less inclined to spend time with her? So many questions and no way of getting answers, really. At least not without asking questions that made her seem way more invested than she was. Or should be.

"I think we beat you, Mama."

Harper's question pulled her out of the rabbit hole of her thoughts. She looked at the flat circles of dough in front of Harper and Sutton, then down at her own barely flattened ball. She let out a chuckle. "I got distracted watching y'all."

"It's easy to see why." Sutton tossed her head haughtily. "We're clearly pros."

She looked again at their dough. Harper's had at least two holes poked in it and Sutton's looked more like a lopsided egg than a circle. "Let's not get carried away."

Sutton seemed unfazed, but Harper giggled. "She usually tells me I'm getting too big for my britches."

Sutton cracked a smile, then. "Well, that's no good. Then your ankles are sticking out and your butt might show and you'd look very silly."

Another giggle from Harper. She was a pretty happy kid most of the time—Kate had been blessed in that regard—but Sutton brought out her exuberance. "Mama buys me new clothes before I really get too big for them."

Sutton continued to smile, but there was a softness to it now. "Sounds like your mama takes very good care of you."

It could have been simply a moment between Harper and Sutton, but Sutton looked up and made eye contact with her. Emotion threatened to swell in her chest. She coughed to clear it. It was being complimented on her job as a parent that got to her, not the fact that it came from Sutton. "So, how about we get these pizzas topped and in the oven?"

"Yeah!" Harper stepped back from the table and pumped her fists in the air, driving away any lingering sentimentality.

Kate grabbed a cookie sheet and arranged the three pieces of dough on it. "Who wants sauce?"

"Me, me, me." Harper raised her hand.

"And me, me, me, too." Sutton mimicked Harper's gesture.

This time, Kate giggled even before Harper. She shook her head, but let herself continue to smile as she added sauce to each of the pizzas. "All right, have at it."

The three of them crowded around the cookie sheet, debating the relative merits of various pizza toppings. Pepperoni was a universal favorite, of course, but when Sutton reached for the bell peppers, Harper wrinkled her nose. "Have you ever even tried them?" Sutton asked.

"I mean, I eat them in stuff." Harper scowled. "Like jambalaya and spaghetti sauce and gumbo. But I don't like them crunchy."

Rather than dismissing her, Sutton nodded. "They get kind of soft on pizza, but fair enough. More for me."

Sutton gave Harper a gentle hip check and added more peppers to her pizza. Harper stared at it for a long moment, then let out a sigh. "Maybe I'll try one."

Sutton teased her with a brief game of keep-away before handing her the bowl. Harper put one slice on her pizza, then a second. "Beauteous," Sutton declared.

Kate slid the pan into the oven and everyone took turns washing hands. She let Harper pour herself a Coke, then turned her attention to Sutton. "Coke or beer? Wait. Wine. You brought wine."

Sutton offered her a smile she couldn't decipher. "I'm okay with beer if you'd prefer it."

"Oh, no. I'm definitely having wine." She didn't hesitate to drink wine by herself, but there was something nice about sharing a bottle with someone. Especially a bottle as nice as the one Sutton brought.

She opened it and poured glasses. It didn't take long for the pizzas to bake, and before she knew it, they sat around the table discussing the general awesomeness of pizza in all its forms. She'd encouraged Harper to save her interview for after supper, so they talked about the weather and Frances and plans for the summer. When they'd finished, Kate suggested they take the cookies out to the back porch.

Sure enough, the storm that passed over while they ate had taken the edge off the day, bringing the temperature down a good ten degrees. Even the worst of the humidity had rolled off, leaving the evening pleasant and only a bit muggy. She took a seat on the swing, expecting Sutton to settle in one of the rockers. But instead Sutton looked at the empty spot, then at her. "Do you mind?"

Kate shook her head and Sutton joined her. It felt, well, it sort of felt like old times. As much as she'd assured Daddy it was nothing like that, having Sutton next to her made her think of the hundreds—thousands?—of afternoons they'd while away the hours on the swing at her house or Sutton's. They'd talk about school or work or the future, including dreams of having a house of their own, complete with a porch swing.

Harper settled on the floor cross-legged, notebook in her lap. Her presence kept Kate grounded in the moment, but it didn't stop her from thinking about how nice it felt. It was silly, really, and she knew better. Still, she could enjoy a moment and not read more into it than was there, right? Right.

"So, what is your job? What's it called?" Harper asked, pen poised.

"I'm a systems implementation consultant, with a focus on higher ed platforms."

Harper blinked, clearly not sure what to do with that many words. She started to write, then stopped. "Could you say that again?"

Sutton laughed. "Let's stick with systems implementation consultant. The rest just means I do my job with colleges and universities instead of businesses."

Harper nodded. "Like LSU?"

"Yes, although I've never had a project at LSU."

"That's too bad. Uncle Bryce works there." Her eyes lit up. "Maybe he could hook you up."

"That would be cool, but my boss usually tells me where my projects are."

"Bosses are like that. Bossy." Harper angled her head toward Kate with about as much subtlety as a cartoon character.

Sutton let out a snort but recovered quickly. "Perk of being the boss. Lots of pressure too, though, so I'm happy not to be the boss."

Harper seemed to mull that over, then scribbled something in her notebook. She then launched into her list of questions. Kate hadn't realized she'd written them out ahead of time and they were quite thorough. Sutton didn't flinch. She talked about how important it was to get computers to talk to each other, for different programs to share information so people could understand the big picture. Definitely a layperson's explanation, but not overly dumbed down.

Despite Sutton's assertions it wasn't the most exciting work, Harper was riveted. She stopped writing at one point, resting her elbows on her knees and propping her chin in her hands. Even Kate was sucked in. It made her realize how many jobs there were in the world that she didn't even know existed. Which in turn made her wonder where along the way Sutton decided this was what she wanted to do.

It gave her a pang for how many years had passed, how little they knew about each other now.

Kate let herself relax and slip further into observer mode—a rare role for her, but one she could enjoy in small doses. Like at the store, Sutton and Harper fell into an easy rapport. It didn't surprise her. Harper could talk up pretty much anyone. The Sutton she remembered could be shy, though, especially around people she didn't know well. But they'd warmed up to each other in a way that went beyond small talk. They'd become friends.

If a piece of her heart melted at that, the rest remained sharply aware that Sutton wasn't sticking around. She didn't worry about losing sight of that herself, but Harper was a different story. Kate wouldn't discourage them from being friends, but she'd need to help Harper manage her expectations.

Because life wasn't about avoiding disappointments. It was about knowing they were inevitable, facing them head on, and getting on with all the good things in life. An unorthodox parenting model these days, at least if her friends with kids were anything to go on. But it was one she'd committed to the day Harper was born and she wasn't about to change her tune now. Especially when it came to the likes of Sutton Guidry.

Chapter Eleven

K ate settled at the picnic table and eyed her daughter's plate. In addition to a hot dog, there was potato salad, pasta salad, baked beans, and a deviled egg. "Why are there no vegetables on your plate?"

"Potatoes are vegetables." Bryce pointed a fork at her. "Technically, beans are, too."

She glared at him. "Not helping."

Harper leaned her head on his shoulder. "He's totally helping."

She shook her head. "You two are hopeless. Harper at least has the excuse of being a kid. I don't know what to say about you."

Bryce gave her an exasperated look. "I eat plenty of vegetables. This is a holiday so we get to eat what we want. Right, H?"

She nodded vigorously. "And I had a ton of carrots and broccoli when we got here."

He shrugged. "I did not."

"And there are strawberries in the ice cream for later." Harper lifted a finger as she made her point. "Uncle Loic let me add them myself."

"Yeah, we both took turns cranking when we got here, so we exercised, too." Bryce winked at Harper like they were in on a secret together, making her giggle.

Uncle Loic's strawberry ice cream had been a highlight of the Prejean July Fourth celebrations since she was a kid. Despite being given a very sleek electric model a few years prior, he held fast to his ancient crank contraption, complete with ice, rock salt, and lots of volunteer arms. And since she wanted to stay as far away from food shaming as possible, she dropped it. "Fair enough." She turned her attention to Bryce. "How's work?"

"Summer sessions are in full swing and we're ramping up for orientation."

"Already?" Harper would be back at school in a little over a month and she so wasn't ready. Now that Harper was old enough to come to the store and not be bored out of her mind, Kate loved having her there and had no desire to rush the start of the school year.

"Hard to believe summer's more than half over."

That got a groan from Harper.

Bryce looked at her with sympathy. "Sucks, huh?"

"Not really. I'm excited to start middle school. We get different teachers for every subject and switch classes every period like they do in high school."

"That's cool."

Harper's face lit up. "And we get lockers."

"Lockers are cool." Bryce nodded, even as he gave Kate side eye. The side eye that came with surviving the horrors of middle school, the one that covertly asked whether it might be better to give the kid a little warning.

Kate paired her smile with a pointed look. "We'll get her schedule in a couple of weeks and there's a fifth graders' day where all the kids get to check out their classrooms and meet the teachers."

"And we get our lockers," Harper said.

Truth be told, she was a little worried. Middle school—with its cliques and hormones and vastly differing stages of development— seemed to have a nearly universal degree of misery baked in. But Harper was resilient. She wasn't a cool kid exactly, but she made friends easily. And she seemed not to take the things mean kids said to heart. If she could hold on to that, she'd do fine.

Harper lifted her shoulders, then let them drop with a sigh. "I wish Sutton was here."

"Why is that?" She made a point of keeping her tone light. Rather than satisfying Harper's curiosity about Sutton, pizza night only seemed to intensify it.

"Because she's super fun and I bet she doesn't have other plans tonight."

"What makes you think she doesn't have other plans?" She'd wondered herself, but inviting her ex-girlfriend to a big family party seemed like a step too far. Or too lesbian. One of the two.

"Because her only family is Mr. Albin and he's laid up."

"She has a point," Bryce said.

She shot him a look of exasperation. It was one thing for him to side with Harper on the matter of vegetables. This was different. Did he want to see her squirm or did he have an ulterior motive? "She has friends, though."

Harper, who'd taken a bite of her hot dog, wiped her mouth with the back of her hand. "Yeah. Us."

Kate handed her a napkin. "We aren't her only friends."

Bryce and Harper gave her matching looks. If they weren't so busy backing her into a corner, she'd find it endearing. Although, to be honest, it wasn't a corner she minded all that much. Which maybe should give her pause, but it was a holiday. And Sutton had been to this exact party more times than she could count. "Fine. I'll see if she wants to come."

Harper let out a cheer and she and Bryce did a fist bump. Kate rolled her eyes. Talk about outnumbered.

She took her phone out of her pocket and pulled up her text thread with Sutton. *What are you up to?*

She didn't expect an immediate reply but one came. *Don't laugh. Watching a ball game with the old man.*

Kate bit her lip, but it didn't hide the smile that crept through. *Which one of you is the old man, again?*

That got her a laughing emoji and a question about her own activities.

Party at the Prejeans, obvi.

Aw.

Kate looked at the sky for a second, then typed, *Harper wants to know if you wanna come over.* Her finger hovered over the send button, but she didn't press it. Not because she was rethinking the invite. No, it was how much she was hiding behind Harper. She moved the cursor, tweaking and deleting. *Wanna come over?*

Seriously?

She rolled her eyes, but didn't stop smiling. *I wouldn't invite you if I wasn't.*

The read notification popped up but a reply didn't, leaving her to wonder if Sutton was checking in with her dad or debating whether or not she wanted to accept. It bugged her not knowing which. It also bugged her to think she was pressing the friend thing too hard. Or that she was enjoying Sutton's company maybe a little too much.

I'll be there in 20.

Well, that was that. No need to overthink the rest.

Kate tucked her phone back in her pocket. Sutton had been over to her cousins' enough times that details and directions weren't necessary. It was kind of nice, spending time with someone who already knew so much about her life.

It made her wonder if Sutton felt the same. If being home felt like home. She'd slipped back into life here with apparent ease, but what Sutton showed the world and what she had going on under the surface weren't always the same thing.

"Well?" Harper stared at her with impatience.

"She's coming."

Another whoop of celebration from Harper. Bryce didn't whoop, but he did give her a look of smug satisfaction. Which was weird, in a way. She would have expected the opposite from him, all things considered, but he seemed squarely team Sutton all of a sudden. Not that there were sides to pick, or teams for that matter. She'd have to ask next time they were alone.

They finished eating, said hello to some of the older aunts and uncles who opted to stay in the air conditioned house, and procured some of the famous strawberry ice cream. She wasn't sure she'd count it as a serving of fruit, but it was definitely in her top five favorite ice creams of all time. And she took ice cream pretty seriously.

Seriously enough that she'd probably have a second bowl when Sutton arrived. Because just like with the cookies—and whether she wanted to or not—she remembered every single one of Sutton's favorites.

❖

Sutton didn't know what she expected from a party made up almost entirely of Kate's extended family, but she found herself surprised by how laid-back everyone was. Not laid back in general. Laid back with her. Oh, there were a couple of raised eyebrows for sure, but they were aimed at Kate more than her.

Maybe enough high school sweethearts had moved on and married other people that it didn't seem all that noteworthy to be friends after so long, especially in a small town. Or maybe people had forgotten they were together in high school. It made Sutton realize she had no idea what Kate's dating history had been for the last decade. Maybe she mostly went out with men and people didn't even think of her as bi. Maybe their relationship had been just a phase and—

"Okay, I'm dying to know what you're thinking right now." Kate handed her a bowl of ice cream and looked at her with curiosity.

"Um, yeah. I'm going to plead the fifth."

Kate raised a brow, giving the curious look a suspicious edge. "That bad, huh?"

"No, no. Not bad. I swear." Kind of bad, but probably not in the ways Kate imagined.

She smirked slightly, making Sutton realize another possible angle was that her thoughts leaned inappropriate. "I mean. I was thinking how long it had been since I'd seen most of these people. And how nice everyone is being."

The smirk grew. "Well, aside from my dad, of course."

Sutton winced. Mr. Chuck had definitely been cool in his greeting. By any standards other than Southern, it might have passed, but they were about as South as South could get and his curtness didn't go without notice. "Of course."

"I hope you don't let that bother you. It's a protective thing. He doesn't actually dislike you, he just feels obligated to."

She licked a bite of ice cream from her spoon, then stuck it in the bowl so she could lift a hand in defense. "Hey, no judgment. Dads have a code unto themselves."

Something passed through Kate's eyes. Sadness? Regret, maybe? It was gone so quickly, Sutton thought maybe she'd imagined it. On its heels, a bright smile. "Agreed."

With dusk setting in, everyone started moving in the direction of the field where the fireworks would be. With Harper off doing sparklers with her cousins, Sutton was left sitting with Kate on an old patchwork quilt as a slew of Kate's extended family set up the fireworks. Being together, but also sort of alone, made her realize how many times she and Kate had spent the holiday like this, as friends even before becoming girlfriends. "This is nice. Thank you for inviting me."

"I feel like I should confess it was Harper's idea."

Part of her wanted Kate to think of her like that, to want to spend time with her on her own. It felt like splitting hairs, though. If Kate didn't want her around—or around Harper—she had every right and every chance to make that call. But the invitations kept coming. "Yeah, but you're the one who texted me. I'm okay with it being a joint effort."

"She's a bit enamored with you."

It was impossible to tell from her tone if Kate considered that a good thing or a bad. "Does that bother you?"

"I need to keep her expectations realistic, but no. I thought maybe it would bother you."

"She's fantastic. I like getting to know her." If someone had asked her a few weeks ago, she'd have given a very different answer. But that wasn't something to get hung up on now.

"Well, the feeling is mutual. And she doesn't have a lot of queer adults in her life besides Bryce and me, so that's good, too."

"I don't get a lot of kid time these days. It kind of makes me feel like the cool gay aunt."

Kate regarded her with curiosity. "Do you want kid time? I thought you were all about being the high-powered executive."

The question, like so many things in the last few weeks, gave her pause. "I love kids. I mean, I still want my own someday." She paused, unsure whether she was opening up or digging a hole. "I guess it's just been easier to focus on the career first."

Kate nodded and looked like she had something to say, but she was cut off by a firecracker going off a lot closer than she expected. She flinched, Kate looked in the direction of the sound, and somebody named Billy got yelled at.

Sutton decided to take the opportunity to change the subject. "Not to sound all uptight and city, but I'm a little terrified someone is going to blow their hand off."

Kate laughed. "It's not because you're uptight, it's because you're an adult."

Despite the nature of the conversation, Sutton's stomach did a little flip. Kate's laugh had always had that effect on her, but it was different now. Both the laugh and the effect. "I think I'm okay with that?"

"Oh, absolutely. Being a grown-up has a lot to recommend it."

It was hard not to look for hidden meanings, but she resisted. At least for tonight. "I'm glad not to be working at a fireworks stand, that's for sure."

Kate turned to her, eyes huge. "Oh, my God. I'd forgotten all about that. That place was so sketchy."

Sutton chuckled at the description because it was accurate. A couple of ramshackle buildings that propped open like the game booths that set up at fairs and festivals. In addition to selling all manner of barely legal explosives, the owner paid her and the other teenagers he hired in cash from the till every night. "Yeah, but the money was good."

Kate wrinkled her nose. "I wanted you to come work at the store so bad."

She smiled at the thought. "Yeah, but I wouldn't have been able to resist making out with you in the stock room and we both would have gotten in trouble."

Kate's shoulders bounced playfully. "It would have been worth it, though."

"You always were the risk taker."

"You liked it."

"Oh, I absolutely did." It was Kate who initiated their first kiss. Without Kate's courage, it might never have happened.

"I'm a bit more boring now." Kate shook her head. "That part is a shame."

"I don't think so."

Kate smirked. "You don't think I'm boring or you don't think it's a shame that I am."

"You're definitely not boring. Perhaps you're a little less impetuous than you once were. But aren't you the one who just said being a grownup had a lot to recommend it?"

Kate tipped her head in concession. "It's true. I did."

It was hard to put into words how much Sutton missed this. Few people in her life teased her, even fewer with this playful edge that made her think even as they made her laugh. "So, you've proven your own point. Being settled and responsible is sexy."

She'd meant it in a playful way, but the look Kate gave her was anything but. Her gaze was slow and assessing and it seemed to travel the full length of Sutton's body. "But don't you, every now and then, want to do something a little reckless?"

Every fiber, every cell, of Sutton's body kicked into overdrive and, in that moment, reckless wasn't the half of what she wanted to do. "I—"

Her answer was cut off by the first of the real fireworks. A sizzle sounded and a swirling tail of fire zipped into the sky. The color—a burst of red—flashed a fraction of a second before the popping sound. Considering she had no idea how to respond, the interruption was more welcome reprieve than annoyance. A cheer went up from the crowd and, for lack of something better to say,

Sutton found herself whooping along with people she'd known for most of her life.

She braved a glance at Kate, who merely smirked at her before returning her eyes to the sky.

Crackling golds overlapped with palms of green and explosions of purple, silver, and blue. Never more than one or two at a time, the show was a far cry from the massive displays in Atlanta. But something about this—the intimacy, the laid-back energy—had its charms. She would have thought so even without Kate's thigh brushing her own. Or Kate's innuendo-laced question hanging in the air like the haze of sulfur from the fireworks.

When was the last time she'd done something reckless?

The fact that she couldn't remember spoke volumes. And she wasn't even racking her brain for something truly dangerous. No, somewhere along the way, she'd lost her ability to goof off. Or maybe it was inspiration more than ability. Whatever the underlying cause, it left her deflated. Talk about boring.

She'd need to do something about that. She didn't know what, exactly, but something.

The finale of the backyard show peaked with a flurry of explosions. The smell transported her as much as anything else. To a time that felt simpler for sure, but also more hopeful. She let her fingers creep across the blanket, brushed her pinkie against Kate's in a way that could be accidental. Only Kate didn't retreat. Her hand came closer, inviting Sutton, teasing her.

She braved another look in Kate's direction. This time, Kate's gaze didn't waver from the sky, but her hand turned over and her fingers laced with Sutton's. Sutton swallowed. She might have held her breath.

She looked from Kate's face, down to their joined hands, then back. Kate turned, almost in slow motion. She smiled, her face illuminated in a veritable rainbow of fireworks.

Sutton leaned in without realizing it. But then Kate did, too.

She knew it was cliché to say time stood still, but that's exactly what it felt like. Mere inches separated them and everything about the moment begged for a kiss. Sutton's body was definitely on board. And if her brain and her heart had reservations, they were keeping quiet about them.

She watched Kate's gaze dart to her mouth. Sutton's did the same. And then their eyes locked and it all felt inevitable and overdue and perfect.

"Mama!"

Kate blinked. Almost as quickly, she pulled back. "Over here."

Sutton struggled to get her bearings, while Kate slipped her hand away and shifted seemingly effortlessly into mom mode. "Mama, can I sleep over at Macy's tonight?"

Kate took a shaky breath before answering. The only tell she'd been as caught up in the moment as Sutton, but Sutton would take it. "Did she already ask her mama?"

Harper nodded. "Yep. She said they were going to hang by the pool tomorrow and I could borrow a swimsuit and stay til whenever."

"All right. What are the rules?"

Harper folded her arms like the mere question was an insult to her good manners. "Please and thank you, don't stay up all hours, and offer to help."

Watching the interaction stirred something in Sutton. A very different thing than what Kate had stirred up only minutes before, but a stirring nonetheless. "Those are good rules."

Harper's eyes got big. "You should come have a sleepover at our house sometime. You don't even have to help with stuff."

Considering the kind of sleepover her imagination had simmering, it took considerable effort not to laugh. "Maybe sometime. You have fun tonight."

"I will." Harper leaned in and gave Kate a kiss. "Good night, Mama."

"Good night, baby. Be good."

She turned to Sutton and flung her arms around her. "Good night, Sutton. I'm glad you came."

Harper ran off, leaving Sutton and Kate in the awkward afterglow of nearly kissing. She fumbled for something light or clever or even coherent to say, but came up blank.

"I'm glad you came, too." Kate's hand returned to hers and gave it a squeeze.

Of course she could read that about a hundred different ways. But even as her brain spun scenarios, she knew better. Kate lived in the moment and pretty much always spoke her mind. So, Sutton did her best to ground herself in the present, too. That included a perfectly starlit night, outstanding company, and the hum of possibility. It might not be as good as a kiss would have been, but it was pretty damn close.

Chapter Twelve

"What do you mean you almost kissed?" Bryce swiveled his head, eyes wide.

"How many interpretations of that statement are there?" Kate wiped at her dripping brow, seriously regretting agreeing to an early morning run.

"A lot. She could have tried to kiss you and you stopped it. Or the other way around. It could have been mutual and you both thought better of it. Or it could have been mutual and something interrupted you and that's the only thing that stopped you."

She'd thought maybe telling him while they were running might spare her the third degree. That he might make a pithy comment and leave it at that. But of course not. One, he was way too nosy for that. Two, he actually liked running and did it often enough that it didn't make him want to die. "I can't discuss this while I'm gasping for breath."

Without breaking stride, he lifted both hands in exasperation. "You're the one who brought it up."

"But I thought if I told you now, we wouldn't have to discuss it."

He stopped dead in his tracks. "Seriously?"

She stopped, too. Only she leaned forward and braced her hands on her knees. She indulged in a few deep breaths before looking up at him. "Maybe."

He narrowed his eyes and seemed to consider his options. "If I take you back to my house and give you coffee, can we talk about it?"

If he was willing to cut a run short, he had to think it was a big deal. She'd almost convinced herself it wasn't, but really, she knew better. "Iced coffee?"

"I have a pitcher of cold brew in the fridge as we speak."

The thing was, he was going to get it out of her—and make her process it—one way or the other. She might as well do it in the air conditioning with a nice beverage instead of on the street in rapidly rising temperatures. "Deal."

"Race you." He poked her in the ribs, then took off.

She groaned and started running. She had no hope of catching him, but if she didn't hightail it at least a little, he'd tease her all day. Which might be preferable to the teasing she'd endure about Sutton, but whatever.

By the time she let herself in the back door, he was fixing their coffees. He threw her a towel and smirked. "Nice of you to join me."

She swiped the towel over her face and neck, then plopped herself at the kitchen island Bryce had built himself as part of his kitchen remodel. "Don't make fun of the old lady. I've birthed a child."

He handed her a tall glass, complete with a metal straw and a perfect layer of foam on top. "You're gorgeous and plenty fit, even if you don't ascribe to my preferred methods of torture."

Kate smiled. She didn't have a lot of insecurity about it now, but it had been hard to have a post-baby body before twenty. Bryce, who'd started wrestling with his own dysphoria by then, became a fierce champion of her self-esteem. Even if she didn't still need it, she could appreciate it. "I'm glad you drag me out now and again. Who knows when I might need to run away from a bear. Or an alligator."

That earned her a head shake and an eye roll. He grabbed his own coffee and joined her at the island. "Tell me everything."

It happened less than twelve hours ago and she'd pretty much not stopped thinking about it since. But when she opened her mouth, nothing came out.

"Speechless, huh? Must have been a damn good almost kiss."

She swatted at his arm.

"So it was bad?" His eyes never stopped laughing.

"Why do I confide in you, again?"

He reached over and covered her hand with his. "Because I love you and I've got your back. Teasing you mercilessly doesn't change that."

He wasn't wrong. That had been their dynamic since birth. "Right."

"So?"

She closed her eyes for a second and let the memory play back through her mind. "It was good. The moment, I mean. Hot summer night, fireflies all around. That sizzly spark you want right before a kiss."

"So, it was mutual?"

She took a deep breath. "So mutual."

"What happened?"

"Harper came running over to ask if she could spend the night at Macy's."

Bryce shook his head. "Kids. The ultimate cock-block."

She wanted to give him a hard time for the crass language, but it was completely true. "Yeah."

"And?"

"And what? That was it. Nothing else happened."

"But how do you feel about it?" He put an almost comical amount of emphasis on the word feel.

She rolled her eyes. "Can't you just act like a guy and not want to talk about feelings?"

"No." He answered without hesitation. "One, I'm your sibling and I'm not going to pass up an opportunity to poke at you. Two, I don't want to be that kind of guy. We've discussed this."

She did appreciate that about him, at least in the grand scheme of things. "Speaking of, how's Jasmine? Is she legit queer?"

"No changing the subject." He lifted a finger. "And don't say legit queer. It undermines people's identities."

Kate groaned. It annoyed her when he pulled out his academic speak on her, more so when he was right. She'd had her own identity questioned or not taken seriously more times than she could count. "Sorry."

"Sorry for trying to change the subject or for saying something our parents would say?"

She groaned again. "Our parents would never say that. They're terrified of the word queer."

He laughed then, a real, from the belly sort of laugh. "Touché."

"So, as I was saying, does our lovely Jasmine identify as queer? Or have—what did you call them?—queer sensibilities?"

Bryce's face softened and he smiled. "She does. It's early yet, but I have a good feeling."

"Aw, that's great." She figured it would take him ages to get over Elena and even longer to find someone who fit the bill of queer femme interested in a small-town trans guy. It was nice to be proved wrong. At least in this case.

"But we're still not changing the subject."

"From what?" She couldn't get away with playing dumb, but she could enjoy the look of exasperation on his face when she tried.

"Your almost kiss. Oh, and your feelings."

She'd been thinking about both plenty, both before falling asleep and since waking up. And in her sleep, too, if her dreams were any indications. Particularly the one where she and Sutton were about to kiss. Only no one was around to interrupt them and they did kiss. And a whole lot more. And she woke up sweaty and aroused and—

"Are you dragging it out for effect or do you really not want to talk about it?"

The question yanked her out of her—at this point, totally overactive—imagination. "I should have been relieved, but I was disappointed, which bugs me."

"I see."

"You know, I was worried that seeing her would be weird and hard. I worried it might stir up all my hurt and anger. Or hers. That we'd have to try to avoid each other and it would suck."

"But you didn't worry about being attracted to her still. Or again. Whatever."

She blew out a breath. "Yeah."

"And obviously that attraction is mutual."

Having Bryce say it out loud made it real in a way she hadn't quite gotten her head around. "This has trouble written all over it."

"I'm not saying I disagree, but why?"

She thought back to the conversation with her mother when she learned Sutton would be coming home for a while. And to their first run-in at the store. And to everything that had unfolded since. "Because we agreed to let the past be in the past and be friends. Because that's kind of nice, actually, and sleeping together would fuck that up."

He nodded slowly. "Because a kiss would obviously lead to that."

"Lead to what?"

"Sleeping together."

Of course she'd just taken a sip of her coffee and of course she choked. When the coughing fit subsided, she glared at him. "Who said anything about sleeping together?"

His eyes narrowed and he looked genuinely confused. "You did."

"No, I didn't."

"Um, yeah. You did."

"Kissing. I was talking about almost kissing her."

He folded his arms and fixed her with a look that reminded her so much of Daddy. "You literally said, 'and sleeping together would fuck that up.'"

Did she? Well, fuck. There was her problem. "Oh."

"I mean, it's not a huge leap. Why would you kiss her if you weren't also considering going to bed with her?"

She could argue she wasn't, but it would be a lie. On some level, at least, it was one hundred percent about that. "Yeah."

"Maybe the real question is why you want to sleep with her."

"Or, how stupid am I?"

He shrugged. "Not stupid. But you should know what you're hoping to accomplish and decide if sex is the answer."

She hadn't wanted to go there, but now that they were in the thick of it, she might as well tap into his slightly more objective take on the situation. "What could I be hoping to accomplish?"

"Revenge. Seeing if it's as good as you remember. Getting her out of your system once and for all. Getting back together." He rattled off the list as though giving her choices for lunch.

"I don't think I like any of those options."

Another shrug. "It's not an exhaustive list. Those were just off the top of my head."

"Could you tell me this has disaster written all over it and to not even consider it instead?" Because at the end of the day, she trusted his judgment. If he emphatically told her not to, she'd most likely listen. And then she wouldn't have to think about it anymore.

"I could. And maybe I should."

"But?"

He waited a long moment before continuing. "All teasing aside, there's something there, between you two. Only you know if it's unfinished business or something new. But I'm guessing ignoring it isn't going to make it go away."

"So, you're saying I should sleep with her and see what happens?" Why did the mere thought of that send a ripple of excitement through her?

"No, that is absolutely not what I'm saying."

Again, she should have felt relief, but was hit with a pang of disappointment instead. She propped her elbows on the counter and covered her face with her hands. "Ugh."

"I'm saying things between y'all ended badly. If this is a chance to change the narrative, maybe you should. But you should figure out what you want and what the risks are. And then whether those risks are worth it."

She lifted her head and studied him. When did her annoying little brother get so wise? "That's actually decent advice."

"I'm not saying it's easy to do, or that it will work out how you want. But if I've learned one thing in my life, it's that pretending something isn't there, or isn't true, doesn't work."

She considered his words—and the hard lessons he'd had to learn along the way—and her heart swelled with a mixture of affection and pride. She rested her head on his shoulder. "Don't let it go to your head or anything, but I'm glad I got so lucky in the sibling department."

He leaned his head against hers. "Same, girl. Same."

❖

"Do you spend this much time staring into space at work?"

"Huh?" Sutton blinked, pulling her eyes into focus to find Dad peering at her over the top of his newspaper.

"You're staring into space. It reminds me of when you were a kid trying to wrap your head around things like astrophysics."

She laughed. She did have an affinity for getting lost in big concepts. "I still wish I had a better understanding of dark matter."

He folded the sports section and set it aside. "I hope you don't spend your time at work doing that or they really are overpaying you."

"I'll have you know that staring into space is an essential component of both systems implementation and project management. How else are you going to see the big picture?" She sipped her coffee and waited for his pithy comeback.

He narrowed his eyes, then gave her the look he usually reserved for when she got overly technical when explaining something. "Is that what you're doing right now?"

"Maybe." She'd told him about the Loyola gig—the one she'd accepted and scheduled to start today so she'd be done before his second surgery. He'd been unnecessarily excited to learn she'd be doing some real work and had even arranged to have his buddies drive him to PT so as to not interfere with her ability to go to New Orleans whenever she needed.

The truth of the matter was she'd been daydreaming about Kate and the almost kiss, but he didn't need to know that. Nor did he need to know the amount of time she'd been thinking about Kate in general. Or Kate's jewelry business and how much satisfaction it seemed to give her. Or how uninspiring Atlanta was starting to feel when she considered going back.

"Well, then, I'm sorry I poked fun. You know more about this fancy computer stuff than I do." He got up from the table and started to clear their breakfast dishes.

Not sure what to make of the abrupt shift, she followed him to the sink and clapped a hand on his shoulder. "Since when do you apologize for giving me a hard time?"

He waved a hand. "You know what I mean. You do big, important work and I'm proud of you."

She never—not in the entirety of her near thirty years—doubted his love or his pride. He wasn't usually sentimental or loquacious about it, but she never doubted it. "You're getting soft on me, old man."

That got her a grumble about being an ungrateful child. She kissed his cheek and headed to her room to finish getting ready. It was strange to put on full business professional surrounded by posters and stuffed animals, to check her reflection in the mirror on the back of the door and see what she'd started to think of as her Atlanta self staring back at her.

In the living room, she stuffed her laptop and the notepad where she'd scribbled notes in her leather messenger bag. Dad made comments about how she cleaned up nice. Now that they'd moved past the sentimental stuff, he laid it on extra thick. She rolled her eyes and groaned, but hugged him and promised to text an ETA when heading home.

She'd just opened the back door when a knock came at the front. She changed directions and opened it to find Kate standing on the other side. "Uh, hi."

"Hi." Kate looked her up and down and her smile faded. "Did someone die?"

Confusion gave way to laughter as she realized the reason behind the question. "No, no. I'm meeting with a client in New Orleans and this is standard work me."

Kate nodded slowly. Was it judgment? Appreciation? "Fancy."

"You look pretty fancy, too. What's up?" The sleeveless top and paisley skirt weren't as professional as Sutton's suit, but they made Kate look even more beautiful than usual.

"I had the morning off and I thought I'd see if you wanted to grab coffee or something."

"I mean, I'd love to, but—"

Kate lifted both hands. "You're busy and on your way out. It's all good. I'm not sure why I decided to stop over instead of texting."

She was wondering the same thing. But even though she couldn't accept, she had a hard time regretting Kate showing up on her doorstep. "I'm sorry because I'd definitely rather spend the morning with you."

Kate waved her off. "That's silly. I won't keep you. I—"

"I really would love to. Rain check?"

Kate's head shook no, almost imperceptibly. "Sure."

"I mean it. I adore Harper. I hope you know that. But it would be nice to hang out just the two of us."

Kate hesitated.

"I'm working this week, but I'll be home every evening. Text me a couple of options. I'll nag you if you don't."

The teasing seemed to get her to relent. "Fine."

"Excellent." Sutton lifted her chin. "So, why are you dressed up?"

Kate's face registered surprise, then embarrassment, then defiance. "No reason. I guess I'm more the type to wear fun things when I don't have to be at work."

It might not have been a dig, but it felt like one. Or maybe it was her own disenchantment with the consultant's uniform. "Well, you look lovely."

In typical Kate fashion, she let out a sniff at the compliment. "Don't let me make you late."

"Don't worry. I'm early."

That got her a laugh. "Of course you are."

"So, you'll text me?"

"I'll text you."

Kate turned to leave and Sutton followed her onto the porch, pulling the door closed behind her. She wanted to ask about the almost kiss, but didn't want to come across as needy or over-processy.

"Good luck with your client." Kate offered a wave and headed to her car.

Sutton did the same, taking her jacket off before climbing in and cranking the AC first thing. God, she hated wearing a suit in the summer. With the air blasting, she backed out of the driveway and started the drive. She needed to get her head into the project, especially after a few weeks away from flexing that part of her brain. But the only thing occupying her mind was the image of Kate on the other side of that door and the idea of what it would have been like to spend the day with her.

Chapter Thirteen

Even after chatting with Kate, Sutton got to New Orleans close to an hour before she was scheduled to meet with Dean Regina Lopez. Since it was far too hot for a stroll, she opted for a drive around campus instead. Tulane was one more of those places she hadn't been in ten years.

It didn't have the cachet of Duchesne as far as memories were concerned, but it was on her short list for colleges. She'd done the tour with Dad, met with a student in the computer science department, and everything. In the end, Emory offered her a better scholarship and financial aid package and that made the decision for her. But as she crept along the oak-lined streets and ivy covered buildings, she couldn't help but imagine how different her life might be if she'd stayed closer to home.

Of course, she couldn't bring herself to wish for that anymore. Not now that she knew Harper. Sutton sighed. It was funny how becoming friends with Kate again made things both so much simpler and so much more complicated.

Impatient and slightly irritated with herself for letting her mind wander, she turned her attention back to her phone and the directions to the lot where she'd been told to park. The walk to the law school was short but oppressively hot. Fortunately, the building was cool and inviting. It was also quiet, that almost eerie kind of quiet unique to schools not in session.

In the dean's office, a young guy greeted her and escorted her to a small conference room. Regina was there, along with a handful of people she imagined were the IT crew. Regina greeted her with a handshake and a warm smile and Sutton relaxed. She settled into introductions and got ready to work.

They talked through the CRM implementation, a newer product but one she'd worked with at least a dozen times before. Then she had them take her through their homegrown systems. A fairly standard project, but it would have its surprises and hiccups along the way. She'd been at this long enough to know they were inevitable. She said as much, adding her standard assurance that it was part of the process, not something to worry over.

They wrapped up and all the tech folks headed to another meeting. With the IT team gone, only she and Regina remained in the room. She could tell Regina had something on her mind, but she didn't know her well enough to guess what it might be. "Are you feeling good about the project and timeline?"

Regina smiled. "I am. Much better than when I wasn't sure you'd be project lead."

"Hard to say no when it's in my backyard." She tipped her head. "And working with someone I've got a good, if small, connection with."

"Not that it's any of my business, but is everything okay? When Jay mentioned you were on a leave, Clara and I worried."

The phrasing, combined with Regina's body language, made her inclined to share, even if it had been something more personal. "Just getting my dad through bilateral knee replacement."

"Ah. My mother lived with us when she broke her hip, so if you need a friendly ear, don't hesitate."

She appreciated the gesture, even if it didn't feel necessary. "It's actually been kind of nice to be home. I love my dad and I don't get back as often as I should."

Regina laughed. "Should and want to are two different animals, though, aren't they?"

She would have made the same distinction a few weeks ago. "Indeed they are. I'm finding myself pleasantly surprised, I guess."

"Well, that's good. But if you change your mind and want to be among your people, let me know. Clara and I would love to have you for dinner while you're in town."

She could have mentioned Kate. But she wasn't in the business of discussing her personal life with clients or colleagues, especially when her personal life felt like one big gray area. She also knew better than to turn down the opportunity to network with a pair of such influential women. "I would love to."

"I'll check with Clara and text you a couple of dates. In the meantime, is there anything else you need from me?"

The scope of the project was pretty basic. Now that they'd established the big picture, she'd be doing most of her work with the IT folks. Which made the prospect of seeing Regina outside of work all the more appealing. "I'll send you updates, but otherwise, I think we're good to go."

"Excellent. It's good to see you, Sutton, and I'm glad you're working with us on this." Regina stood and extended a hand.

Sutton shook it. "Same. On both counts."

She showed herself out and, on the way to her car, called Jay with a status report. He joked about being relieved she hadn't lost her touch out in the boonies and they agreed to check in again end of week. She texted Dad and started home.

As she drove, her thoughts went to Kate, though not in the usual ways her mind drifted these days. She thought about Kate in the context of Regina's invite. Kate fit the bill of being "her people," at least in the way Regina meant, but there was more to it. What would it be like to do stuff together, beyond casual hanging out, as adults? Would Kate like people like Regina and Clara or would she find them stuffy and unrelatable? Would she enjoy a glimpse into the world of academia or would it make her resent not ever making it to college herself?

And, maybe most importantly, did Kate ever think about doing such coupley things with her?

❖

Kate wiped her hands on the back pockets of her jeans and looked around. She'd almost left the skirt on for work, but thought better of it in the end. She could certainly pass an entire shift at the store without doing any heavy lifting, but she didn't like not having the option. Especially on a day she was the manager on call. It was a good decision, since Owen called in with a sore throat and a shipment of push mowers came in and needed to be sorted and stacked.

She'd roped in Bryce—who'd popped in on his way home from work—and now the task was done instead of waiting for morning. "Thank you for the help. I owe you one."

He looked down at his now dirty clothes and shook his head. "You're welcome."

"Come on, a little manual labor is good for a body."

"I'm not saying it isn't, but I prefer to do it in slightly less expensive pants."

She smirked at him. "You're such a diva."

"A diva would have watched you struggle with boxes bigger than you are."

"Okay, fair point. And I should be nice to you since you helped me."

"Or you could be nice to me in general."

She lifted a shoulder. "Eh?"

He rolled his eyes, but laughed. "Yeah, that would get boring."

"Exactly."

He followed her to the office, where she added the invoice to the stack waiting to be entered and reconciled. She flopped in the desk chair that had seen better days and he leaned against one of the old filing cabinets. "Well?"

"Well, what?"

"I didn't stop by to help you move stuff. You made it sound like something was up."

She'd texted him after her awkward encounter with Sutton that morning. Though now that several hours had passed and he was standing right in front of her, she felt less inclined to talk. "I got there as she was leaving. I felt silly. That's pretty much it."

"Mm-hmm. And where was she going again?"

"She's doing some project in New Orleans this week, which I didn't even know she was doing, so the whole thing made me look like an eager puppy whose owner is heading off to work and leaving her behind."

Bryce scrunched up his face and angled his head. "Wait, are you annoyed she was going to work or annoyed she didn't tell you?"

"Both." Kate groaned. "Neither."

"Oh, you're annoyed with yourself for being annoyed." He was so right.

"Ugh."

"I mean, it's not surprising."

"What is that supposed to mean?" To her, it made no sense.

"You've been thinking about kissing her and she's been thinking about work. That doesn't sit well."

"Okay, that's pathetic."

He winced, then waved a hand back and forth. "No, no. I didn't mean it like that."

"Pretty sure there's only one way to take it." And it meant she was pining for Sutton and Sutton wasn't giving her a second thought.

He shook his head now, conciliatory. "You're not much of a daydreamer and Sutton has you daydreaming. You're not crazy about it and having it not be mutual adds insult to injury."

"That's slightly less pathetic." Barely, but she'd take what she could get.

"And who says work precludes daydreaming? I daydream all the time at work." He shrugged like that was the most obvious thing in the world.

She pressed her fingers to her forehead. "It's none of my business whether or not Sutton daydreams on the job."

"I think if she's daydreaming about you, it's absolutely your business. Especially since you went over to her house to kiss her."

Kate groaned. Again. "I didn't go to her house to kiss her. Her father was there."

"Yeah, but you got pretty and were putting out feelers because you want to kiss her."

She could argue, but there was something icky about making a case against something she knew in her heart to be true. "Ugh."

Like the groan, it was the second time she'd said as much in as many minutes. Bryce didn't even try to hide a snicker. "Why are you fighting this?"

"Why are you so on board with it?" It came out more accusation than question. "The last time we were together, it didn't end well."

He shrugged, a little more casually than she thought the situation warranted. "I told you. There's some sizzly, chemistry thing between you two. I think, if you don't find out what it's about, you'll regret it."

"Yeah, but I can't tell if you think we need closure or if we're supposed to get back together."

Another shrug. "I don't pretend to know one way or the other."

She pointed at him and made tiny circles with her finger. "You're advising me."

"I am not." He frowned, but it was more a pout over being caught.

"You're doing, like, reverse psychology."

He rolled his eyes. "That's not what reverse psychology is."

It was her turn to lift a shoulder. "Oh, sorry. I don't have multiple degrees like you do."

That got her a withering stare. "You're like a thousand times smarter than me. Don't pull that shit."

"I was teasing you about being overeducated, not me being under."

He let out a sniff. "You're trying to distract me with insults. It won't work."

She knew it wouldn't. In addition to having a graduate degree, he was smart. Like, intensely smart. Sparring with him satisfied more than the innate need to antagonize one another as siblings. It reminded her she was smart, even if she hadn't made it to college in the long run. "Can't you humor me this one time?"

"Nah."

She reached over to smack him but was interrupted by her phone pinging. And not just any ping, either. It was the sound she'd assigned to Sutton. She grabbed her purse and dug around for her phone.

"Girlfriend?" Bryce asked, suddenly innocent.

Sorry again I had to take off this morning. Definitely want to get together. Name the day. And then, a second later, *Maybe not Clotille's?*

Bryce's mouth fell open for a moment before he started in. "Oh, my God. It is her. I was kidding but I can tell from the look on your face."

"You're insufferable when you're gloating. You know that, right?"

"Being right doesn't mean I'm gloating."

"No?" It sure felt like gloating to her.

"But I am right? It's Sutton? Is she asking you out?"

"Maybe." She made a show of holding the phone close to her chest.

"Tell me. I want to know exactly what she said."

Because he'd be truly insufferable if she didn't, she read the text aloud. "I have to go to Houma this weekend for a few things. Maybe she'd want to tag along?"

"Seriously? You're going to run errands on a date?"

"It's not a date."

"Isn't it?"

"Pseudo date. At best."

"Look, I know I give you a hard time, but I'm honestly confused. You almost kiss. Then you go over to her house for no specified reason. Now you're making plans but making them as un-date-like as possible. What's going on?"

Kate blew out a breath. He could be a pain in her ass, but he wasn't wrong. "I don't know."

He nodded affably. "Okay. That's a starting point."

"I kind of want to know what it would be like, even though I know it probably isn't a good idea."

"Not unreasonable, all things considered. Here's my question."

When he didn't continue, she waited. When he still didn't, she caved. "What, Bryce? What is your question?"

"Do you want to kiss her or do you just want to know you can?"

It was, by all accounts, a completely obnoxious question. At the same time, completely relevant. Since it was Bryce—her best friend as much as her brother—she decided he deserved the truth. "Pretty sure it's both."

"Oh, Kate. I do love you. I don't envy you, but I love you."

"Does that mean you're going to stop meddling?"

He grinned. "Not a chance."

She returned her attention to her phone. Despite Bryce's teasing, the prospect of having a meal and a conversation with Sutton somewhere other than one of the two dining establishments in Duchesne had a certain appeal. And since Harper had a birthday party sleepover, Saturday was going to be the one afternoon and evening she had entirely to herself. She said as much to Sutton, who agreed instantly and enthusiastically. She showed the screen to Bryce and stuck her tongue out for good measure.

He tipped his head in a show of concession. "Does this mean you're going to kiss her? Or let her carry your bags?"

Kissing wasn't the sort of thing she liked to plan in advance, but it was hard to imagine not wanting to. And, as Bryce said, wanting to know she could. Whether she followed through with it remained to be seen. And even if Sutton had been occupying her thoughts, she refused to obsess about it. "I haven't decided."

"Fair enough. Just promise me that, if you do kiss, you'll do at least a little telling afterward."

She and Bryce were open books with each other when it came to relationships, so this shouldn't be an exception, even if it was Sutton. "You'll be the first to know."

CHAPTER FOURTEEN

K ate finished updating the inventory database and plugged the iPad in to charge. With Daddy on closing tonight, she could duck out early. She and Harper could stop at the store on the way home and pick up something fun for dinner instead of having the leftovers waiting for them in the fridge. That would be nice, since they wouldn't have dinner together the next day.

She looked at Harper, who sat curled up in the old comfy chair in the corner of the office reading a book. "I need to go ask Pawpaw something, but how about we head out early?"

Harper looked up, not seeming to care one way or the other. "Okay."

"Burgers for supper?"

That did the trick. Harper's eyes lit up. "And tater tots?"

"Tater tots and carrot sticks."

Harper nodded slowly, like she was considering her options. "Tater tots, carrot and celery sticks, and ice cream."

God, she loved her kid. "Deal."

Harper jerked her shoulders back and forth in what was either a happy dance or a victory dance. She stopped abruptly, face serious. "Blue Bell. Cookie dough."

It wasn't her least favorite flavor, but it wasn't her favorite by a long shot. But they compromised on a lot, so she wasn't inclined to haggle. Maybe she'd splurge on a couple of pints instead of a half-gallon and they could both get what they wanted. "All right."

Harper resumed her dance and Kate headed to the front of the store. Thinking about getting what she wanted made her think about Sutton. Was there a chance they could both get what they wanted, too? Not that Sutton's wants were her responsibility, but she wasn't selfish or detached enough not to care at all.

Sigh. That meant she'd have to figure out what Sutton wanted in the first place. She'd told herself she wasn't going to go there, but if she was contemplating kissing—or more than kissing—perhaps that ship had already sailed.

She found Daddy at the front register, hunched over a pile of something small and shiny. "Why do you look like you're performing surgery?"

He looked up from the counter, revealing a pile of washers in various sizes. "It feels like surgery, I'll tell you that. Damn drawers got all mixed up."

She bit back a smile. "You know you can pay someone with younger eyes to do that for you."

"My eyes are perfectly fine, thank you."

She felt bad about teasing him, especially when she was there to ask favors. "Do you want help?"

He waved her off. "Nah. It's good for me."

She knew better than to argue. "Inventory is done. I thought Harper and I might scoot out now if you don't need anything else."

"That's a fine idea. With your mother out of town, I'm in no rush to get home."

Realizing he was going home to an empty house every night this week gave her a pang of guilt. "Do you want to come over for supper?"

He waved her off again. "I've got a hot date with the Braves and a six-pack."

She chuckled. He didn't get much bachelor time and he made the most of it. "Okay. Well, you know you can change your mind."

"Y'all are still coming Sunday, right?"

"Wouldn't miss it."

He beamed. "Well, there you go."

She almost thought better of asking him the other favor. She could rope Bryce in instead. But he'd probably be hurt if she didn't ask. And, truth be told, the only reason she hesitated was who her plans were with. "Could you also do me a favor?"

"Of course, baby girl. Anything for you."

"Harper is at her friend Lily's tomorrow for a slumber party. I'm going to Houma to run some errands and grab a bite to eat with Sutton. Since Mama is in Gulf Shores, can you be my backup if something happens and Harper needs to be picked up right away?"

His eyes narrowed. She should have left out the Sutton part. "What do you mean you're going out with Sutton? Like a date?"

She still hadn't settled on whether or not it was a date. She certainly didn't want to parse out the nuances of it with her father. "I'm not asking you to weigh in on my plans, I'm asking if you can be backup."

Daddy frowned. "Of course I'll pick Harper up. Just because your mama hogs all the grandparent responsibilities doesn't mean I'm incapable."

"Thank you. You probably won't even have to. I just don't like being an hour away without someone else close by."

"But seriously, what are you doing with Sutton?"

She sighed. His protectiveness came from a good place, even if it drove her crazy. "I need to run some errands and we talked about getting together somewhere other than Clotille's. I'm killing two birds with one stone."

The explanation did little to appease him. "You invited her to Fourth of July, you're letting her spend time with Harper. I don't like it."

He didn't know the half of it, but still. "You're being dramatic."

"I don't understand why you would let her back into your life after she abandoned you."

It might have felt like being abandoned ten years ago, but she didn't think about it that way anymore. "We were teenagers. We broke up. Because I slept with someone else, if you recall. It was a long time ago. There's absolutely no need to be enemies now."

He sniffed. "I saw the way she was looking at you at the party."

That made her wonder if he'd seen them almost kiss or if he was reading into some other moment they'd shared over the evening. Part of her wanted to play dumb, but he deserved better than that. Besides, she wasn't a good liar and he'd probably see through her anyway. "There's a spark. I'm not going to pretend it isn't there. But I know what I'm doing."

"Do you, now?"

She bristled at the paternalistic tone. Heart in the right place or not. "Yes. I'm an adult and I can weigh pros and cons and make decisions all by myself."

That, more than telling him it was none of his business, got his attention. "I know you can take care of yourself."

"Thank you."

"It's just that I don't see her sticking around and I don't like the idea of you getting attached again."

In spite of her irritation, she softened. "I know."

"You deserve better than some cut and run woman who decided she was too good for you or this town."

It was more complicated than that. She knew it and he did, too. "I've let it go, Daddy. If I have, don't you think it's time you did, too?"

"Oh, no." He shook his head emphatically. "A father's statute of limitations has no expiration."

Time to try another tactic. "Okay, then. How about you trust me?"

"It's not you I don't trust. It's—"

"Daddy?"

He glowered but didn't continue.

"I love you. And I love that you're looking out for me. I got this."

Considering how much stock he put in her ability to handle anything, there wasn't much he could say to that. "I know you do. I just don't want to see you get hurt."

There was every possibility getting involved—any kind of involved—with Sutton would go sideways. But like Bryce had said, ignoring it wasn't going to make it go away. And knowing the risks, not to mention knowing herself, changed things. Since she couldn't say any of that to Daddy, she settled on, "I promise I won't do anything stupid."

And because he'd raised her to be smart and independent, that was the end of that.

❖

Sutton pulled into Kate's driveway and told herself to relax. Again.

She had no grounds to think of this as a date. They were grabbing dinner, as part of running errands no less. It was, at best, a hangout. Even if she spent more time than she should have getting ready. Or hadn't been able to stop thinking about almost kissing Kate under the fireworks. What might have happened if Harper hadn't interrupted them. What might happen with Harper not around this time.

She shook her head. She needed to chill out.

And then Kate stepped onto the porch. After pulling the door closed, she turned Sutton's way with a wave. The gesture included a subtle toss of her hair, which she'd left down. And she was wearing a dress. Not a fancy dress, but a softer, flirtier look than even the skirt she'd worn the other morning. So much for chilling out.

She barely resisted getting out of the car to open the passenger door.

Kate climbed in, seemingly unaware of the flurry of thoughts parading through Sutton's mind. "Hey."

"Hey." She cleared her throat. "You look nice."

Kate smiled. "You, too."

She wanted to deflect, but attempting to would only make her look awkward and uncomfortable. "Thanks."

Kate's smile gave way to a frown. "I have to say, I feel weird making you run errands with me."

Sutton reached over the center console and patted Kate's knee, to reassure and because she longed to touch her, even casually. "It's not weird at all. You needed to go to Houma and I wanted to have a meal with you someplace where we didn't know literally everyone in the restaurant."

Kate grabbed the seat belt and secured it over her. "Yeah, okay. I guess it's fine. It's not like we're on a date."

She'd spent the better part of the day wondering. No, not wondering. Hoping. Hoping it was a date. She pulled her hand back, praying the disappointment wasn't obvious on her face.

"At least not that kind of date."

She braved a look at Kate and found a playful expression on her face. "That kind of date?"

"The kind where we're just getting to know each other and trying to make a good impression."

Did that mean they were on a different kind of date? She quashed her need to know, to have everything clear and sorted. One, because Kate would tease her for it. Two, because she wanted to be in the moment and not need all the answers for a change. "I wish you'd told me sooner. I wouldn't have ironed my shirt."

That got her a full smirk. "You do look nice."

Something in the comment made her think there was more to it. "But?"

"But nothing. I was thinking how I liked this kind of casual dressy better than the power suit, but I didn't know if you'd take that the wrong way."

She could have, but didn't want to. "The suits are a bit much."

"Don't get me wrong, you looked hot. It just seems like a lot for everyday."

"Yeah." She laughed. Kate always had a way of telling it like it was. "Hot, huh?"

Kate gave her an incredulous look. "You know you rock it."

She always felt polished, but that wasn't the same thing as hot. "How about we change the subject to something else?"

"Like what?"

Sutton rolled her eyes. "Like anything."

Kate laughed, turning Sutton's embarrassment into a completely different, not entirely bad, sort of discomfort. "You're cute."

"See? That's a downgrade from hot. This is why I asked to change the subject. I'm trying to quit while I'm ahead."

Another laugh. This time Sutton let herself enjoy it. "Okay, okay. Um, let's see. Oh, I know. How's your work thing?"

"Really? That's the best you could come up with?"

Kate shrugged. "Come on. It's not like I'm asking about your love life."

God. Just the thought of discussing her love life—or lack thereof—sent a shiver of dread through her. "When you put it that way."

"See? Everything is relative. So?"

"It's good. It's at Tulane. They're implementing a CRM that works with the university's student information system, but not the one in the law school. Or their admissions system."

"I don't mean to sound dumb, especially since I was there when you explained your job to Harper, but what's a CRM?"

Ugh. She lapsed into jargon when she was nervous or trying to prove a point. And Kate definitely made her nervous. "Not dumb at all. I forget how much IT shorthand I use without thinking. It can be annoying."

"Not annoying. Nerdy, sure, but that's okay."

She explained client relationship management tools, but then made a point of shifting gears to talk about the personal connection to Regina and how nice it was to work with a female in senior leadership. Kate asked questions that seemed more genuine interest than small talk and the next thing she knew, they were rolling into the relatively bustling metropolis of Houma.

They started at Target, where Kate needed a second bookshelf for Harper's new and improved bedroom. Sutton decided to pick up some new sheets for her room at Dad's and they debated the relative merits of laundry hampers versus baskets. The whole experience proved so casually domestic, it left Sutton more than a little unsettled. Next stop was an art supply shop, where Kate bought the glass rods she turned into beads, and a craft store for wire and several items Sutton would have no idea what to do with. The whole operation took less than two hours.

"Thank you again for carting me around," Kate said.

"My pleasure. Thanks for letting me tag along. And for having dinner with me." She pulled into the restaurant parking lot and found a spot.

On the walk in, she resisted the urge to rest her hand in the small of Kate's back. Pseudo date or no, it didn't feel like they were on that page. She did hold the door, though, and Kate didn't even tease her for it.

Kate ordered a glass of wine, so she did, too. She considered the blackened redfish, but when Kate went for an oyster po-boy, she opted for fried catfish instead. She'd just have some vegetables the next day to even things out.

Conversation meandered while they ate, with Sutton doing her best to keep things focused on Kate more than herself. She asked about Kate's role at the store—if she had hopes of buying it when her parents retired—and whether she'd ever consider pursuing her jewelry business full-time. They might not have been trying to impress each other, but it sure as hell felt like a date to Sutton. And if the way Kate eyed her over the rim of her glass was anything to go on, Kate was feeling it, too.

She talked Kate into sharing a slice of lemon icebox pie. It was Kate's favorite, after all. Even if the real motivation was extending the evening a little bit longer. When it came, Kate scooped up a forkful and held it up. Sutton did the same and they tapped their forks gently together. It was how they'd toasted things as teenagers.

Sutton brought the bite to her lips, loving the way sweet and tart played off each other on her tongue. With her bite, Kate closed her eyes and sighed, making Sutton smile. She always did know how to savor things.

"Thank you for today. I'm not sure if it's what you had in mind when you stopped by the other morning, but I've had a really good time."

A look passed through Kate's eyes she couldn't decipher. "Not exactly, but close. And I'm not going to lie, adult conversation with someone other than Bryce or my parents is nice."

"Is it hard to date?" If she could have kicked herself under the table, she would have. Where did that come from? "Sorry, that's probably overstepping."

Kate shook her head. "It's fine."

"You still don't have to answer." And if she wanted this to be a date, it was probably better Kate didn't.

"I think it was hard when Harper was little. Now, she's more than happy to spend the night with my parents or at a friend's house. I don't even need to pay babysitters. It's just…"

When Kate didn't continue, Sutton offered, "A lot of work?"

Kate laughed. "Exactly. Driving to Baton Rouge or, God, New Orleans to meet someone I might have absolutely zero chemistry with doesn't feel worth it."

She didn't know how she would have expected Kate to answer, but that wasn't it. "Yeah. I feel you."

"But you're in a huge city. There must be thousands of eligible lesbians within a stone's throw of where you live, where you work."

But none of them are you. The thought came to her unbidden and she shoved it away. Not because she knew better than to say such a thing to Kate, but also because it wasn't true. At least not entirely. "Not to be obnoxious, but I swear sometimes that makes it harder."

Kate's face made it clear she found that assertion beyond obnoxious. "Seriously?"

"And maybe I'm a bit of a workaholic." Which was definitely part of it.

"Okay, that I'll believe."

Sutton blew out a breath. "I'm not saying I'm proud of it."

"No? Big fancy career. Wasn't that the whole point?"

She frowned. "No. I mean, career, yes. But, I guess I'm not sure how I let things get so unbalanced."

Kate let out a sigh of her own. "I can't fault you for that because I'm guilty of it, too."

From where she sat, Kate was about ten thousand steps ahead of her in that department. "You seem to be doing okay. Job, parenting, side hustle."

"Yeah, but I've been reminded recently I don't have enough fun."

"Really? I thought I was the only one who needed that advice."

Kate finished her wine and tipped her head slightly. "Maybe we can remind each other."

Sutton's stomach flipped over. She still wasn't sure what kind of date this was—or even if it was one—but there was no mistaking Kate's flirtatious smile. Or the look in her eyes. Whether or not they ever got there, she knew in that moment Kate's thoughts were as much on kissing Sutton as Sutton's were on kissing her. Well, kissing and maybe more. A whole lot more.

Chapter Fifteen

Kate unbuckled her seat belt, but didn't move to get out of the car. The air between them seemed to crackle, the way it did right before a thunderstorm. All trapped energy with nowhere to go. Based on the way Sutton wouldn't make eye contact, she felt it, too.

Sutton cut the engine. "I'll give you a hand."

"You don't have to—"

"I want to. Let me." Sutton looked at her. "Please."

It was more reflex than not wanting help, or another minute with Sutton. "Okay."

They climbed out of the car and gathered her purchases from the back seat. At the door, Sutton took everything while she fished out her keys. Inside, she set down her purse and flipped on a light. "You can put everything on the coffee table and I'll sort it out later."

Sutton did, then stuffed her hands in her pockets. "It was cool to spend the day with you. I mean, don't get me wrong. I adore Harper. It's just—"

"This is different." She finished the sentence, hoping to convey not just that she understood, but agreed. "She needs time with other kids and I need time with other adults. It's good for everyone."

Sutton offered her a sheepish smile. "I'm glad to be one of those adults."

"Do you want a drink or something?" She wasn't sure why—or what, exactly, she expected to happen—but she wasn't ready for Sutton to leave.

Sutton didn't answer right away and Kate imagined her running through whether or not she should, what it might mean, and probably a dozen or so other questions.

"No pressure, but it's early still. And I don't have to be at work until ten tomorrow." Hard to tell if it was Sutton she was trying to convince, or herself.

"That sounds great."

"I have beer in the fridge and some chardonnay I think."

"Beer would be good." Sutton sounded about as nervous as Kate felt. That should have made her feel better, but it only intensified the weird energy and sense of anticipation she couldn't put a finger on.

"I'll be right back." She headed to the kitchen and opened the fridge. When she turned, a bottle in each hand, she bumped right into Sutton.

"Sorry, I—"

"I didn't realize you—"

Before either of them finished a sentence, Sutton's mouth was on hers. Hot and wanting and maybe a little desperate. Or maybe it was Sutton's hands in her hair that gave it the trace of desperation.

Sutton pulled her mouth away and dropped her hands. "I'm sorry. I shouldn't have done that."

Kate took a shaky breath. That answered that. She set the beers down. Instead of responding to Sutton's apology, Kate kissed her back. Nothing gentle or questioning or anything a kiss probably should have been, given their past. No, it was hard and hot and now had a trace of her own desperation thrown in. Desperation she hadn't realized she was holding, but that burned bright and suddenly threatened to consume her.

Sutton somehow turned them around so Kate's back was against the counter. The press of Sutton's body against hers was familiar but not. Bigger and stronger than she remembered and yet exactly what she wanted. Needed.

Sutton's mouth went to her neck, kisses interspersed with noises that went from Kate's ears right to her clit. She fisted one hand in Sutton's shirt and slid the other around the back of Sutton's neck, guiding their mouths back together. By the time Sutton pulled back a second time, they were both panting and Kate had a throb between her legs she hadn't felt in a long time. Sutton's gaze went from her eyes, to her mouth, then back. "This is probably a terrible idea."

"Yep." And yet the thought of stopping, of not going further, seemed next to impossible.

"Well?" Sutton asked.

She could end this before it got out of hand. Be the responsible adult she invariably was these days. But she didn't want to.

"To be fair, I've wanted to take you to bed from the moment I saw you in the hardware store."

Kate swallowed, desire and something else—something she didn't dare name—pulsing through her. "Is that so?"

Sutton made the tiniest nod. "I've mostly been able to keep it under control, but being here with you, the taste of you on my lips. I'm at the breaking point."

Suddenly, they weren't playing anymore. Or maybe they were and somehow Sutton had snared control of the game. Whatever it was, she was completely and utterly under Sutton's spell. "I think you should take me to bed."

Bryce's words echoed in her mind, the ones about there being something between Sutton and her that she couldn't ignore away. It might be a terrible idea and she might regret it come morning. But the thing was, some of the best things in her life had come from choices she might otherwise regret. It was a truth she never lost sight of and it gave the notion of regret a whole different meaning.

Sure, there were things she wouldn't—couldn't—risk. Things like the security of her family or Harper knowing how very much she was loved. But the only thing on the line here was her heart. It had taken batterings and bruisings she wasn't sure she'd survive and yet she'd come out happier and stronger than before. She had no idea what would happen with Sutton, or what the fallout might be, but she had no doubt she could handle it.

Sutton stared at her with unwavering intensity. "Even though it might be a terrible idea?"

There was every possibility she would regret whatever came next, but she knew that going in. Knew she could weather it. "I'm okay with that."

Sutton swallowed but didn't speak.

Kate licked her lips. If they were going to do this, it had to be mutual. "Are you?"

Sutton gave an almost imperceptible nod. "I never stopped wanting you, Kate."

She could take that a thousand different ways. And though it was her nature to press, to find out exactly what Sutton meant, she resisted. It wasn't her business. It wasn't her responsibility, either. "Then I think we should put that wanting to good use."

Without waiting for a reply, she grabbed Sutton's hand and dragged her in the direction of her bedroom. They didn't even make it to the hallway before Sutton was kissing her again. Tugging at the strap of her dress. Biting her shoulder. She went to work on Sutton's shirt, needing to feel her skin, taste it. They left a trail of discarded clothing in their wake, somehow making it to the bedroom but not even bothering with a light.

She worried Sutton might be overly gentle, bordering on reverent. That being together after so long might be weighed down with memories or significance or feelings. But the only feelings Sutton seemed interested in were the physical sort. Her hands roamed over Kate almost aggressively, her kisses raw with passion.

The back of Kate's legs brushed the mattress. The next thing she knew, she was flat on her back, with Sutton braced over her. She couldn't help but smile. "Smooth."

Sutton lifted a brow. "Are you complaining?"

She shook her head. "Oh, no. No complaints here."

"Good."

Sutton kissed her again. Her mouth, right below her ear, the spot where neck blended into shoulder. Kate arched against her, aroused and impatient. "Yes."

Sutton's mouth didn't stop, but her hands started to roam. Down Kate's torso and back up, over her breast. Sutton pinched her nipple through the lace of her bra. "Sit up for me."

"Huh?" The words registered, but her brain definitely wasn't firing on all cylinders. Sutton took her hand and tugged, pulling her into a sort of upright position. "Oh."

Without letting go of her hand, Sutton reached around and flicked the clasp of her bra. Despite Sutton's assertions about not dating much, it was clearly a practiced move. It managed to be hot and stir up a tiny flare of jealousy at the same time.

Before she had a chance to process that, Sutton's hand slid between her legs, stroking her through the silky fabric of her underwear. A sound escaped her throat—something between a whimper and a groan—equal parts pleasure and need. Sutton let out a hum of pleasure and continued the languid strokes that managed to feel like heaven and yet made her throb for more.

"Please. I need you."

Sutton shifted, getting to her knees. Without speaking, she yanked Kate's panties down her legs. Just as quick, she was back, braced over Kate and with her hand between Kate's legs. This time, when Sutton's fingers slid over her wetness, there was no barrier. Just skin against skin and pure, unfettered pleasure.

"I need you, too." Sutton plunged into her with none of the hesitation or adoration of their first times together. This was hungry, possessive, and raw. Kate wouldn't have said she needed that, but as Sutton filled her again and again, it was like finding the missing puzzle piece that made her feel whole.

She managed Sutton's name a few times, along with a few expletives. She wasn't celibate by any means, but this made her realize how little sex she was having these days. Either that or Sutton had gotten really, really good.

Maybe it was both.

Instead of analyzing the possibilities, she sank into how good it felt. She grabbed Sutton's shoulders, squeezed her fingers, and met her thrust for thrust. The orgasm rumbled through her, spreading through her entire body and making every muscle tremble. She screamed, loudly, before collapsing back on the bed. "Oh, my God."

Sutton shifted to the side, but remained propped on her elbow. "You're amazing. And gorgeous."

She blinked a few times with purpose, willing her eyes back into focus. "I think I'm supposed to say that."

Sutton chuckled. "You still can."

She'd been joking, but it only seemed fair to say it back now. Not like it wasn't true. "You're amazing. And gorgeous."

Sutton grinned. "Thank you."

"I mean it. I haven't been fucked that well in a long time." Maybe ever.

"I'm glad you approve." Sutton kissed the top of her head with what felt like almost casual affection.

A little piece of her wanted to ask about Sutton's relationships over the years. Sex, sure, but had Sutton fallen in love with other women? She hoped so, even as the prospect of Sutton with someone else gave her a pang of jealousy. But like Sutton's feelings on risk or regret, it wasn't her place to worry about it.

So instead of opening that door, she propped herself on her elbow and dropped a line of kisses down Sutton's arm. "Oh, I more than approve. It was crazy hot. Strong and confident suits you."

Something passed through Sutton's eyes that Kate couldn't decipher. But it disappeared as quickly as it arrived, leaving her to wonder if maybe she'd imagined it. She shifted, rolling and then bracing herself over Kate. "I've grown up, that's for sure."

Kate opened her legs wider and Sutton settled between them, pressing her pelvis deliciously against Kate's. "I like grown up you."

"I'm just getting started."

Sutton kissed her. It didn't have the edge anymore. Instead, it was—what? Intentional. Sutton kissed her with intention and purpose and maybe a touch of swagger. Could a kiss have swagger? She wouldn't have thought so, but this one definitely did.

Paired with the movement of Sutton's body, Kate's own responded, ratcheting up all over again. She ran her hands up Sutton's arms and down her chest, only to have Sutton stop kissing her. She encircled each of Kate's wrists with her fingers and slowly pinned them over Kate's head.

"Let me." Sutton looked at her with the same intensity as she had in the car when they got home. "Please."

Kate nodded, sensing a need she couldn't fully understand. In herself, but in Sutton, too. And then Sutton went about pleasing her.

Slowly. Methodically. With that trace of swagger. Under her hands, and her mouth, Kate came undone.

After coming the second time, she stretched, a long and languid extension of every muscle she could move. A purr escaped before she could stop it. She really, really should have sex more often.

"So, what does this mean?" Sutton looked at her with expectant eyes.

She couldn't decide whether to find it sweet or irritating that Sutton looked to her for answers. She settled on sweet, if for no other reason than it was less work. "I think we've fully made up?"

Sutton offered a slow smile. "Well, I should hope it means that at the very least."

Kate lifted a shoulder. Better to keep the conversation light. "I don't know. I hear angry sex has a lot to recommend it."

Sutton shook her head, eyes serious. "I don't do angry sex."

No, she wouldn't. She was too romantic for that, too sensitive. "I wasn't suggesting we try it."

That seemed to help her relax. She opened her mouth, but closed it, as though thinking better of whatever she'd been about to say.

"What?" Kate asked.

Sutton hesitated. She trailed a finger down Kate's arm, sending a shiver up her spine. "Don't answer that question."

"What question?"

"The one I asked a minute ago, about what this means."

"Oh." Please don't let her get all moody and sullen. Or, worse, mushy and sentimental.

"It wasn't fair and there's probably not really an answer anyway."

The thing with Sutton was she always tried to be fair. To a frustrating degree sometimes, but also something Kate had always loved about her. "You're probably right, on the second part at least. But I can say I'm glad you're here, and I don't regret what we did."

Sutton took a deep breath and for a second Kate worried she'd said exactly the wrong thing. But then Sutton nodded. "You always were good at pulling me back from the edge."

That was true, too. Sutton had always been the one with bigger, more intense feelings. Or, at least, she'd always been better at expressing them. Another thing Kate loved about her, even if it was part of the reason they'd imploded all those years ago. She let out a chuckle. She'd been teasing Sutton about being precious and here she was dissecting all the things she loved about her.

"What?"

She blew out a breath. "I think we might both be overthinking things now."

That earned her a big smile. "I can think of a few better things to do with our time."

"Is that so?"

Sutton nudged Kate onto her back and braced herself over her, settling one of her legs between Kate's thighs. "Yeah. Would you like a demonstration?"

"You know, I think I would."

Sutton leaned in for a kiss. She slid her thigh up and down, creating a hint of friction against Kate's clit. Despite being sated and spent a moment before, a thrum of arousal made its way through her. And she'd yet to have her turn. As much as she liked being pleased, she had every intention of touching—and tasting—every inch of Sutton before the night was through.

Maybe it wasn't the smartest idea to be doing this with Sutton, but it probably wasn't the worst, either. She'd been through the worst and come out the other side. This time, she knew better than to put her heart on the line. And damn it all to hell if it wasn't the best sex in as long as she could remember. She had no reason not to enjoy it. She knew what she was doing, after all, and she had no illusions about where it might go.

Chapter Sixteen

Sutton lingered just long enough the next morning to have a cup of coffee with Kate. She drove home slowly, enjoying the quiet streets and crepe myrtles in full bloom. After pulling into the driveway, she sat for a long minute, simply basking in the afterglow. She had plenty to think about and wonder about and worry about, but she could get to that later. Now, with the smell of Kate still clinging to her skin, she let every detail of the night play through her mind.

Kate's playful laugh. The sound she made when Sutton slipped inside her. How slipping inside her felt like coming home. The way Kate came—passion and joy, unbridled and completely in the moment.

All the things Sutton had spent the better part of a decade telling herself she didn't need and could live without. Things that would be a whole hell of a lot harder to live without after last night. She chuckled to herself. So much for not overthinking.

She found Dad in his easy chair, doing a crossword. He looked up and peered at her over the top of his reading glasses with a look that reminded her of the times he caught her breaking curfew.

"What?"

He cleared his throat and made a point of looking back at his puzzle. "I didn't say anything."

"You didn't have to. You gave me the look."

He gave her the look again. "What look?"

She pointed at him. "That one. It's stern and a little judgmental."

He shook his head and, again, looked down at his puzzle. "I have no idea what you're talking about. You're a grown woman and can come and go as you please. I'm not about to tell you what to do with your time. Or with whom."

Ha. "There. Just by saying that, it's clear you're thinking the opposite."

He set down his pencil and shoved his glasses to the top of his head. "I'm just saying you should be careful."

"What's that supposed to mean?"

"I have a pretty good idea of who you spent the night with. That's what I mean."

"Kate's a grown woman. With a child. It's not like we were up to anything nefarious."

He sniffed, though she couldn't tell if it was the content of her comeback or that she was talking back in the first place. "Kate's built a good life for herself and Harper. And you have your own life to think about. Forgetting that is playing with fire."

"Okay, Dad."

He set the crossword aside and got to his feet. Even in the midst of this conversation, she couldn't help but notice he seemed to have an easier time of it than before the first surgery. "I think some parts of the past are better left there."

Sutton blew out a breath. He wasn't wrong, at least when it came to some things. And he obviously had her best interests at heart. But in this case, regardless of what did or didn't happen with Kate, she disagreed. She needed last night—more than she'd known and certainly more than she would ever disclose to her father. "I'll be careful, okay? I don't want anyone to get hurt."

He sniffed again, clearly unconvinced, but didn't say more.

"Have you had breakfast?"

"Of course I've had breakfast. It's practically nine in the morning."

She lifted both hands in defense. "All right, all right. No need to get testy."

"I mean, if you were going to make pancakes or something, I could probably manage to choke down a couple."

She nodded. "I see. And if I said I was just going to have cereal?"

He lifted a shoulder and gave her a look that reminded her of Duke when he was denied something from the table. "You do whatever you want."

He might be a pain in her ass sometimes, but she really did love this man. "I think pancakes are a fantastic idea."

He returned to his easy chair and picked up the folded newspaper. "Put on another pot of coffee, too, will ya? I drank the first one."

She retreated to the kitchen and started with the coffee, as much for herself as him. She went through the motions on autopilot, mulling over his words in addition to her own questions about what it all meant and what she was supposed to do next.

She topped off his cup and filled one of her own, then set about making breakfast. She wasn't a fancy cook by any means, but she enjoyed the process. It made her feel centered and, if she was being honest, in control of her surroundings. Not that she specifically needed that after last night, but her brain and her body were still trying to make sense of it all. She called Dad to the table and snagged his crossword to take a pass at the ones he hadn't gotten yet, filling in a handful of answers.

Dad buttered his pancakes and poured cane syrup over them, gesturing at her with his fork. "You always get the science ones. And the pop culture. I miss having you around for that."

She filled in tsetse and shrugged. "I'm pretty sure I'm becoming less hip by the day, but I do what I can."

"You're plenty hip, at least compared to an old fart like me."

"Low bar, Dad. Low bar."

They ate in silence for a few minutes. She couldn't come up with the actor from the vampire movies, but she did manage to remember what cosine was. Her thoughts drifted back to Kate, so she hovered the pencil over a blank space and let herself enjoy for a second.

"I didn't mean to ruffle your feathers, you know."

She looked up, worried she'd missed something. "Huh?"

"When you got home. I didn't mean to give you a hard time." He shrugged and looked more uncomfortable than the first time his painkillers wore off after surgery. "It's the two of you. I don't know. Seems like borrowing trouble."

He was looking out for her. Hard to blame him, considering she'd already entertained all sorts of ways things with Kate could go badly. The problem was, she didn't care. Well, it wasn't that she didn't care. More like Kate was some kind of daredevil activity and she'd become an adrenaline junky. She knew she was risking her heart, but she couldn't seem to stop herself. "I know your heart's in the right place."

"Well, you've got your career and your life to get back to. You can't lose sight of that."

Sutton sighed. She wasn't looking to give up her career. But she also didn't find herself missing Atlanta. Like, at all. Not the closeness of her neighbors or the generic, perfectly manicured lawns of her development. Not the traffic or the noise or even the restaurants, and there were some spectacular restaurants. "I'm not quitting my job to become your live-in nurse. Don't worry."

He scowled, like he was worried about her doing exactly that. "I know you're being a smart-ass, but I'm serious. You didn't work as hard as you did to get where you are, only to blow it all away and come back here."

The vehemence in his voice gave her pause. She tried never to lose sight of how much he sacrificed for her to go to college, but it surprised her he still carried that level of feeling about it. "We both worked hard. I promise I don't take that for granted."

"Okay, then." He busied himself with another pancake.

She was pretty sure he had more on his mind, but he wasn't sharing and she wasn't in the mood to nudge him. They finished eating and he insisted on cleaning up, literally shooing her down the hall. Hugh, who'd been sound asleep on her bed, looked happy to see her, but generally unconcerned about her absence. It made her smile just how at home he felt in the house.

In the bathroom, she pulled off the clothes she'd worn the day before. Whether it was the rustling of fabric or exposing her skin, she couldn't be sure, but she'd swear she could smell Kate. She closed her eyes, shoved the worries and what-ifs aside, and let herself enjoy.

Not knowing if or when they'd spend the night together again made her reluctant to get in the shower, but she couldn't not. She climbed in with a sigh. After a quick shampoo, she grabbed a bar of soap and worked the lather over her body. It didn't take much for her imagination to conjure Kate's hands, her mouth, moving restlessly over her skin. God, she hoped they had occasion to spend the night together again.

Back in her room, she pulled on clean clothes and wondered if texting Kate would be thoughtful or clingy. She picked up her phone and realized she didn't need to. Kate had already texted her.

Thanks for last night. My body is still humming.

Sutton stared at the words. It was a compliment, to be sure, and a relief to know Kate found the experience even half as satisfying as she had. But something in the "thanks" gave her pause. It made the whole thing feel—what? Transactional, maybe. Like she'd helped Kate out of a jam or given her a thoughtful gift.

She shook her head. Overthinking. *Humming, huh? That sounds nice.* See? She could play it cool.

Nice doesn't even begin to describe it. Before Sutton could respond, a second message came through. *We okay?*

Crap. *Um. I thought so? You?*

I'm fucking fantastic, but it seems like the kind of thing you'd analyze to death so I thought I should ask.

Sutton laughed. Like a genuine LOL. Not only was Kate the best sex she ever had, Kate seemed to know her better than anyone. Still. *I'm okay.*

Not super convincing, pal.

She stared at the ceiling for a moment before constructing her reply. *Reflective but avoiding rabbit holes.* There. Lighthearted but honest.

I'm impressed, all things considered.

Sutton frowned and tried to think of a clever comeback.

I'm working today, but Harper is with Bryce. If you want to talk, we could grab coffee or something when I'm on break.

Wanting to see Kate warred with wanting to avoid those rabbit holes she'd alluded to. But it was probably better to talk and process and stuff and get it over with. *I'll swing by this afternoon after Dad's PT. Can I bring you something? Iced mocha?*

You trying to get me back into bed? ;)

The obvious answer was yes. With a side of I never stopped loving you. But she knew better than to go there—in general but especially in the afterglow of sex. *I'll let you know when my body stops humming.*

Instead of waiting to see how Kate would respond, she stuffed her phone in her pocket and headed to the living room. Dad had his shoes on and a baseball cap perched on his head. "There you are. I was about to send a search party to the bathroom."

"Ha ha." She swept a hand up and down. "Looking this good takes time, you know. It can't be rushed."

They used to have competitions over who could get ready faster, so that got a laugh out of him. "I'm so glad you took after me and not your mother."

She grabbed her keys and slung an arm around his shoulder. "You and me both."

❖

Sutton had texted an ETA, but seeing her stroll in holding a pair of iced mochas sent a ripple of pleasure through Kate. She told herself it was the promise of a much-needed mid-afternoon coffee, but it had everything to do with Sutton. She'd showered, of course, and her hair was somewhat tamed. It made Kate's fingers itch to mess it up. Again.

Sutton caught her eye and headed over, complete with that thousand-watt smile. She held out one of the drinks. "Hey."

She took the coffee and didn't wait to take a long sip. "I should warn you this is the sort of thing a girl could get used to."

"I can think of worse things."

"Seriously, though, it's such a treat. Thank you."

Sutton took a sip from her own cup and lifted a brow. "You sure are thanking me a lot today."

"Huh?"

Sutton smirked. "The first text you sent me this morning was thanking me for last night."

"Oh." She let the word drag, then lifted her cup. "Well, this is good, but it has nothing on last night."

"That's a relief."

Was Sutton honestly worried there was any comparison? Or was she teasing back? She was pretty sure it was the latter, but not certain. She hated feeling so rusty when it came to flirting, or to reading Sutton's thoughts. "Let me call Owen and we can go sit outside."

"No rush." Sutton shrugged and took another sip of her drink. "I technically have all day."

Less than a minute after paging him, Owen appeared. She loved his promptness almost as much as she loved his head for math and affable personality. "Can you cover the front while I go on break?"

"All righty." He tipped his hat slightly.

"Thank you. I'll be back in thirty."

She led Sutton through the store, into the stock room, and out the back door. It made her think of all the times they did that as teenagers. Sutton would stay after school to do tutoring or go home for chores, then show up at the store in time for Kate to take her break. She'd only get fifteen minutes because her shifts were short on school nights, but they'd make the most of them—talking and kissing and dreaming about the future.

"I didn't know if the picnic table would still be here." Sutton regarded it with wonder, clearly on a similar trip down memory lane.

"Oh, it's as much a fixture as the awning out front, at least for those of us who work here."

"I love that."

"Though I'm not sure it sees much making out these days."

Sutton smiled. "Well, that's a damn shame."

"Agreed." Kate hopped up on the surface, feet on one of the benches, just like she used to. Sutton sat, straddling the bench, just like she always did. Part of her wanted Sutton to scoot closer, to run a hand up her leg and rest her head on Kate's thigh, but that would sort of defeat the purpose of getting together to talk.

"So, how are you?" Sutton looked vaguely uncomfortable, a stark contrast to the flirty and confident energy a few minutes before.

"I'm good. More than good. How are you?"

Sutton nodded. "Same."

"No regrets?" She hated having to ask, but if Sutton was regretting what happened, best to get it out in the open.

Sutton, who'd been unduly interested in the lid of her coffee, looked up. The intensity in her eyes was enough to make Kate's breath catch. "I could never regret being with you."

Relief came first, followed by a different sort of worry. "Okay, good."

"You?" Sutton looked like she maybe didn't want the answer. "Do you regret what happened?"

"Absolutely not. I might have been caught up in the moment, but I knew exactly what I, what we, were doing."

Sutton nodded, her own relief palpable. "Yeah. Same. For sure."

"And it was good." Kate closed her eyes and let a couple of choice images dance through her mind. "Like, really good."

"But?"

"But nothing. Sex can be an end unto itself. Amazing sex is like a little gift from the universe. It's good for the body and the soul."

Sutton frowned.

"That's not a bad thing."

"No, you're totally right." Sutton's words didn't match her expression.

"I just don't think either of us is in a position for it to be anything more than that." Even if a few of her daydreams begged to differ.

"I agree."

"If you agree, why are you frowning?"

Sutton rolled her eyes. "Because my brain can't resist going down a thousand different paths. You know this. You pretty much cited it in your invitation to talk."

Kate couldn't help but smile. Sutton's brain could be a source of endless fascination, as well as endless frustration. She had this constant need to think—and worry—ten steps ahead, making it virtually impossible to let go and be in the moment. At the same time, her ability to spin out possibilities made Sutton a dreamer as much as a worrier. As someone with the tendency to be overly concrete, rooted in the moment, Kate often relied on Sutton for that, to think about what might be and not just what was.

Sutton put a hand on her knee. "I'm trying, though. I promise. I know it doesn't make sense to get bogged down in the what-ifs. Especially now."

"Okay, good. I had fun. I know you're only around for a couple of months, but I'd like to keep having fun, too, if you're interested." She knew it was the right thing to say even if a tiny part of her longed for that girl who once made her think anything was possible.

"If that's on the table, I'm interested." Gone was Sutton's frown. In it's place, a wicked grin that had the potential to get Kate into all sorts of trouble.

As tempting as it might be to simply go with it, she needed to lay out the rest. "I don't want it to mess things up. I'm glad we're friends again and I'd like to keep it that way."

Sutton took a deep breath and nodded. "I agree. I definitely don't want to lose that."

"So, friends with benefits?" It felt so weird to say, but that's pretty much what they were agreeing to.

The phrase seemed to land funny with Sutton, too. "I guess?"

She shrugged. "Well, it sounds better than fuck buddy."

Sutton choked on her coffee. "Could you maybe warn me when you're going to say something like that?"

It broke the tension, if nothing else. "Sorry."

"You're not. I can tell."

It was strangely exciting that Sutton could still read her so well. "A little bit sorry."

"Likely story." Sutton took a longer sip of her coffee, then cleared her throat. "Okay. Friends with benefits."

She had this odd sensation they should be shaking on it. Instead, she nodded and made a point of looking Sutton in the eye. "Friends with benefits."

Sutton nodded, too, but then frowned. "But you have to let me take you on a real date at least."

Kate laughed. "Real date? I'm not sure we've ever been on a real date."

Sutton covered her mouth and seemed genuinely horrified by the idea. "We haven't, have we?"

"It's not like a couple of teenagers in a tiny town could do much in the way of real dates."

Sutton shook her head. "I'm still sad I didn't get to take you to prom."

Most of their friends, and even a lot of the adults in their lives, had known they were together and were supportive. Or at least accepting. A lot better than other teenagers fared, especially a decade ago. But going to prom as a couple had seemed a step too far, so they'd done the group thing for Sutton's senior prom and, well, they never made it to Kate's. Sutton had broken up with her and she was five months pregnant. She shook her head. "It's probably for the best."

"Will you let me make it up to you now?"

The idea of Sutton making things up to her sent an uncomfortable flutter through her chest. "What do you mean?"

"I mean, let's do something nice. A night in New Orleans, maybe?"

When was the last time she'd had a fancy date? Um, never. At least not in the way Sutton was talking. It was the sort of thing people with money did or, maybe with something special to celebrate. Neither fit the bill of her life.

"Too much?" Sutton regarded her with concern.

"No. Just weird."

Sutton lifted a brow. "Weirder than saying fuck buddies?"

Chapter Seventeen

Sutton's alarm woke her out of a sound sleep. Unlike the morning of Dad's first surgery, she didn't have the nerves jangling around—over the surgery or the inevitability of seeing Kate. She knew what to expect, on both fronts, and the outcomes had exceeded her expectations.

They piled into her car and started the drive to New Orleans, picking up the interstate as the sun rose. Dad grumbled about being prohibited from having even a single cup of coffee and Sutton did her best not to taunt him with her travel mug. With less apprehension about how the day would unfold, she let herself enjoy the scenery: sugarcane fields giving way to swamps, the cypress trees jutting from the water, dripping with Spanish moss.

She wouldn't go to campus today, but she had her laptop to make productive use of her time in the waiting room. At the hospital, they went through the intake process and Dad got wheeled off. She was grateful he got to be first on the schedule. It meant things ran on time, but also that he wouldn't have much time to doomsday before getting put under.

She situated herself in one of the uncomfortable chairs and got to work. Well, sort of work. She managed to make her way through her inbox before getting sidetracked by planning her date with Kate.

She shouldn't go overboard, but it was hard not to. In part it was her own unfortunate tendency not to plan fun things. Without a steady girlfriend, she just couldn't drum up the enthusiasm for even the most basic of getaways. Not that Kate counted as a girlfriend, but it was the closest she'd come in a while.

Kate still had to confirm the date, but she went ahead and booked a suite at the Crowne Plaza on Canal. Since she could use the obscene amount of reward points she'd accumulated with all her work travel in the last few years, she could assure Kate it cost practically nothing and she'd be telling the truth. With that justification, she made dinner reservations at a nouveau Cajun restaurant she'd seen written up in *Food and Wine* and did some research on romantic spots for pre- and post-supper cocktails.

She imagined Kate sitting next to her in a plush booth in some dimly lit bar. Candles on the tables and a jazz trio turning out one sultry number after another. Kate's hand would rest on her arm just so, inviting Sutton's hand to slip under the hem of her dress. Kate would lean in and her perfume would tease Sutton's senses, make her want to find out where exactly she'd sprayed it. She'd kiss Kate's neck and Kate would whisper in her ear about going back to the room.

"Ms. Guidry?"

Sutton's head jerked at the sound of her name. "Huh? Yes?"

It was Dr. Braverman. Oh, God. Did something go wrong?

"I didn't mean to startle you. I wanted to let you know your father is in recovery."

Already? How was that possible? What time was it? "Sorry. I just wasn't expecting you. I must have lost track of time."

Dr. Braverman offered her a kind smile. "Always a good thing when playing the waiting game. He came through like a champ. Should be a similar recovery to last time. The nurse will let you know when you can see him."

She got up to shake Dr. Braverman's hand. "Thank you so much. You've made this whole process so much less stressful than it could have been."

"It's my pleasure. I'll see you both when I do rounds this afternoon, I imagine. I don't see any reason we'll keep him more than overnight."

She wanted to ask questions, but knew another patient was probably prepped and waiting. "Absolutely. Thank you again."

She went on her way and Sutton checked her watch. The surgery hadn't gone fast. She'd spent the better part of three hours planning a single date. She chuckled at herself and chalked it up to getting sucked into a good distraction. And since no one but her needed to know, she could leave it at that.

❖

Kate studied the schedule hanging in the break room. She'd actually scheduled herself to work extra hours while Harper was away, but planned Friday off for herself. So all she'd need to do was get someone to cover her Thursday shift, since she'd told Sutton that would be easier than Saturday.

It was cowardly, maybe, but she started with Owen. Unfortunately, he was already working Thursday and had a family thing Saturday. That left Mama and Daddy, since no one else on staff could handle the closing and deposit duties. Ugh.

"Well, that's quite a puss you're wearing. What's wrong?" Mama's voice came from behind her.

She laughed. Speak of the devil. "I'm not wearing a puss."

"Could have fooled me." Mama's hands went to her hips. She did not appreciate being lied to, even in the context of making faces. Or maybe it was especially in that context.

"I was thinking about if I could get a day off, but it's kind of short notice." The truth, if not the whole truth.

"I can do it."

The fact that she offered without any details made Kate's heart swell with both affection and a trace of guilt. "Would you? I was thinking Thursday, but it could also be Saturday. I'm flexible."

"Hmm. Thursday would be better. The Catholic Daughter bake sale is Sunday and I have to make three cakes for it."

Of course she did. "Thursday would be perfect."

"Please tell me you're doing something indulgent for yourself."

Mama had made the case for that when she first confirmed Harper's camping trip. She'd waved off the idea at the time, mostly because she figured she'd wind up working in her studio instead of at the store. "I am."

Mama clapped her hands together, clearly delighted. "I love it. What are you doing? Spa day?"

"When have I ever done a spa day?" Pretty much never.

Mama shrugged. "You could. At least hair and nails. That place in Thibodaux is doing massages now."

It didn't sound terrible, but it so wasn't her speed. "Not this time."

"Well, what then?"

She'd sort of backed herself into a corner. But even if she didn't tell her mama everything, she made a point of not lying. "Sutton asked me to spend the day in New Orleans with her."

"Sutton? Is something wrong with Albin? I thought his second surgery was this week. Does he have to go back to the hospital?"

"No, no. He's fine. It's just, we've been hanging out a little and she asked if I wanted to go have a fun day."

Mama narrowed her eyes. The same look she gave Kate when she was a teenager trying to get away with something. The one she'd honed and now gave Harper for the same reason. "A fun day? You two have been spending an awful lot of time together. What's going on, Kate? Are you falling for her again?"

Of course not. I'm just sleeping with her. Not exactly the sort of thing a mother wanted to hear. "It's not like that."

"Really? What is it like, then?"

"We're trying to be friends." With benefits.

"I don't understand why you'd do that. What are you trying to prove? That you can?"

It was funny. It started out that way, proving she wasn't pining, or holding a grudge. Now, it just felt—what? Nice. It felt nice. Even without the sex, spending time with Sutton reminded her of all the reasons they'd been best friends in addition to being girlfriends. It had been so hard to lose both. If she could get the friend part back, she'd take it, even when Sutton went back to her life in Atlanta. "We're friends, Mama. We were friends first and we're trying to be that again."

She didn't look convinced. "And you don't think that line is going to get blurred?"

If Mama had any idea how much it already had, she'd be squawking like an angry crow. "I know what I'm doing. Trust me." Mama let out a sigh and put a hand on each of Kate's shoulders. "I do trust you. I trust you to take care of yourself and your family where it matters most. But I think you might be underestimating the potential to get bruised along the way."

When Sutton left—both to go to school in the first place and then when she said she'd never come back—Mama had been the shoulder she cried on pretty much every day for months. In addition to being her cheerleader and her biggest champion, she'd been Kate's role model. Her ability to do the right thing, to love even when it hurt, was something she tried to emulate in her life. Not to mention something she worked to instill in Harper. She wondered if her mother had any idea how profound that impact was. "I might get a little bruised, but life isn't for sitting on the sidelines, right?"

Mama tucked her tongue in her cheek and nodded. She'd used the saying with Kate almost from the time she was old enough to walk. "Mm-hmm."

"You'll still cover for me?"

"Honey, I wouldn't take that back just because I don't approve of what you're doing with the day off."

Kate frowned. "So, you don't approve."

Mama patted her cheek and smiled. "I don't approve, but I don't disapprove."

Kate blew out a breath. "I'll take it."

Day off secured, she texted Sutton and got to work, reconfiguring the roofing aisle to accommodate a new line of eco-friendly products. After, she updated inventory and placed a few orders, then covered the registers so Cliff could go to the dentist. The hours flew by so much that when Bryce stopped in on his way home from work, she had to double check her watch.

Bryce laughed. "Don't be like Dad. It's six, I promise."

"No complaints here." She was looking forward to picking Harper up from Macy's and having a low-key night at home.

"You and H want to come over for supper? I was thinking I might grill."

"Aren't you supposed to have a date tonight?" They'd not hung out much in the last couple of weeks, mostly because things were going so great with Jasmine.

He shook his head. "Nah."

Something in his tone caught her. "Nah, you don't have plans or nah, something is up?"

"The second."

"Aw, buddy. I'm sorry. What happened?"

Another head shake. "I don't want to talk about it."

Knowing he'd probably change his mind eventually made it easier not to push now. "Okay. No pressure. You know I'm here, right?"

"Yeah. Thanks. So, supper?"

"Absolutely."

That seemed to perk him up a little. "Don't say yes because you feel sorry for me."

"I'm saying yes so I don't have to cook."

That got a smile. "Good enough for me."

"Can we bring anything?"

He made a face. "Dessert?"

"Always." She considered their options, then decided to get a feel for how bad the Jasmine situation was. "Is it a snag the ice cream from the freezer kind of day or a stop at the bakery for the craziest thing in the case kind of day?"

He closed his eyes and sighed. "The second."

"You got it. I'll grab a six-pack, too."

"You're the best."

She winked. "I know."

He rolled his eyes. "And so humble."

"That's me. Oh, not to change the subject, but do you think Frances could stay with you next Thursday night?"

"Yes?" The word and the tone didn't match.

"Are you not sure or surprised?"

"I'm sensing a theme today. The second."

"Harper is going to be at camp, so I'm going to take advantage and spend the night away."

"You're going away?" Bryce raised a brow like they were discussing some high-level intrigue. "Do tell."

It was Kate's turn to roll her eyes. "Go easy on me. I already got the third degree from Daddy the other day and the 'are you sure you know what you're doing' from Mama today."

Bryce laughed at the description, probably because he'd been on the receiving end of both plenty of times himself. "Give me the details and I promise I won't give you more of either."

"I don't want to make this all about me if you're having a bad day."

"Don't do that. That's not how it works and you know it."

She wanted to process with someone who understood and he was her go-to. Of course, that meant she was going to have to tell him about hooking up with Sutton in the first place. She looked around to make sure they were alone and took a deep breath, wanting to get as much out as possible before he interrupted. "After Sutton and I had dinner the other night, we went back to my place and had sex. And yes, it was mind-blowing. We talked about it the next day and agreed to keep things light, but she asked if I would go on a real date with her, which is going to be a night in New Orleans."

The play of emotions across Bryce's face was almost comical. His mouth opened and closed like a fish and she was pretty sure he couldn't decide between a tawdry joke and genuine concern. "I…"

When he didn't continue, she smirked. "I don't leave you speechless very often."

He shook his head. "Go back to the beginning. Tell me more than you think you should."

She blew out a breath. "It was that night—"

Before she got any further, Mama strolled up from the back. "Well, this is a pleasant surprise."

Kate bit her lip and shrugged. "I'm going to go close up. I'll catch you up later. Promise."

He gave her a look but had the decency not to press. She knew better than to think she was off the hook, but she'd prefer to have this conversation where a random customer—or one of her parents—couldn't wander into earshot.

CHAPTER EIGHTEEN

K ate set a plate of French toast in front of Harper before snagging her own and the bottle of syrup from the fridge. "On a scale of one to ten, how excited are you?"

"Mmm…" Harper looked at the ceiling. "Twelve."

She smiled. "Good. And you're not nervous at all?"

Harper gave her a look of exasperation. "I'm not a baby. I have sleepovers all the time."

"I know." She resisted the urge to ruffle Harper's hair, if for no other reason it would mess up the matching French braids Harper had requested for her camp hair.

"What about you? Are you nervous? Are you going to miss me?" Harper squirted syrup onto her toast and dug in.

"Of course I'm going to miss you. You're my favorite."

"Are you going to be so bored?" she asked around a mouthful of food.

Kate had gone back and forth about telling Harper about her plans with Sutton. It was one thing to omit, but she did her best not to lie. "I made some fun plans of my own so I wouldn't be too bored or too lonely."

Harper seemed only mildly interested. "What'cha doing?"

"Sutton asked if I wanted to go to New Orleans with her."

That got Harper's attention. She set down her fork and looked at Kate with something resembling betrayal. "You're going to New Orleans with Sutton? I want to go."

"You're going to camp."

Harper scowled. "But why do you have to go when I'm gone?"

She'd been looking forward to the four-day adventure with her Girl Scout troop for months, so no way was Kate going to let her back out now. "Because we're going to do grown-up things that you wouldn't find fun."

Which wasn't a lie. Even if Harper didn't need to know what those things were.

She thought Harper might pout or have bit of a tantrum, but she got quiet. Almost eerily quiet. When she kept her head down, Kate put a finger under her chin and tipped her face up. Harper let out a sniff, and a pair of matching tears rolled down her cheeks. Unlike the crocodile tears she'd gotten alarmingly good at turning on at the drop of a hat, these were real and they tore at Kate's heart.

"Oh, baby, it's okay." She got up from the table and wrapped her arms around Harper.

"It's not fair."

Kate returned to her seat. She might feel like a heel, but she knew better than to let Harper see that. "It's not fair that I have fun while you're off having fun?"

"But you're going to New Orleans. We never go to New Orleans. And you're going with Sutton."

It was hard to tell whether Harper was struggling more with the New Orleans part or the Sutton part. "You got to see Sutton a few days ago. And we'll all do something fun when you get back."

"Not New Orleans." Harper grumbled the words more than she spoke them.

"I know you're disappointed, but no pouting. You're about to go on a very big, very fun trip."

Harper's face fell, but she said, "I know."

"That's better. Now finish up your breakfast so we can get going."

"Yes, ma'am."

She spent the rest of breakfast wondering if she'd made the right decision. But, much like letting Harper become friends with Sutton in the first place, she wanted Harper to understand that life came with ups, downs, and plenty of disappointments. Not so Harper wouldn't be hopeful or dream big, but so she wouldn't give up the first time she fell on her face. She reminded herself of that while she did the dishes and Harper brushed her teeth and, by the time they were packing the car, she felt better.

It took three trips to get all of Harper's supplies loaded into the back of the car. "That sure is a lot of stuff."

Harper lifted a shoulder. "It's just what was on the list."

What was it about her little girl putting on a brave face that melted her heart more than any meltdown possibly could? "Well, I think you have enough sunscreen and s'mores supplies for a month in the woods."

That got her a half smile, but nothing more. She double-checked they had everything, then sent Harper back inside to use the bathroom and tell Frances good-bye. She used the moment alone to convince herself not to feel guilty and to check her phone. Of course she had a text from Sutton waiting for her.

Good luck with drop off. Tell Harper to eat all the s'mores for me.

In spite of herself, she smiled. *I will. But I made the (bad?) decision of telling her about our plans and I think it's put a damper on the excitement for camp.*

Aw. That makes me so sad.

Kate shook her head, but continued to smile. *Sucker. You didn't even see the tears.*

Sutton's reply was immediate. *We should do a day in NOLA the three of us.*

Something about that being Sutton's response—instead of questioning why she told Harper in the first place—made her heart do this flippy thing in her chest. *You don't have to say that.*

I'm serious, though. Can we? Can you tell her now to cheer her up?

As much as she didn't want to be the mom who caved every time her kid was disappointed, she also didn't want to be the one who'd let her kid head off to camp with an unnecessary cloud hanging over her head. And Harper didn't whine or pout about much. *You're sweet. I will and it will make her day.*

Sutton replied with several variations on the happy face and a thumbs up, then *I'm not overstepping, am I?*

On one hand, she absolutely was. Harper was getting far more attached to Sutton than she should probably allow. But at the same time, it sort of felt like that ship had sailed. Spending a day together wasn't going to be the make or break point in how sad Harper would be when Sutton went back to Atlanta. And she'd already said yes. *All good.*

Harper emerged from the house, pulling the door behind her. She walked down the steps slowly, not trudging, but close.

"You all set?"

Harper nodded. "Yes, ma'am."

Kate bit her lip and tried not to smile. Harper wasn't quite at the age where she'd mastered passive-aggressive, but she could lay on the forlorn obedient child routine with razor precision. "Door locked?"

"Yes."

"Sutton texted to say she hopes you have a good time."

Harper nodded, but didn't say anything.

"I may have mentioned how disappointed you were to be missing the chance to go to New Orleans with us."

"I understand. You need adult time. And you can't have that when I'm around." When Harper looked up, the tears were gone. The pout was, too. In their place, far more wisdom than any nine-year-old should have.

"That's true. But there's no reason we can't go for a day after you get back and before school starts."

"Really?" Hope replaced dejection immediately. God, she loved how resilient kids were. "And Sutton can come, too?"

She smiled. "Well, it was her idea, so it would be rude not to invite her."

And just like that, the switch flipped. Harper's typical buoyant demeanor returned and she spent the entire drive to Belle River chatting alternately about camp and spending the day with Sutton. It might come at a price later, but she didn't doubt she'd done the right thing.

They pulled into Camp Good Friends just as the troop leader and a couple of Harper's friends arrived. There were hugs and hellos, along with some debate about whether wildlife tracking or foraging was going to be more fun. Kate listened and smiled, mostly out of relief she'd be in charge of neither.

After getting all—all—of Harper's things situated in the cabin she'd be sharing with five other members of her troop and a chaperone, she hugged Harper good-bye and started home. As she drove, she thought back to last year's drop-off. She'd held it together until getting in the car, but spent the entire ride sniffling and feeling sorry for herself. It had been Harper's first time spending more than one night away from home, not to mention more than a few minutes away.

This time, she fully expected the pang of they grow up so fast and didn't even try to talk herself out of it. She had no plans to have another child, especially as a single parent, but a part of her missed those first few years. And it made her sad to think Harper would never have a sibling.

When the waterworks started, she laughed at herself instead of wallowing in self-pity. A baby was the absolute last thing in the world she should be thinking about right now. For one thing, her daughter was almost ten. On top of that, she had a very rare few days to herself and a grownup, no strings attached weekend on the horizon. That was where her focus should be.

And because that was how her mind worked, she made it that way.

❖

"You look like you're in the middle of a very pleasant daydream."

The sound of Regina's voice pulled Sutton back to the present—to Regina and Clara's beautifully appointed living room, to the impossibly delicious gin cocktail Clara had served, and to the fact she was supposed to be walking that fine line between socializing and networking. Yet she'd been left alone for thirty seconds and couldn't stop her thoughts from drifting to Kate. "Sorry."

Regina laughed. "Don't apologize. I'm the one who left you alone in the first place."

She had, technically. Clara called for help from the kitchen, leaving Sutton to her own devices. But again, for like thirty seconds. "It wasn't very long."

Regina waved a hand, clearly still finding the apology unnecessary. "May I ask what delightful path your mind wandered down? You looked awfully happy, so I'm guessing it's not my implementation."

A wink reinforced Regina was teasing. Sutton relaxed. "I was thinking about how nice it's been to be home."

Clara returned to the room, cocktail in hand. "Sorry about running off like that. I cook just often enough to be more ambitious than I should when there's company."

Sutton chuckled at the description. "I hope you didn't go to too much trouble."

"Trouble is relative." Clara lifted a shoulder in a careless way that seemed out of step with her role as a provost, a fact that made Sutton smile. "So, what are we talking about?"

Clara sat next to Regina on the couch and Regina draped an arm around her shoulders. "Sutton is happy to be home."

"Oh, that's lovely." Something about the statement made Clara's South Carolina drawl all the more pronounced.

"Seems like it might be more pleasant surprise than forgone conclusion," Regina said.

That was one way of putting it. As restless as she'd started to feel in Atlanta, she hadn't arrived home with any confidence it would be the answer. Even without the unknowns of seeing Kate and what that might stir up. "Something like that."

"How long have you been away?" Clara asked.

She blew out a breath. "A decade."

Clara scoffed. "You barely seem old enough for that to be possible."

"I'm going to take that as a compliment, given I did an implementation for you almost four years ago."

"Was it really that long?" Clara sipped her drink and stared at the ceiling. "My, how time flies."

She was probably close to half Regina and Clara's age, but the sentiment resonated. The more time she spent in Louisiana, the more it felt like she'd wasted a third of her life. "It does."

Clara shifted her gaze to Sutton. "If it's not too personal, what made you leave in the first place? I've come to think most of us who do are either running to something, or running from something."

"You don't have to answer that if you don't want to. Clara doesn't think of you as a colleague anymore, but I know you may think of one or both of us that way." Regina gave Clara's knee a squeeze as she spoke. A subtle gesture, but it made Clara smile and tip her head slightly.

Not only did Sutton notice it, but it filled her with a profound longing for that kind of intimacy with a partner. She sighed. She could take the out Regina was offering, but she found herself drawn to both women, to the prospect they might become friends. And friendship required vulnerability. "I left for school, somewhat reluctantly I confess. After my first semester away, the girlfriend who I thought was the love of my life and I broke up."

Regina shook her head and Clara's face softened into something that felt almost maternal. "You poor thing," Clara said.

"I did not take it well, so I definitely fall into the running from category."

Clara set down her drink. "What happened?"

She'd never told the story to anyone. The rest of her freshman year, she retreated into herself, focusing on her studies. Then she had her year of sleeping around, trying to get Kate out of her system. She certainly never confided to any of those girls. And even though she dated and had made friends, she always glossed over what had happened—more her own unwillingness to talk about it than any lack of interest or trustworthiness on the part of anyone else. But for some reason, that no longer felt like the case. She hoped her new friends didn't regret asking. "She got lonely and slept with someone else. Unfortunately, the someone else was a guy and she got pregnant."

"Oh." Clara came forward in her chair, leaning on her crossed legs. "Oh, no."

"At eighteen, that felt pretty impossible to forgive."

Clara shook her head slowly, riveted. "Wow. So, what's changed? Has she moved away? Do you just not feel anything for her anymore?"

As she so often did, she thought back to the anguish of that day, of those first few weeks after she'd learned about the baby. Harper. The memory remained, but the feelings, the ones she'd been holding on to for so long, had softened. "She's still in town. I was nervous to see her, but it went better than I thought it might. We, well, I guess you could say we made up."

Regina, who'd stayed quiet during most of this exchange, leaned forward. "Did you make up or did you," she paused, "make up?"

The shift in her tone made the meaning of the question clear. But acknowledging that, much less answering, felt like a step too far. "We agreed to be friends again."

For all her lip service to respecting privacy and professional boundaries, Regina was clearly not impressed with that answer. "Friends with benefits?"

Hearing the dean of a prestigious law school say "friends with benefits," without losing it, would have been a tall order on the best of days. On the tails of her very real, very recent conversation with Kate—complete with that exact phrase—she didn't stand a chance. She choked and fell into a coughing fit so loud and so graceless it bordered on mortifying.

Clara poured her a glass of water from a pitcher on the nearby table. Regina regarded her with amusement. Neither helped—the coughing or the embarrassment. When she was finally able to take a breath, she attempted a "sorry," but it came out as more of a wheeze than a word. She took a few deep breaths and tried again. "Sorry."

"No, no. We're sorry." Clara elbowed her wife. "Aren't we, Regina?"

Regina nodded. "Yes. Sorry."

A shrill beeping came from the kitchen. It sounded more like a smoke alarm than an oven timer. Clara winced. "Shit."

Sutton lifted a hand. "I'm going to go with saved by the bell."

Clara hustled off to the kitchen and a laughing Regina followed her. Sutton remained in the living room, in part because she believed in the notion of too many cooks. She also could use a hot minute to collect herself. The beeping stopped and Regina appeared in the doorway. "If you're not looking for the escape hatch yet, supper is served."

She took a deep breath that, honest to God, made her ribs ache. "I'm great."

Despite the hiccups along the way, Clara's pork tenderloin and roasted sweet potatoes were spectacular. Sutton apologized again for her dramatic reaction and, so there would be no chance of hard feelings, explained why she reacted the way she did. Up to and including her negotiation with Kate about finding the notion of friends with benefits more palatable than fuck buddies. Clara and Regina seemed a mixture of amused and empathetic—to her past heartache as well as her current plight. She'd take both over pity or judgment any day.

She attempted to change the subject with questions about how the two of them met. Whether they always shared the hijinks of the early years of their relationship with casual acquaintances or were indulging her after her own disclosures, she couldn't know. But by the time she left their house at a quarter of ten, her stomach hurt from laughing and she was pretty certain she had a pair of friends for life.

CHAPTER NINETEEN

Sutton pulled into Kate's driveway. It felt strange not to have Harper bounding down the front steps to greet her, but Kate appeared on the front porch before she even got out of the car, so she wasn't about to complain.

Kate started her way, purse over one shoulder and a small duffel bag over the other. Sutton popped her trunk and took the bag. "Is that everything?"

"Fancy tonight and casual tomorrow, right?"

She smiled at the description. "Yep."

"Then yes, that's everything."

She set the bag next to hers and followed Kate to the passenger door. She placed her hand on the handle, but pulled it away without opening it. "So, you put yourself completely in my hands?"

Kate folded her arms and shot her a look of exasperation. "I already said yes."

She lifted a finger. "No, you said you'd let me be in charge of planning. Putting yourself in my hands is different."

Kate's eyes narrowed. "What? You planning to tie me up or something?"

The thought of Kate literally tied up, for Sutton to touch and tease and please as long as she wanted, sent a lightning bolt of desire through her. "I mean, that does have a certain appeal, but it's not what I meant."

"So, what did you mean?"

She hesitated, wanting to be honest but also not wanting to make things that weren't things, things. "I mean, I want you to relax and trust me and have a good time. I may have gone a little overboard, but that was my choice."

Kate frowned. "This is about money, isn't it?"

As much as she didn't want to have this conversation, she'd rather get it over and done before they left instead of letting it get in the way later. "Maybe a little. I don't want you to pay for anything and I don't want you to be weird about it."

"I make decent money, Sutton. I don't need you taking care of me."

Sutton closed her eyes, hoping she wasn't ruining their weekend before it started. "I know you don't. But I'm paid almost stupidly well for what I do and I don't spend it on fun stuff very often. You're inspiring me to let loose and I'm hoping you'll indulge me in that."

Kate let out a sigh that might have also been a growl. "Fine."

"And you won't argue with me?"

Kate's scowl became a smirk. "Well, I can't promise not to argue with you at all."

That broke the tension. "Since that's probably as good as I'm going to get, I'll take it."

She opened the door and held it while Kate got herself situated, then rounded the hood and settled into the driver's seat. She pulled onto the road, not even bothering with GPS. Between Dad's surgeries and commuting to Loyola the last few weeks, she'd made the drive to New Orleans more in the last month that probably the entirety of her childhood.

"Are you going to tell me what you have planned?"

"Not all that much, really. I made dinner reservations for tonight, thought we could get a swanky cocktail somewhere. I wanted there to be time for anything you want to do. Speaking of, is there anything you want to do?"

Kate chuckled, clearly appeased. "I know it's going to be sweltering, but I'd love to walk around some. I get to New Orleans so rarely, I almost feel like a tourist."

"That can definitely be arranged. Do I get to talk you into one of those cheesy caricature drawings of us?" It was blurring the line of friends versus couple, but she couldn't resist asking.

Kate wrinkled her nose. "Maybe."

Sutton grinned, happier than the reply warranted. "Again, I'll take it."

The drive passed quickly, with Kate talking about Harper's camp and Sutton telling stories about her evening with Clara and Regina. At the hotel, she pulled under the awning and up to the valet podium, putting the car in park.

"Exactly how overboard did you go?"

She gave Kate what she hoped was a confident smile. "Not very."

"Could have fooled me."

"I travel a lot for work. I have a massive number of hotel points. Promise."

Kate narrowed her eyes and Sutton got the impression she was weighing whether or not to argue. Eventually, she shrugged. "All right."

Might as well grease the skids now. "And since I'm not paying for the room, I got a little extravagant with our dinner reservations. I hope that's okay."

Another moment of consideration. "I appreciate what you're doing and I don't want to ruin it with haggling. So I won't. Let me take you to breakfast in the morning at least?"

She had fantasies of room service in bed but wasn't about to deny Kate anything. "Deal."

She handed her keys to the valet, assuring him they wouldn't need the car until morning. They grabbed their bags and headed inside. Kate wandered the lobby while Sutton checked them in. She might claim discomfort, but Kate looked as beautiful and at ease in a four-star hotel lobby as she did helping customers and stocking shelves at the hardware store.

It hit her how much she loved both sides of Kate. Though really, there were far more than two sides. There was Kate in mom mode. Playful Kate. All grown up and amazing in bed Kate. Sutton loved each and every one of them. Not that she had any business being in love, but it was more forgone conclusion than decision at this point.

Key card in hand, they headed up the elevator. After asking how much time they had, Kate made a comment about freshening up and disappeared into the bathroom. Sutton stood at the window, telling herself there was absolutely no reason to be nervous.

When Kate emerged, she wore nothing but a cerulean lace bra and a pair of matching panties. Yanking back the duvet, Sutton resisted her instinct toward reverence and practically tossed Kate onto the bed. They made love in the daylight, complete with giggles and squeals of delight. It made her feel young and utterly adult at the same time.

They dressed for dinner side-by-side, the way a real couple might, and walked the few blocks to the restaurant for supper. She'd wanted time for a leisurely drink at the bar, but she couldn't bring herself to complain. After a brief argument about the cost, Kate settled in and spent the remainder of the meal in unbridled bliss. Sutton, too. She'd read about the upscale take on Cajun classics, but hadn't been before tonight. It was everything she wanted in a meal. Though, for her, it was more about the company than the food.

❖

After dinner, Kate let Sutton talk her into a drink at the Carousel Bar, one of those places she'd seen in movies and never imagined herself going. Sutton made it seem like no big deal, and they literally walked by it on the way back to the hotel. They tucked into a booth rather than sitting at the bar and, between the live jazz and the to die for Vieux Carré, she felt a bit like a movie star. Or maybe it was the way Sutton stared at her—a heady mix of desire and something she couldn't name. The combination of that and the cocktail had her skin tingling.

The feeling, and the intensity of Sutton's gaze, didn't wane on the walk back to the hotel. They rode the elevator up with another couple and it was all she could do to keep her hands to herself. In the room, Sutton adjusted the thermostat and slipped off her shoes. Part of her wanted to yank Sutton's clothes off and tumble into bed. But for some reason she couldn't quite explain, she held back.

She wanted Sutton to take the lead, the way she had with the plans. She wanted to turn off that part of her brain that had to know what was happening at all times, make sure everything was as it should be. And maybe just as much, she wanted to see if Sutton would take charge.

"How are you feeling? Would you like another drink?"

Sutton's questions came off as confident more than eager, which turned her on more than she cared to admit. "I'm good, I think."

"Are you tired? Would you like to take a shower? Or a bath?"

They'd almost crossed the line into caretaking. She would have expected that to chafe, but it didn't. "Actually, a shower sounds lovely."

Sutton's smile came with a trace of swagger. "Would you like company? I could scrub your back."

There was no logical explanation for her body to be responding the way it was. She wasn't even tipsy. "That would be nice."

"I'll let you get started. Holler when you're ready."

The urge to get Sutton naked and in bed surged again. It took more effort to resist than before, but she did. "All right."

She went to the bathroom, closing the door part way but not all. She undressed, studying herself in the mirror. She didn't think too much about being attractive, being an object of desire. But something about the way Sutton looked at her—whether or not they were in bed—made her feel beautiful. Wanted. She wouldn't say she needed that sort of thing, but it was certainly nice to have.

She got the water going, adjusting the temperature and fiddling with the different settings of the showerhead. "I'm getting in," she called as she stepped under the spray.

She'd just finished soaking her hair when Sutton joined her. Sutton's arms came around her waist and she kissed her jaw. "Hi."

Kate smiled. "Hi."

"Would you like me to wash your hair?"

Of course Sutton would remember how much she like having her head massaged. "I can't turn that down."

"Nor should you have to." Sutton squirted shampoo from the tiny hotel amenity bottle into her hand. "Turn around."

She did as instructed, finding an odd tingle of pleasure at being directed. Sutton's hands ran the length of her hair, then her fingers went to work rubbing the shampoo into her scalp. A groan of pleasure escaped before she could stop it.

"I wondered if you still liked that."

She laughed. "Um, yeah."

Sutton continued the massage for another minute. "Rinse."

Conditioner followed, then body wash. It was a sensual pampering, its effect potent. Sutton let her reciprocate and she took her time, enjoying the way Sutton's soap-slicked skin slid over hers.

She thought Sutton might take things further, but no. Sutton cut the water and stepped out, handing her a towel for her hair and another for her body. The sweetness, the attentiveness of it, threatened to play with her heart more than her body. "Take me to bed."

Sutton angled her head, eyes full of mischief. "Yes, ma'am."

Sutton took her hand and led her to the bedroom. Before coming to the shower, she'd tidied and turned down the bed and adjusted the lighting to romantic perfection. Kate couldn't decide whether it made her happy or uncomfortable. "You don't have to woo me, you know."

"Does it feel like I'm wooing you?"

Was that a trick question? "I don't know. Maybe?"

"And do you not like it or are you not used to it?"

Definitely a trick question. "I don't not like it."

Sutton smiled that confident smile. "How about if I do something you don't like, you ask me to stop and I will?"

On one hand, it was a basic, logistical, consent sort of question. On the other, it implied Sutton had ideas—plans, even—that went beyond falling into bed and fucking. Anticipation rippled through her. Not uncomfortable, exactly, but more than she bargained for. "All right."

"Excellent. How do you feel about massages?"

"You already gave me a massage in the shower."

"I'd like to think I was just getting started."

Was this how Sutton was with women now? Or maybe this was her way of doing a night away. Kate steered clear of deconstructing every little thing but couldn't help but wonder. "Do I get to reciprocate?"

Sutton shrugged. "Maybe."

She opened her mouth to argue, but Sutton merely shook her head.

"Lie down and roll over."

She wouldn't have said being told what to do was a turn on, but Sutton's command sent a jolt of arousal through her. She sat on the edge of the bed. "You don't have to—"

"Roll. Over." Sutton nudged her shoulder, her tone playful but firm.

She lay back and rolled to her stomach. The mattress shifted as Sutton joined her, her knees straddling Kate's thighs. "Mmm. That's nice."

Sutton's hands—warm and slick with lotion—traveled the length of her spine, all the way up to her neck, then across her shoulders and back down. On top of that, the motion had Sutton's pelvis pressing into her backside. Sutton was hot and wet, and feeling it against her ass made her pussy clench with wanting. "Fuck."

"Oh, I intend to. Just not yet."

She shook her head, not quite able to reconcile the confident assertiveness with the Sutton she knew. Or, at least, the Sutton she thought she knew.

Sutton's hands stilled. "What? Is something wrong?"

Ah, there it was. "No. Sorry. This is perfect."

The massage continued, but more slowly. "Are you sure?"

The only way to ease Sutton's concerns at this point would be to tell her the truth. "I was just thinking I like this side of you."

"And what side is that?"

Sutton's thumbs followed the line of her shoulder blades with the perfect amount of pressure. She moaned before she could stop herself. "Um, the assertive one."

"Really? That more than attentive to your every desire?"

How could she explain in a way that wouldn't dismiss that attentiveness? "It's just that I already know that side of you. This other side is new."

"Ah."

Sutton continued to knead her muscles, but she got the feeling she'd said the wrong thing. "I mean, I like both. I—"

Sutton's laugh cut off her fumbling attempt to backpedal. "Don't apologize. Just enjoy."

"Okay." She made it sound so simple.

CHAPTER TWENTY

S utton hadn't planned to give Kate a massage, but once she started, she had a hard time stopping. Kate might tease her about liking this assertive side, but she knew she bordered on the reverent. She would happily spend hours like this, appreciating the perfection that was Kate.

But that wasn't part of the agreement. They'd agreed to be friends. Friends with benefits. Adoration didn't come with the package. Neither did being hopelessly in love. But as she continued to glide her hands over the smooth skin of Kate's shoulders and back, the backs of her thighs and her calves, love was the word that rang through her mind like the peal of church bells on Christmas morning.

"If you keep that up, I'm going to melt into a boneless puddle." Kate's voice was muffled by the pillow.

"I can think of worse things." And not too many better.

Kate shifted, rolling partway onto her side. "But if I'm a puddle, how am I supposed to make all your sexual fantasies come true?"

Sutton's breath hitched and she was pretty sure her mouth fell open. "Uh."

Kate grinned. "I'm glad you're not all confident and bossy. I like it, but it might get boring."

"How do you make my heart stop and my pulse race at the same time?" It came out like a line, but she meant it.

Kate's grin became a smirk. "Magic."

It sure as hell felt like magic. "I see."

"Though, I think you should let me work a little of my magic on you."

"You really don't have to—"

Rather than letting her finish, Kate rolled the rest of the way over. The movement sent her thigh gliding over Sutton's very wet, very sensitive center. Kate glanced down at the wetness streaked across her leg. "Oh, I think I do."

"I just meant—"

Kate sat up. "Do you want me?"

She nodded, hopefully not too dumbly.

"Good. I want you, too. I want you to fuck me halfway to next week. But I want to go down on you first, because that really turns me on. Is that okay with you?"

Another nod. No words. So much for being the assertive one.

Kate pressed a finger to Sutton's chest and she let herself be nudged onto her back. Kate straddled her and her entire body convulsed with the sensation of Kate's pussy pressing into her. Kate angled her head playfully. "Now."

She blinked. "Now?"

"Now." Kate smiled. "No one is saying you can't be in charge."

"No?"

"I think you should tell me exactly what you want me to do and how you want me to do it."

Oh. Ohh. "Okay."

Kate leaned in, her hair falling forward and tickling Sutton's shoulders. She kissed Sutton's neck. "Do you like it hard?" Another kiss. "Soft?" Kiss. "Fast?" Kiss. "Slow?"

At the rate things were going, she'd be lucky not to come the second Kate touched her. "You. I just need you."

Kate started a tortuously slow slink down her body. Her breasts grazed Sutton's abdomen and the tops of her thighs. She sprinkled kisses all over Sutton's torso. Sutton opened her legs. Kate settled between them and offered a teasing smile. "You've got me."

Under normal circumstances, that sort of comment would send her brain into overdrive and she'd have to tell herself—chide herself—not to read too much into it. But these were anything but the normal circumstances of her life and Kate didn't give her mind the chance to get ahead of the rest of her. She pressed her tongue into Sutton's wetness and effectively shut her brain off entirely.

Sutton groaned and her head fell back into the pillow. Kate licked her slowly, languid strokes that seemed to touch each and every nerve ending. When she pulled away, Sutton whimpered. "Are you going to tell me what you want?"

You. This. However you want. Forever. Knowing she couldn't say any of that had her shaking her head.

"No, you're not going to tell me or no, this isn't what you want?"

"You. I just need you." It made her feel foolish to repeat herself, but she didn't trust herself to say more.

"All right."

It was impossible to know if Kate found her lack of direction amusing or if she sensed something more going on. But she didn't ask more questions. Instead, she wrapped her arms around Sutton's thighs and, without words, gave Sutton exactly what she needed.

Not that she was in any hurry about it. No, she absolutely took her time. She worked her way through every possible combination of soft and slow and hard and fast there was until Sutton thought she might literally die from pleasure and Kate's expert way of bringing her to the edge but keeping release at bay.

She lost track of time, of the number of times she mumbled Kate's name. She wound her fingers into Kate's hair and trembled at the way Kate's hum of pleasure reverberated through her.

And then she came. Like an unstoppable wall of water spilling over the top of a levee, it swept her up in its path and carried her away. She had no footing, no purchase, but she didn't care. All that mattered was Kate and this moment and wanting it never to end.

She had no idea how long it took to come down, for her mind and body to merge back together and be aware of the mattress under her, of Kate's head resting on her thigh. "I…yeah…okay."

Kate lifted her head and smiled. "Yeah?"

She laughed, both at her own incoherence and Kate's response. "Yeah."

"Good." Kate kissed the inside of her thigh before crawling up the bed to collapse, half next to her and half draped across her torso.

"Very, very good."

Kate grinned. "I've been wanting to do that. Thank you."

The comment caught her off guard. She hadn't been trying to keep Kate from going down on her, she'd just been so caught up in trying to get her fill of Kate that it hadn't felt like a priority. She swallowed the explanations and caveats and looked right into Kate's eyes. "No, thank you."

And just like that, the need returned. The need to touch and to taste, to etch every inch of Kate into her memory, took over. She rolled onto her side, then braced herself over Kate. She looked down at Kate's satisfied expression and smiled. "But let's not kid ourselves. You were very much in charge of that."

One of Kate's shoulders twitched. "I don't know what you mean."

"Yes, you do." Sutton kissed her. "I'm not complaining, mind you. You seemed to know exactly what I needed, and then some."

"Your body is very expressive. Words, not so much."

That was putting it mildly. "Maybe you'll let me make up for it now."

Kate arched a brow. "How so?"

"The being assertive bit. You may have addled my brain, but I have some very clear thoughts on what I'd like to do to you."

"Really?"

If she only knew. "Yes, really."

"Mmm."

"Which isn't to say I don't want to know exactly what you want, exactly how you want it."

Kate's smile became a smirk. "Well, if the other day and this afternoon are anything to go on, you seem to have a pretty good handle on what I like."

Her fingers skimmed over Kate's stomach and hips, settled at the apex of her thighs. "I think it's like you said. Your body is very expressive."

Kate shifted, opening for her. Inviting her in. She slid her fingers over Kate's folds, coating them in her wetness. She closed her eyes for a second and reminded herself to breathe.

"See, that right there? That's nice." Kate's nails scraped lightly over her shoulders. "But you know what I really need."

She plunged her fingers into Kate and her own body's response was on par with any orgasm. This was what she needed. What she craved.

Kate's body bucked against hers. "Yes."

She slid out and plunged in again. Not possessive, she reminded herself. Kate belonged neither to her nor to anyone. But she could meet Kate where she was, worship and please her and if she let a bit of her heart fall at Kate's feet in the process, so be it.

"God, you feel good." Kate's grip on her shoulders tightened.

Kate moved with her, against her, rising to meet each thrust of her hand. She matched her pace to the rhythm of Kate's body, hypnotic and perfect.

She used the thumb of her free hand to stroke Kate's clit. Kate's body clenched around her even tighter, pulled her in even deeper. Kate let go of her shoulders and her fists gripped the sheets. Only to have her let go and grasp Sutton once again. Her eyes closed and her head listed from side to side. Each breath came with a yes.

She longed for Kate to say her name, but hated herself for thinking it in such an otherwise perfect moment. "That's it, baby. Come for me."

Whether it was her words, or the sound of her voice, or something entirely different, she'd never know. But Kate exploded for her in that moment, a flood of heat that coated her hand and dripped down her wrist. Sutton's entire body tightened in its own kind of release.

Kate's arms fell away and her whole body went limp. Sutton situated herself next to her and pulled her into her arms. She gave in to the urge to kiss the top of Kate's head, to stroke her hair. If this moment didn't deserve a bit of reverence, she didn't know what did.

"Holy fuck."

She couldn't help but smile at the expletive, and the fact that it instantly lightened the mood. "I hope you don't cuss like that in front of Harper."

Kate lifted her head, angled it playfully. "We have an agreement."

"Really? What's that?"

"She can cuss, too, just not in front of other people."

"I love that." Maybe she almost slipped and said, "I love you," but she didn't.

"It seems to work for us, especially now that she's older. I mean, I try to rein it in a little around her, but I've had a foul mouth for a long time."

Sutton laughed. She'd been so nerdy in middle school and Kate had made it her personal mission to get Sutton to loosen up. It was funny how, for all the things that had changed, some hadn't. "You definitely taught me a thing or two about creative swear words."

Kate propped herself on her elbow, a look of mischief dancing through her eyes. "Is that all I taught you?"

"I'm pretty sure that list could go on for days."

"You taught me plenty, too." Kate poked her lightly in the ribs.

She could feel herself teetering on the edge of seriousness, but she didn't want that tonight. Not for Kate or for herself. So she nudged Kate onto her back and nipped her jaw. "I'd like to learn a couple more things from you tonight."

Kate lifted her chin. "Like what?"

"Like how many times I can make you come."

"I see." Kate nodded slowly.

"I mean, unless you know the answer and want to just tell me."

"I think we both might stand to learn something."

The idea of spending all night finding out sent a tremor of lust through her. "Well, then, we better get started."

Sutton kissed her, slowly at first. As she worked her way down Kate's body, she wondered how many people Kate had been with since they broke up. But rather than filling her with a sense of dread or jealousy, it made her hope that Kate had been loved, that she'd been with people who cared about her—about her pleasure, but also about her wants and needs and hopes and dreams. Even if she'd wanted to be that person for so many of those years. Even if part of her wanted to be that person again.

❖

Kate lay in the darkness, the fragrance of the high-end hotel body wash and lotion clinging to her skin. She'd actually lost track of how many times she came and was pretty sure Sutton did, too. When she finally tapped out—sweaty and sated and spent—Sutton had coaxed her into a cool shower. It was an extra layer of luxury, a way to wind down, she didn't even know she needed.

She wouldn't want this to be her everyday life. She loved Harper, obviously, but she also loved their little house and their low-key routine that was more about simple pleasures than luxury. Still, indulgence had its place. It wouldn't be hard to get used to getaways like this once or twice a year. The problem was, as clearly as she could envision it, she couldn't imagine doing it with anyone but Sutton.

Foolish, given Sutton's temporary presence in her life. She'd have to rope Bryce into some sort of adventure. Or maybe Delia. They could do a girls' weekend sometime. No mind-blowing sex, but they could still have fun.

Feeling better, she let her mind follow her body into relaxation. She shifted her legs back and forth, enjoying the caress of the impossibly high thread count sheets. And, if she was being honest, the feel of Sutton pressed against her.

She woke to the same feeling—the sheets, the press of Sutton's body, deep relaxation. Only they'd shifted somehow in the night. Instead of tucked into Sutton's shoulder, her back was curved against Sutton's front, Sutton's arm wrapped around her middle. More possessive than the way Sutton held her when they were awake. And although she might not want to admit it, it felt really, really good.

She stretched and wiggled, wanting to wake Sutton gently. Sutton responded with an extra squeeze and a neck nuzzle she could so get used to. It didn't take long for lazy cuddles to lead to wandering hands, for wandering hands to take on a sense of urgency. She thought she might be sore, but her body felt loose and limber and Sutton knew each and every button to push.

They showered together, again, and ordered coffee in the room. "I have half a mind to extend the reservation, just so we can have a few more hours."

Tempting, but her practical side kicked in. "That's silly. We should enjoy the city while we're here."

Sutton hung her head for a moment, but ultimately smiled. "Fine."

Since they'd missed the window on breakfast, they settled on an early lunch at Drago's, a casual affair at the bar that consisted entirely of charbroiled oysters and an obscene amount of warm French bread. After, they spent the afternoon wandering the French Quarter like a pair of tourists, admiring the art of the street vendors and tossing a few dollars into the can of a trio of kids—who couldn't be a day older than Harper—banging on a bunch of buckets with more precision and rhythm than musicians she'd paid good money to see.

They collected the car, but instead of heading home, Sutton asked if they could go to City Park. After gorging themselves on beignets at Morning Call, they strolled the park. She hadn't been there since an elementary school field trip to Storyland. Even for someone who spent the entirety of her life in Louisiana, the oak trees—with their branches dipping all the way to the ground and rising again—had a certain magic to them. She let go of Sutton's hand to climb over and around the biggest one, letting her fingers caress the tendrils of Spanish moss. Sutton followed, kissing her against the tree's massive trunk.

Kate's heart thudded in her chest. "I had so much fun last night. I'm not exaggerating when I say it might be the best meal I've eaten in my entire life. But I think I like this more."

Sutton's eyes searched her face. She tucked a piece of hair behind Kate's ear. "Me, too. It's more us."

Us. She'd not used that word to talk or even think about Sutton and her for so long. But, in this moment, it felt right. "It is."

"I suppose I should get you home."

The reluctance in Sutton's voice made her smile. "Probably. You know, you could come home with me."

"Not bored of me yet?"

She didn't have words for just how not bored of Sutton she was. "Not yet."

"I like the sound of that." Sutton took her hand as they headed to the car.

Kate studied their entwined fingers. She didn't yearn for the past; she'd given that up a long time ago. She rarely longed for the future, either, preferring to live in the moment. But a tiny part of her imagined what it might be like to be with Sutton for years and not just a few weeks.

She sat with that on the ride back to Duchesne. Sutton was quiet, too, making Kate wonder where her thoughts were. Probably better not to know, given her sentimental state. But when Sutton pulled into her driveway, Kate hesitated to move.

"Thank you for today, and last night." She put feeling into the words, but they landed like a platitude in her ears, completely insufficient to capture either her appreciation or her emotions.

Sutton offered her a slow smile. "You're welcome."

"I mean a lot more than thank you, I just don't seem to have the words right now."

"You don't need more words. I'm glad you let yourself enjoy it. I have to say I can't remember a better twenty-four hours."

"Stop." Surely this was the sort of thing Sutton did all the time. Okay, maybe not the sex part, but the travel—plush hotels and fancy restaurants in city after city.

"I mean it. I travel for work. I don't want to think of myself as a stick in the mud, but it's not like this." Sutton grabbed her hand. "It's never like this."

Kate swallowed the lump in her throat. It was possible she and Sutton would never share that kind of night again. Even though that was the sort of thing she tried not to dwell on, she couldn't seem to help herself. "Yeah."

"So, Harper isn't home until Sunday?"

She smiled, pretty sure she knew where Sutton's mind had gone. "That's right."

"But you have to work tomorrow."

"Yes. And Sunday morning."

Sutton nodded. "Yeah. I know we joked about me coming home with you, but if you need some alone time, I totally understand."

Of course Sutton would think of that. "I wouldn't say no to some company in the evenings. Assuming you can leave Albin, of course."

Sutton smirked. "I make him wear the Life Alert when I leave the house."

She laughed. "I'm sure he hates that."

"He does. It's good for him, though."

"So…" She trailed off, not sure whether they'd decided or if she should invite Sutton in.

"So, I'm going to pop home to check on Dad and take care of the animals. Can I pick up supper on my way back? Something easy and light?"

Again, Sutton's unyielding thoughtfulness struck her. "I've got cold chicken and salad makings in the fridge."

Sutton's smile was quick and easy. "That sounds perfect. I'll be back in about an hour. Is that okay?"

None of this fit her guidelines for a friend with benefits. Not that she had a playbook. But as she thought about a quiet night in—supper on the sofa with an old movie and tumbling into bed with Sutton once again—she couldn't bring herself to resist. "It's perfect."

Chapter Twenty-one

Sutton woke to sunlight streaming in and Kate's warm, naked body pressed against hers. It was the third morning in a row she'd had the pleasure, and it took everything she had not to imagine what a lifetime of waking up next to Kate would be like. Kate stirred, doing that stretching thing with the little noises that managed to be sexy and cute at the same time.

"Hi." She gave Kate a squeeze and kissed the top of her head.

"Morning." Kate stretched again, turning the end of the word into a squeak.

"Is it okay if I'm both glad Harper is coming home today and kind of sad I won't get to wake up with you like this again tomorrow?"

Kate sighed against her. "Yes."

Why did she have to go and say that out loud? "I'm sorry. That was probably the wrong thing to say. I'm mostly glad Harper is coming home."

Kate sat up and Sutton scrambled to do the same. "You don't have to say that."

"I mean it though." Whether she admitted it to Kate or not almost didn't matter. She had no illusions of how hard she'd fallen for Harper.

"I'm not sure I believe you, but I'm not going to argue. Coffee?"

"Yes, please. Although, I'm happy to make it, if you'd like. Assuming you trust me in your kitchen."

Kate made a show of looking her up and down. "If you're making me coffee, you can do whatever the hell you want in my kitchen."

She bowed slightly. "At your service."

Kate flopped back, spreading her arms wide. "I'll wait here."

"I'll be back shortly."

Sutton headed to the kitchen. It didn't take much riffling to find the coffee—in the cabinet above the coffeepot—or the mugs. She got it going and pulled out the flavored creamer she'd noticed the last time she was there. While the coffee brewed, she leaned against the sink and wondered how often Kate got coffee in bed. Harper didn't seem quite old enough to do it. And Kate, for whatever dating she did, didn't seem keen on bringing too many people into her home.

Did the prospect of Sutton doing it now make her uneasy? Not if her playful response was anything to go on. But did she think about it beyond the luxury of the moment? Probably not, at least not in the way Sutton did. She would happily bring Kate coffee in bed every morning for the rest of their lives.

If Kate had any idea that's where her thoughts were, she would likely laugh or send Sutton packing.

She shook her head. She couldn't help being the person who always thought about the what-ifs. She just had to make sure thinking about them didn't get the better of her. She had no idea how long things with Kate would last this time around and she didn't want to waste a minute.

Speaking of wasting time, she'd been so busy daydreaming she missed the coffee finishing. She prepped two cups and returned to the bedroom, finding Kate exactly where she'd left her. "For you, madame."

Kate let out a contented sigh and sat up. "Thank you."

They sat in the bed cross-legged, facing each other. Sutton sipped her coffee, let out a hum of pleasure. She needed to enjoy the moment and not worry about anything else.

"A girl could get used to this."

So much for that. "I'm sorry it isn't a little luxury you get every day."

Kate shrugged. "I don't usually have the patience to linger in bed, but I can see how it has its perks."

"What time do you have to be at work?"

She wrinkled her nose. "Nine, so I can leave at three to go pick up Harper."

"Would you like company for the ride?" She hadn't meant to say that, but the words tumbled out before she could stop them.

Kate looked skeptical. "Really? That's what you want to do with your Sunday?"

She tried not to take the question personally. "I mean, if you'd rather go solo, that's fine. But hanging out with you and seeing Harper sounds like more fun than trying to watch a baseball game while Dad snores in his recliner."

Whether Kate wanted her company or not, the juxtaposition seemed to soften her. "When you put it that way."

"Exactly. But, really, no pressure."

Kate hesitated and Sutton wanted desperately to know what was going on in her head. Was she tired of spending time together? Did she want that time alone with Harper after so many days apart? "That would be nice."

"You don't seem sure."

"No, it would be nice. I'm just—" Kate shook her head. "You know what? Never mind."

"Come on, what is it? You'd never let me get away with saying that."

That got a laugh. "You're right. Sorry. I just wondered if it was weird to spend this much time together, but why not, right?"

It was hard to say whether that explanation made her feel better or worse. "Yeah. I mean, I have to work most of next week, so I figure I won't be seeing much of you."

"Yeah. Totally." Kate seemed to appreciate that rationale.

Sutton smiled. She was past the point of trying to rationalize wanting to spend time with Kate, but Kate didn't need to know that. "I'm happy to drive if you want. I can pick you up at the store."

"Mmm." Kate made a face. "I can't promise there won't be some gnarly things coming home in her stuff."

"Not a problem. Promise."

Kate studied her for a long moment before she said, "You really like hanging out with her, don't you?"

Sigh. "Yeah. I do."

Kate nodded but didn't say anything else.

"Does that bother you?"

"No, but it makes me think about what's going to happen when you leave."

If a tiny part of her had started to wonder what it might be like if she didn't leave, she knew better than to say so. "I have a feeling I'll be spending more time here moving forward."

That seemed to land well. "That would be nice."

"Besides, a very smart woman I know told me to stop getting ahead of myself. I'm trying to take her advice."

Kate smiled then. "That sounds like an excellent idea."

❖

Kate rarely found work to drag, but today was one of those days. The weather was dismal—rainy but still sweltering—and customers few and far between. She got a jump-start on the week's orders, tidied and stocked the entire plumbing department, and cleaned and reorganized behind the front counter. And still she found herself both restless and bored, sighing and drumming her fingers on the worn laminate surface.

It got so bad, Daddy asked if she wanted to go home early, forcing her to admit Sutton would be picking her up. He didn't lecture her, but his look conveyed his displeasure plenty. She brushed it off, reminding herself it wouldn't be an issue for much longer anyway.

Sutton showed up at exactly 2:55. She'd showered and changed and, despite the amount of sex they'd had in the last three days, all Kate wanted to do was drag her to bed and get her dirty again. She resisted, because she genuinely missed Harper as much as she was required to pick her up at five, but the hum of desire lingered.

Despite the amount of time they'd been in each other's company—in and out of bed—they spent the drive chatting. Sutton talked about Albin's progress with physical therapy, then asked her about her jewelry and how she'd made the decision to turn it into a business. She seemed genuinely impressed, which surprised her, given Sutton's job.

Sutton shook her head. "But this is your own business. You're creative, but you also market yourself and keep the books and manage your inventory. It's a big deal."

She didn't consider herself modest, but something about the awe in Sutton's voice had her blushing. "I don't think of it that way, I guess."

"Well, you should. I mean, I like my job but it feels downright uninspired compared to what you do."

"You could do it, too, you know."

Sutton guffawed. "I don't have a creative bone in my body."

She had a flashback to high school, when Sutton would doodle in the margins during class and sketch birds and flowers from the swing on the front porch. "You draw."

"That was just goofing around. I haven't drawn anything in years."

"Why not?"

Sutton frowned. "I want to say I was too busy, but it's not true. I don't know why. Maybe because I never felt all that good at it."

"You don't have to be good at it, or do it for money."

The frown intensified.

"I mean, I heard you were stupidly well paid, so money should be the last thing on your mind."

Sutton continued to frown, but she nodded slowly. "Maybe."

"It's okay to do things simply because they bring you joy."

"You're right."

Kate had meant to drive home her point, but Sutton looked to be on the brink of tears. "I'm not sure I should be giving life advice or anything, but—"

"You have every right to give life advice. You've made more of yours than I have of mine," Sutton said.

She reached over the center console and gave Sutton's knee a squeeze. "Hey, don't talk like that. You're really successful."

Sutton seemed to catch herself, pull back. Watching it play across her face made Kate inexplicably sad. "Sorry. I shouldn't be complaining. I'm very fortunate."

She left her hand where it was. "You can appreciate where you are and what you have and still decide you want something more, or different."

Sutton blinked a few times, then seemed to literally shake off where her thoughts had gone. She turned to Kate with a bright smile. "You're right. Again."

Part of her wanted to press, to see if Sutton would open up about the undercurrent of unhappiness they'd uncovered, but they were minutes away from Harper's camp. So instead she filed it away. Maybe they'd revisit the subject, maybe they wouldn't. It might not be any of her business in the grand scheme of things, anyway.

She pointed out the turn and they joined the line of cars making their way up the gravel drive. After finding a spot in the grassy parking area, she led them toward the group of cabins that had been home to Harper's troop. The ten or so girls remaining sat in a circle, engrossed in some sort of game. When she called Harper's name, her head popped up and she scrambled to her feet.

"Sutton!" Harper's face registered delight and she ran right to her, flinging herself into Sutton's outstretched arms.

Kate stared, not quite in disbelief, but something akin to it. "What am I, chopped liver?"

"Sorry, Mama." Harper released Sutton and threw her arms around Kate.

"That's better."

Harper let go and looked at her, suddenly serious. "It's just that I knew you were coming and Sutton was a surprise."

She smiled. "I know, baby."

"I'm super excited to see you both. It's been so fun, but I'm ready to be home."

Sutton started to laugh, but covered it with a cough. Kate didn't bother trying to hide her amusement. "You sound like such an adult when you say that."

Harper shrugged. "I am almost ten."

That seemed to catch Sutton's attention. "When's your birthday?"

Harper beamed. "August twenty-sixth."

Sutton closed her eyes for a second and Kate imagined her doing the math, subtracting nine months. She opened her mouth to say something, to divert her attention, but Sutton didn't give her the chance. "That's really soon."

"Will you still be here? Will you come to my party?"

By her calculations, Sutton would be back in Atlanta by then. It was why she hadn't mentioned it, to either of them.

"I'm not sure yet, but if I am here and your mom is okay with it, I'd love to come."

A diplomatic answer, and one Kate couldn't find fault in. But for some reason, it left a hollow feeling in her chest. Not used to the sensation, and not liking it one bit, she shifted the conversation. "Are you all packed up?"

"I am. I made some cool stuff, too. A candle poured into a deer track I found and a collage out of stuff from our nature walk and a wind chime and a jar of jelly."

"Wow." Whether or not Sutton was legitimately impressed, she put on a good show.

Kate caught her eye. "Told you there'd be stuff."

With the extra pair of hands, loading up took no time at all. Harper hugged her friends good-bye and they were off. They hadn't been on the road ten minutes when Harper declared she was starving. She should have mentioned to Sutton she expected that to happen. But before she could gauge Sutton's thoughts on the matter, Sutton said she was, too.

"Really?" She gave Sutton an incredulous look.

"What? Was that the wrong answer?" Sutton made a face. "You're going to give me a line about having two kids on your hands, aren't you?"

She laughed, both at Sutton's sheepishness and her accuracy. "Shall we stop for supper on the way home?"

"Yeah!" Harper's arms went up in triumph.

"Yeah." Sutton's echo matched Harper's enthusiasm, even if she only let go of the steering wheel for a second to approximate the gesture.

Kate shook her head, amused but not wanting to show it. "I guess that settles that."

They let Harper decide, which meant a chain restaurant with chicken tenders on the menu. Not exactly what she would have picked, but Sutton didn't seem to mind. Harper regaled them with stories of swimming, picking blackberries, and barely missing a patch of poison oak on one of the trails. But by the time they were sharing a cookie sundae—because why not—her focus shifted.

"When are we going to New Orleans?" Harper asked.

"What happened to being ready to be home?" she asked, not as a stall tactic exactly, but sort of.

Harper didn't miss a beat. "I am ready to be home. That doesn't mean I'm not also ready for another adventure. Besides, school starts in like two weeks."

The declaration ended with a groan, which got a laugh out of Sutton. "Well, I have to work this coming week, but I'm free after that."

Harper looked at her expectantly. "Well?"

"I'll look at my work schedule." Though, other than the back-to-school orientation night, she could probably make anything work.

"Do you have requests? Things you want to do?" Sutton asked.

"Can we go to the aquarium?"

It wasn't a huge ask, but something they hadn't done before. Given Harper's interest in marine biology, it gave her a pang of guilt not to have made it happen. Sutton, to her credit, looked Kate's way before responding. She nodded.

"I think that's a brilliant idea."

After a bit of haggling, Sutton let her pick up the check. They piled back into the car and spent the rest of the ride home discussing the sundry specimens of sea life they might have the opportunity to see. Sutton needed no help carrying the conversation, so she let her mind wander—from an entirely different sort of trip to New Orleans to the start of the school year and the fact that her baby would be in middle school.

All the while, the conversation with Sutton from earlier hovered at the edges. It hadn't occurred to her that Sutton might not be happy with the life she'd chosen. And even though it might not be her place to worry or to interfere, she'd let Sutton back into her life. They might not be getting back together, but it didn't mean she didn't care. What to do about it, however, was another matter altogether.

CHAPTER TWENTY-TWO

Sutton finished the project at Tulane a day ahead of schedule. Regina was thrilled, particularly to have everything up and running before fall classes started. She was almost as pleased as Jay, who promised her a bonus for taking on the project and begged her to hurry back. She hadn't hinted an intention to do otherwise, but he seemed squirrelly as her leave entered its third month.

To be fair, she was feeling a bit squirrelly herself. Not that she had plans to up and quit, but the longer she spent in Duchesne, the more she found herself wondering if she could make it work as a home base. How often did she need to be in the office, anyway?

Fortunately, she had a few more weeks before she would need to broach that subject with Jay, or make any sort of decision. A few more weeks to see how things unfolded with Kate. Her mind was doing that what-if thing again, only this time it was colored with shades of happily ever after.

Too soon. She chided herself—again—as she pulled into Kate's driveway.

Harper didn't disappoint, bounding down the porch steps before she even put the car in park. Kate was right behind her, so she didn't even bother cutting the engine. She rolled down the window as Harper approached. "Nice shirt."

Harper glanced down and grinned. "Thanks."

She couldn't decide what she liked more—the sparkly manatee or the caption "Real mermaids have curves." Harper got in behind her and Kate climbed into the passenger seat. "Hi."

Kate, in a more subtle but totally sexy green-and-white striped sun dress, smiled. "Hi, yourself."

"You look gorgeous."

Kate smirked, but she also tucked a piece of hair behind her ear and looked down. "Thanks."

Fighting the urge to kiss her, Sutton glanced in the rearview mirror. "Everyone buckled in? Can't have you jostling around back there."

"I'm not jostling," Harper declared as she tried to get the belt to catch. "And I always wear my seat belt."

"Good. I like people who follow the rules." She winked, which earned her an eye roll but also a giggle. Then she turned her attention to Kate. "All set?"

Kate looked a little unsure, but she smiled. "All set."

The drive to New Orleans flew by in a flurry of conversation about sea creatures, beignets, and the relative merits of big Mardi Gras parades versus smaller local ones. She navigated to the garage she'd scouted ahead of time and they made the short walk to the aquarium. "I got tickets online so we wouldn't have to wait in line."

Harper let out a woo-hoo, but Kate frowned. "That was thoughtful. I hope you'll let me pay you for ours."

"How about you treat us to beignets or something when we're done?"

Kate narrowed her eyes. "As a start."

Considering she expected more of a fight, she'd take it. They bypassed the ticket line and headed inside. The cool air and dim lighting was such a contrast to the outdoors, it took her senses a moment to adjust. By the time they did, Harper practically vibrated with excitement.

"I want to see the sharks and the sea turtles, but can we start with the tunnel? I saw the pictures online and it looked so cool," Harper said.

Kate looked at Sutton expectantly. She wasn't sure if it was the right thing to say or not, but she lifted a shoulder and said to Harper, "I think you get to be in charge while we're here."

They spent over three hours wandering the various tanks and exhibits. A lot had changed since the field trip her high school biology class took back in the day. Harper's enthusiasm and energy felt limitless, spilling over and making her feel a bit like a kid herself. It made her wonder if the same thing happened to Kate or if she had some sort of parental immunity.

"You seem to be having almost as much fun as Harper," Kate said.

She smiled. "Are you reading my mind now?"

Kate paused. She'd meant the comment as a joke, but maybe it didn't land quite right. "I just meant you look like you're enjoying yourself."

"Oh, I definitely am. But I was thinking how Harper's joy seems to rub off. It's hard not to be a little giddy around her."

"That's sweet of you to say."

"I mean it. Are you exempt because you spend so much time with her or is it a mom thing?"

She sighed and felt herself soften. "I still get caught up in it. Just not enough to be excited about slimy and bitey things."

Sutton gave her an imploring look. "Come on, not even the turtles?"

"Fine. The turtles are cute." They moved to the next station, an open tank with the chance to get up close and personal with a stingray. Harper joined the line to pet her, and she and Sutton stepped off to the side. "Thank you for today. This might not be my thing, but it's so Harper's. I know she requested this specifically, but it's clear you pay attention when she talks."

"Of course I do." Sutton looked offended by the very idea she might not.

"She has a lot to say. It's easy to zone out from time to time."

Sutton chuckled. "She's more interesting than half the clients I work with, I promise."

"I'm not sure if that's a compliment to Harper or an insult to your—"

"Hold on one sec." Sutton stepped away, just in time to snap a photo of Harper's turn with the stingray on her phone. "Sorry. Didn't want to miss that."

She wanted to tell Sutton not to apologize, to thank her for capturing the moment. But her heart had lodged itself somewhere in her throat, and the rest of the sentence got lost in Harper's squeal of delight as she ran back to them. By the time Harper finished telling them what it felt like—in excruciating detail—the moment had passed. When her phone pinged a moment later with the photo, she settled for a simple thank you instead.

As they made their way toward the exit, Sutton leaned close. "Instead of eating at some place in the Quarter, I thought we could ride the streetcar and have supper out that way. Do you think Harper would like that? Would you?"

"You thought of everything, didn't you?" Just like the night Sutton had planned for the two of them. That she would plan, essentially, a family day affected her even more than the romantic escape.

Sutton's smile seemed almost shy. "I like to plan. I don't want it to feel like I'm trying to take over."

She could see how it might, if they were trying to negotiate a life together. That wasn't what this was, though. It was Sutton being thoughtful and thorough. And it felt nice to be out of the driver's seat for once. "I'll let you know if I'd like to exercise veto power."

The shyness vanished and the playfulness returned. "I have no doubt."

They meandered past the casino and over to Canal Street to pick up the streetcar. She and Harper had ridden it once when they came up to go to the zoo, but Harper's memory of it was foggy. Sutton pointed out parts of the Tulane campus they passed, along with Loyola. Harper giggled at the number of Mardi Gras beads still hanging in the trees and listened to Sutton with rapt attention. Sutton told Harper when to pull the cord to signal their stop and Kate let herself smile over Harper's delight in doing it.

They were seated right away—definitely a bonus of leaving the Quarter—at a table with a view of the oyster bar. She perused the menu, but found herself distracted by the sounds and methodical movements of the petite blond woman shucking oysters. She'd never seen a female shucker before. Not that she had any desire to do it herself, but she liked knowing that such women existed.

Sutton tipped her head in that direction. "Share a dozen with me?"

"You don't have to ask me twice." And since she wasn't driving, she ordered a frozen French 75 to go with them.

They ordered everything at once, but the oysters came out first. Sutton leaned forward and inhaled deeply. "I don't get fresh oysters enough."

Kate smirked. "Nice to know there are a few things you miss about home."

Sutton looked into her eyes and, without missing a beat, said, "More than a few."

Since it wasn't the time, or the place, to think about what Sutton might mean by that, she focused her attention on topping an oyster just so and slurping it down. "You know, I live here and I don't get fresh oysters enough either."

Sutton doctored hers—lemon and hot sauce—and lifted the shell in a toast. "Cheers to seeking out simple pleasures."

Now that was a sentiment she could get behind. She topped a second one with cocktail sauce and mirrored the gesture. "Cheers."

Harper, who'd been staring at the whole process, wrinkled her nose. "Ew."

Kate expected Sutton to shrug it off, but she didn't. She set the empty shell down, rested her elbows on the table, and leaned forward. "Have you ever tried one?"

Harper shook her head. "They look like boogers."

"Harper." She was past the point of worrying Sutton would react badly to kid-isms, but that didn't mean she stepped out of mom mode.

"Sorry." Harper looked down for a moment, but then back at Sutton. "They do, though."

Sutton lifted a hand. "It's a fair point. But aren't there other things that look a little weird that are completely delicious?"

"Hmm." She seemed to consider the question.

"How about figs?" Kate asked. Harper had been obsessed with them pretty much since she started eating solid food.

Harper nodded. "They are weird."

"And squishy," Sutton said.

"Yeah." Harper agreed with enthusiasm, but then frowned, like she realized she was now arguing against herself.

"You don't have to try one. I'll be honest, I didn't like them until I was like twenty." Sutton offered a casual shrug. "I just thought you might be more adventurous than I was at your age."

She had no way of knowing whether Sutton's comment was calculated, but it landed with absolute precision. Harper's whole expression changed. "I'm adventurous."

Kate smirked. "You might as well have double dog dared her."

"I swear that wasn't my intention," Sutton said.

Kate almost believed her. "You can try one if you want to, but no theatrics about how gross they are if you don't like them."

Harper looked from her to Sutton to the tray of oysters in the middle of the table. She swallowed visibly.

"You really don't have to try them. I won't think you're less cool." Sutton's voice was earnest, but it was too late. The ship had sailed.

"Can I have the littlest one?" Harper asked.

Sutton smiled. "Absolutely. I like lemon juice and hot sauce, but you can have cocktail sauce, too."

Harper seemed to weigh her options. She liked hot sauce, but had yet to jump on the horseradish bandwagon. "I want it like you do it."

Of course. Sutton eyed the tray and picked the smallest specimen. She doctored it up and set in on Harper's plate. "You can use the little fork or you can dump the whole thing in your mouth."

Harper nodded, her face fixed with a look of intense concentration. "Do I chew it?"

"You can. I like to let it slide right down my throat."

Harper looked genuinely alarmed by the prospect.

"Don't focus on the texture, just the taste."

Harper nodded. Kate considered chiming in but liked that this was between Sutton and Harper. And not only because she expected it to go badly. Harper picked up the shell. She eyed the contents, looked at Sutton, then stared the oyster down once more. Then, without further hesitation or contemplation, she shut her eyes and knocked it back.

Eyes still closed, Harper winced, swallowed, then gave a full body shudder. Kate braced herself for histrionics. But when Harper finally looked her way, all she saw was excitement. "Wow!"

"So, good?" Sutton asked.

Harper considered. "I don't know if I'd say good, but cool. Weird. So weird. And they taste like when you go swimming in the ocean."

Sutton grinned. "Does that mean you want another?"

Harper pressed her lips together and shook her head. "No, thank you."

The rest of the food arrived and the oyster excitement faded. Sutton asked Harper about her favorite exhibits and parts of the day, then about what she was hoping to squeeze into the rest of her summer and what she was looking forward to at school. But as much attention as Sutton showed Harper, it felt like she was just as inquisitive with Kate.

It reminded her of high school, when Sutton's introverted nature often came across as shyness. But the second she felt comfortable, she was the most interested and attentive conversationalist around. It was one of the things she'd loved about Sutton then. She'd thought her days of basking in it were long gone. And while she wouldn't have said she missed it, she couldn't deny how good it felt to soak it in once more.

Stuffed to the gills, they took the streetcar back to the Quarter, piled into Sutton's car, and started the drive home. Harper was chatty at first, but by the time they'd cleared the city, she'd gone quiet. When several minutes passed without Harper saying anything at all, she glanced behind Sutton. Sure enough, Harper had completely conked out. "I think today was a win."

Sutton glanced her way briefly. "I had a really good time."

She'd been so focused on Harper, she hadn't given much thought to herself. But it had been an amazing day all around. "I did, too."

"Thank you for agreeing to it. I know you think I'm a big softy."

Did she? Maybe. "You're the fun one only in town for a little while, not the stuffy mom who has to say no a lot of the time. You get to be a softy."

Sutton frowned at that.

"I don't mean it in a bad way. Bryce is the same. My parents, too, for that matter."

"Does it ever feel hard, doing the parent thing by yourself?"

Oh, that. She looked back to make sure Harper was still sleeping. "Only sometimes. I worry about being the one to make all the decisions and making the wrong one. I'm lucky, though. I have so much help and support, I rarely feel like I'm going it alone."

Sutton nodded, but got quiet, leaving Kate to wonder at the trajectory of her thoughts. Her own had ventured in the direction of how nice it was to spend time with someone who seemed to genuinely enjoy Harper. Not that she dated enough to have many bad experiences on that front, but still.

When Sutton pulled into the driveway, Kate couldn't help but sigh.

"You okay?" Sutton asked.

"Just tired, I think." The tired part was true, even if she just might not be.

"It's been a very full day." Sutton put the car in park. "Do you want help getting Harper inside?"

Even if she did, the prospect of having Sutton in the house, then having her leave, left a bad taste in her mouth. "We're okay. Harper? Wake up, we're home."

Harper mumbled for a moment, but came around quickly. Before Kate could tell her it wasn't necessary, Sutton got out for hugs and good-byes. Harper thanked her without being prompted and Sutton promised she'd see them again soon.

Sutton waited for them to get inside before leaving. A small gesture, but one Kate noticed. She sent Harper to brush her teeth and get ready for bed, but lingered at the window so she could watch Sutton pull away. And maybe, for the tiniest moment, she let herself be sad Sutton wasn't staying.

Chapter Twenty-three

Sutton walked into the house, her state of happy exhaustion jarred by the sound of television gunfire. "Dad, I'm home."

"In here."

She chuckled. Obviously. She hung her keys and headed to the living room, where a *Law & Order* rerun was on much louder than it needed to be. "Miss me?"

Dad muted the television and looked her way. "Well, I'm glad you're not letting your invalid old man cramp your social life."

"You know, I asked if you needed me to come home earlier to take you to PT."

He waved her off. "I'm just yanking your chain. I don't need you carting me everywhere. I've got friends."

"In low places, even."

Dad rolled his eyes, making her chuckle again. "Did you eat yet?"

"I did. Did you?" She'd left roasted chicken in the fridge, but worried it might have been too healthy to tempt him.

"Benny and I picked up po-boys after my appointment."

Of course they did. "Do you need anything else? Fresh beer? Slippers and the newspaper?"

"No, thank you, nursemaid. I can get everything I want on my mandated walkabouts."

"I know you can get what you want. What about what you need? Did you take your pain pill this evening?"

He grumbled. "I'm done with those. They make my skin crawl."

She imagined it was a pretty wretched side effect to have, but it didn't mean she liked the idea of him in pain. "How about a half?"

He grudgingly agreed. She got it for him and a beer for herself and settled on the couch to watch some crap TV with him. But instead of turning the volume back up, he lifted his chin in her direction. "So, what's going on there?"

She looked at the television, then around the room. "Where?"

"With you? The little getaway to New Orleans. Now the family day. What are you doing?"

She set her beer on the coffee table and leaned back, lacing her fingers behind her head. "Nothing."

"Oh, no. You are most definitely doing something. I just want to know what it is."

Ever since the tense conversation the morning after she stayed at Kate's the first time, Dad had kept his mouth shut. It had been a relief, really. So much so that she'd lulled herself into thinking it was no big deal. "Kate and I are reconnecting. I'm not sure what else to say."

"Reconnecting." He let out a derisive snort. "Is that what the kids are calling it these days?"

"Dad." She absolutely, positively was not discussing her sex life with him.

"Are you in love with her?"

She blew out a breath. "I mean—"

"Wait, wait. That's not my question, since it's more obvious than a hound dog in heat you are." He looked at her with more worry than judgment in his eyes. "How in love are you?"

"Not hopelessly." In fact, she had quite a bit of hope.

"Sutton. You aren't a kid anymore. Your actions have consequences."

She laughed before she could stop herself. "The woman I thought I was destined to marry and grow old with is living here and raising a child as a single parent. You think I don't understand consequences?"

"And you come along and sweep her off her feet and then what? What happens when you leave?"

Sutton scrubbed a hand over her face. "What if I didn't leave?"

He sat up straighter, as straight as his twenty-year-old recliner would allow. "That's crazy talk."

"Is it?"

"Your career is in Atlanta. Your life is in Atlanta."

She shrugged. "The truth of the matter is I don't have much of a life. I've had more social engagements here in the last two months than in the last year. And my job is wherever my clients are. I hardly spend any time in my office."

"You worked hard for what you have. You're going to throw it all away because you and your high school girlfriend are having some fun?" Worse than angry, he sounded disappointed.

"I'm not throwing anything away."

He didn't look convinced.

"Don't you like having me around?"

That seemed to soften him a little. "Of course I do."

"I'm sure you'll get tired of me underfoot, but what if I lived down the street and not ten hours away?"

The moment of softness passed. "You're too good for this town."

"I like this town. I like being close to you. I like having friends and bumping into people I know. I like the space and the quiet." She took a deep breath and let herself say it. "It's home."

He huffed out a breath and stared her down. "That's all nice and flowery and whatever. What if things with Kate don't work out? Then what?"

She hadn't gotten that far in the thinking yet, much less the planning. "I have no idea if they will. Or if I'd want to stay either way. I'm just starting to realize my life isn't as satisfying as I wanted to believe and maybe now is the time to do something about it."

He shook his head. "I thought you were happy."

"I'm not saying I've been miserable. I'm saying I think my priorities have been off and I want to shift them."

"Mid-life crisis, huh? Aren't you a little young for that?" He raised his brow in a way that took any sting out of the question.

"Seriously?" Leave it to her father to get her all riled up and then break the tension a second later.

"Did you buy a sports car you haven't told me about?"

She groaned. He laughed.

"You know I just want you to be happy, right? It's all I've ever wanted." His voice was thick with emotion.

"I know, Dad. I know." She got up from the sofa to give him a hug.

He gave her a few firm pats on the back and cleared his throat. "Maybe I will take that fresh beer."

She chuckled, not quite as relieved as he probably was to bring the heart-to-heart to a close, but close. "You got it."

❖

Kate looked up from the pair of earrings she'd been crafting to find Harper hovering in the doorway. "Hi, baby."

"Hi, Mama."

When Harper didn't continue, or come into the room, her spidey sense tingled. "Do you need something or are you just saying hi?"

"Are you ready for the Sugarcane Festival?"

She'd been stockpiling inventory for a couple of months. It wasn't a huge event, but it accounted for a substantial chunk of her retail sales for the year. "Almost. Are you?"

Harper nodded with enthusiasm. "I can't wait. I'm going to have cotton candy and a corn dog and go on all the rides."

"I'm going to check with Macy's mama to see what day they're going and if you can tag along with them." Since she spent most of the festival working, she needed backup on the fun front.

"I thought maybe I could go with Sutton."

"Sutton?" The delivery surprised her more than the ask itself.

"Please, Mama. Pretty please." Harper looked at her with pleading eyes.

"Harper Ann, what do I say about begging?"

Harper huffed out a breath. "That it's childish and rarely the way to get what I want."

"And what are you doing right now?"

"I was almost begging, but I know better, so I'm laying out a logical argument for why my plan is the best plan."

Kate scratched her head and did her best not to laugh. "Logical argument, huh?"

"Yes. Hear me out. One, I know Sutton wants to go because she said so at the store the other day."

She lifted a finger. "But wanting to go and wanting to spend the whole day with you is not the same thing."

Harper nodded decisively. "Exactly. But she did say she wanted to go on rides and play games, and a kid is the best company for that sort of thing."

Even if she didn't agree that was always the case, she gave Harper points for logic. And finesse. "That's maybe true."

"Two, Uncle Bryce has to work so that means either Mawmaw or Pawpaw would have to take me and you know they don't like rides."

She smiled. "I'll give you that one."

"Three, you know I'll want to spend some of the time hanging out in the booth with you, so Sutton can do whatever she wants while I'm doing that."

"I'll think about it."

Harper folded her arms. "I'm not finished."

It bordered on sass, but she was having too much fun to mind. "Sorry."

"Four, I already asked her."

"What?" More than Harper asking Sutton in the first place, it bugged her that this was the first she was hearing about it—from Harper or from Sutton.

"When we were talking about it, I was telling her how you have a booth and sell your jewelry and she said that was cool and asked me if I helped and I told her I did, but not all day because I got bored and then got on your nerves."

"Stop. Take a breath."

Harper did, more dramatically than was necessary. "And then she asked what I'd do the rest of the day and I said you'd get a babysitter and then I asked if she wanted to be my babysitter."

It didn't surprise her that Harper hatched such a plan. Sutton agreeing without talking to her did. "And she said yes?"

"She said yes, but we'd have to ask you first."

"I see."

Harper grinned. "And I said I'd take care of it."

Kate pinched the bridge of her nose. She didn't like being manipulated and she liked Sutton being privy to it even less. "I don't like that you went behind my back."

Harper looked genuinely confused. "I didn't mean it like that, Mama. I was trying to help."

There would be a time, probably in the not too distant future, when her daughter would lie to her and she wouldn't be able to tell. She was grateful that time had not yet come. She was even more grateful Harper wasn't lying now. "Even if that's true, do you see how doing it all without telling me isn't the best idea?"

Harper cringed. "I was trying to surprise you?"

"Which I appreciate, but generally surprises are better if they're for the person you're surprising and not something you want for yourself."

"Yeah." She hung her head. "So, does that mean the answer is no?"

She'd need to talk to Sutton, make sure she both understood and wanted what she'd volunteered for. Or been roped into. But something told her Sutton didn't mind. Which was perhaps another problem entirely, but not one she needed to sort out today. "It's a maybe."

Unlike we'll see, maybe meant probably, which Harper knew. She also knew it meant she wasn't in trouble for meddling. Her face broke into a wide grin. "I'll take it."

"You talk to me first next time, okay?"

Harper nodded. "Yes, ma'am."

"Now give me a hug."

Harper flung her arms around her and squeezed. She let go, her expression serious. "Don't be mad at Sutton."

Talk about another problem entirely. "I'm not. And I'm not mad at you, either."

"Cool." Having got what she came for, Harper skipped from the room.

Kate returned her attention to the earrings, but put her tools down as quickly as she'd picked them up. She snagged her phone from the corner of the worktable and pulled up her text thread with Sutton. *A little birdie tells me you made plans for the Sugarcane Festival.*

When Sutton didn't immediately respond, she went back to work, finishing the earrings and starting a bracelet with the same beads: blue teardrops with a swirl of gold. She needed to figure out what to do about Harper's friendship with Sutton—not to mention her own—but she sank into the work. That intense, almost mindless focus was one of her favorite parts of making jewelry. Even more than the creativity, it stilled her mind in ways she heard other people talk about meditation.

When she surfaced, having used all the beads she'd fired in the last week, over an hour had passed. Her speaker had run out of juice and she'd missed a slew of texts from Sutton.

Tentative. We agreed we had to ask you first.

I want to go anyway and going with a kid is way more fun than going solo.

Unless I could convince you to ride the Ferris wheel with me and kiss me at the top.

I hope you're not mad. I really wasn't trying to step on your toes.

Any irritation evaporated. If a tiny needling took hold in the back of her mind—something in the whole nother problem category—she ignored it. *Not mad. Just want to make sure you know what you're signing up for.*

I was told junk food, games, and rides. Is that not accurate?

She was alone in the room but laughed out loud. *That sounds about right.*

Sign. Me. Up.

Why did Sutton have to make everything so damn easy? *The job is yours. Fair warning, Harper can eat a lot of cotton candy. Also, afraid of heights.*

Sutton's reply couldn't have been more perfect. *I accept these conditions. Also happy to help out in any way I can.*

She might have been talking about the festival—taking care of Harper, carting her around, maybe even helping at Kate's booth—but Kate got the impression it was more of a blanket offer. And while her first instinct was to brush off offers of help that didn't come from family, a tiny part of her liked the way Sutton helped. The ways she kept showing up.

It was nice to have an adult she could count on that wasn't Bryce or her parents. It was nice to have someone in her corner whose company she actually enjoyed. Enjoying sleeping together was total bonus.

But if she was being honest, it was more than that. It was the fact that it was Sutton. Sutton, who'd bolted when she learned about the pregnancy, was showing up for her and for Harper in ways Kate couldn't have imagined a few months prior. Even if she knew it was a temporary arrangement, maybe Sutton wouldn't bolt this time. Maybe they could stay friends in some shape or form. Because even if it was weird in some ways, she liked having Sutton back in her life. And even though she was all about living in the moment, thinking about Sutton in her future made her happy.

Chapter Twenty-four

Sutton pulled into the driveway just as Kate closed the back hatch of her car. Harper turned her way with an enthusiastic wave. Kate mirrored the gesture, if with slightly less exuberance. She parked next to Kate and got out. "I'm not late am I?"

"Right on time. I thought I'd get everything loaded so I could head out when you got here."

"I was hoping to be on time to help, but I should have known you'd get an early start."

Kate smirked. "If you're trying to early bird shame me, it isn't going to work."

"Oh, no. I'm laughing at myself because I was ready half an hour ago and didn't want to be one of those obnoxious people who shows up before they're told to."

Of course Sutton would consider that. "Well, now that we're all running early, I have time for coffee. Can I interest you in a cup?"

"Always. Though, I was thinking we could come with you and help set up instead of coming later."

"That's a long day you're signing up for." More than she was sure either of them were up for.

"We don't have to if you think it's too much for Harper, but I'm game. And I thought it might be nice to have one car."

"I'm standing right here," Harper said with an air of mock indignation.

She looked at Harper, then at Sutton, then back to Harper. "Okay, Miss Opinionated, what do you want to do?"

Harper seemed to weigh her options. "We should definitely all go together."

Sutton grinned. "I guess we're decided."

"Wait a second. Did you two plot this ahead of time, too?"

Both Sutton and Harper shook their heads with vigor. Not scheming now, but they might as well have been. It gave her a flash of what it might be like to live with both of them under the same roof. Yikes. Where did that come from?

"No, really. We didn't." Sutton looked at her with concern.

She chuckled. "I believe you. How about we take our coffees to go and that way we can be leisurely when we get there?"

"If you mean chocolate milk instead of coffee, I'm in," Harper said.

"And if by leisurely you mean we can get funnel cake for breakfast, I'm in."

She planted her hands on her hips. "How did we go from it being your idea to all go together to now I'm the one talking you into it?"

Sutton shrugged, all innocence. "I'm very convincing."

That got a giggle out of Harper. Kate rolled her eyes, but with amusement. "All right, all right. If we're going to do it, let's get this show on the road."

They filed back into the house and she fixed three travel mugs—two of coffee and one of chocolate milk. She let Frances out one last time and promised Pawpaw would be by to visit in the afternoon. Then the three of them piled into her car, with both Sutton and Harper holding boxes of inventory on their laps.

The drive was short and setup took practically no time at all, between three pairs of hands unloading and it being an indoor venue that didn't require her to bring her own tables or a tent for cover. Since she was particular when it came to the arrangement of her displays, she sent them off in search of funnel cakes with assurances she didn't need any, not this early at least.

They came back a couple of hours later, having shared a funnel cake but also bearing lunch. Harper seemed particularly proud of the fact that she not only picked out a gyro for her, but had settled on that for herself, too, instead of a corn dog. They discussed the afternoon's agenda—rides, games, the parade—and she sent them on their way again.

Business picked up after lunch, so much so that she lost track of time. She also lost track of how depleted her displays were getting. After finishing a sale, she rooted around under the table for inventory to replenish what she'd sold in the last few hours. She'd no sooner gotten the new items situated when a woman around her mama's age strolled by and, in a matter of minutes, bought eight pairs of earrings.

"Can't hurt to get ahead on Christmas, can it?" The woman offered a shrug as she handed over her credit card.

She swiped the card and started boxing up the woman's purchases. "It most definitely can't."

Even though it was still August, early Christmas shopping made up a lot of her sales at the festival. Perhaps it was because most of her customers were older folks who made their way to the air conditioned VFW hall for a cup of coffee and a reprieve from the heat and noise outside. She'd initially been worried about the craft show being tucked indoors, but she'd come to appreciate both the flow of people and the fact that she didn't have to spend twelve hours in the heat with nothing more than a pop-up tent for shade.

Gifts in hand, the woman continued her loop of the booths. Kate jotted down a few notes about what to make extra of for the holiday season to come. As always, it seemed she couldn't do enough in purple and gold, especially the new technique she'd devised of swirling gold dust into translucent purple glass.

"Mama!" Harper's yell carried from several booths away.

Harper came to a halt right in front of her stall. Kate lifted a hand to signal her to take it down a notch. "Hi, honey."

"Mama, we rode the Ferris wheel and it stopped right at the top." Harper's voice was quieter now, almost breathless.

"You did?"

"I was scared, but Sutton said the flip in her tummy was the coolest feeling and I decided maybe it was cool and not scary." Despite her longstanding fear of both heights and Ferris wheels, nothing but enthusiasm came through now.

Sutton, who'd been a few paces behind and not running, joined them. She offered Kate an almost sheepish smile. "Hey."

Kate experienced a tummy flip of her own, but after returning the greeting, shifted her focus back to Harper. "And was it?"

"I was still scared, but Sutton said she'd ask the guy to stop if I wanted to get off. I almost did. But Sutton held my hand and that made everything better."

Kate stole a glance at Sutton, who continued to look sheepish. "Having a hand to hold does make everything better."

Sutton folded her arms. "For the record, it was her idea."

Harper nodded with enthusiasm. "We went on the Scrambler and the bumper cars and then I asked Sutton what her favorite ride was and she said the Ferris wheel and it didn't seem fair to go on my favorite rides and not hers."

"It is nice if everyone gets to do their favorite thing."

"I told her I hoped I could convince you to go on it with me later." Sutton winked. "You know, so there wouldn't be any pressure."

"Nuh-uh. You want to go with Mama so y'all can do the kissy kissy." Harper rolled her eyes.

Kate snorted before she could help herself, but poor Sutton looked absolutely horrified. "I didn't say that."

Harper's face became one of disbelief mixed with pity. "Uh, it's pretty obvious y'all do the kissing."

Sutton looked to her with pleading eyes. She shrugged, then said to Harper, "So, you're a yes on the Ferris wheel and a no on the kissing?"

Harper wrinkled her nose. "Definitely a no on the kissing."

"But you'd do the Ferris wheel again?"

She nodded with enthusiasm. "Oh, yeah. Sutton says we should go at night when everything is lit up."

She'd been gently prodding for the last several years. Not that there were many opportunities in Duchesne to work through a fear of heights, but still. And somehow Sutton had managed to vanquish it in the span of a single afternoon. "I think that's a fantastic idea."

Sutton tipped her head toward the booth. "I can cover here if you want."

"No need. The craft fair closes up at seven."

"Do you need to pack up everything tonight?"

"Nah. They lock up the building. I just put everything away."

"So, maybe we could all have supper together?"

Kate tipped her head. "You already brought me a gyro for lunch."

Sutton grinned. "Yeah, but it's the fair. There are so many fried things."

"And things on sticks," Harper added.

They were like two peas in a pod. "Well, when you put it that way."

"Would you like a little break now? Bathroom, stretch your legs, sno-ball?"

She and the woodworking guy in the booth next door had a bathroom arrangement worked out, but the prospect of getting out of the booth for a little while had a certain appeal. "You wouldn't mind?"

"Why don't you two go walk around for a bit? I'm happy to watch the shop." Sutton looked at the tables of merchandise and the makeshift register. "As long as you tell me exactly what to do."

She gave Sutton a tutorial on the products in case there were any questions, then the credit card swiper and other payment options. It was weird to leave someone other than Mama in charge in her absence, but at the same time not weird at all. She already trusted Sutton with Harper, after all.

After giving strict orders to call or text if she had any issues, she and Harper strolled out of the building and into the sunshine, hand in hand. "Sounds like you're having a good day."

"Mama, Sutton is so fun."

Yeah. Only she could keep track of short-term fun versus the long haul. "It's going to be hard when she goes back to Atlanta, isn't it?"

Harper let out a heavy sigh. "Yeah."

"I'm thinking she might come back for visits."

Harper shook her head. "It won't be the same, though."

"I know. And I don't want to ruin the fun of today, but I don't want you to forget that's what's happening, either."

Harper remained subdued until they hit the midway. Fortunately, the bright colors and aroma of sugar and deep fried treats, not to mention the music of the rides and sounds of the games, proved adequate distraction. Harper gave herself over to having a good time and Kate said a prayer that at least a piece of that easy-going attitude stayed with her as her teenage years unfolded.

❖

Sutton added to her notes of what had sold and smiled with satisfaction. Kate hadn't asked for a detailed account, but she figured it couldn't hurt. Given how Kate tracked inventory at the store, she probably had some impressive system.

"Why do you look so pleased with yourself?"

She looked up to find Kate smirking at her. "I've managed five sales in your absence and I'm pretty sure I didn't mess any of them up."

Kate tipped her head. "Well done."

She looked around, but saw no signs of Harper. "I don't mean to question your parenting skills, but you appear to have lost your child."

Kate gave her a you're not as funny as you think you are look. "She ran into her cousins, who were going to ride some more rides then go back to my cousin Laurie's for a swim."

"Tossed aside for a pool party. I'm devastated." She pressed a hand to her chest and dropped her head.

"I confess I encouraged her."

"You did?"

Kate's smirk softened into a more suggestive smile. "Yeah. If she spends twelve full hours here, she'll be beyond cranky."

"Ah." That made sense. She lost track sometimes that Harper wasn't even ten yet. She seemed more mature than Sutton imagined for that age.

"We'll have to pick her up on the way home, but it means you and I will get to walk around a little bit just the two of us."

The idea definitely appealed. "Does that mean you'll ride the Ferris wheel with me?"

"I think that could be arranged." Kate reached over the table and trailed a finger down the front of Sutton's shirt. "The least I can do for the person who got me five whole sales."

The teasing made Sutton smile and, in some ways, felt more intimate than any suggestive comment might have. "There was this woman who was eighty if she was a day. I think my charm helped close the deal. And she bought earrings for all four of her granddaughters."

Kate pressed a hand to her chest, more a be still my beating heart move than the wounded look Sutton had gone for a moment ago. "My hero."

She laughed, then, and imagined being Kate's sidekick at other events. Maybe make it so she could do bigger shows in Baton Rouge or New Orleans. Would Kate like that? Or was she, as usual, getting way ahead of herself?

"What? You don't like being called a hero?"

"Oh, no." She shook her head vigorously. "I absolutely do. I was just…"

Kate folded her arms playfully. "You what?"

"I was thinking about kissing you on the Ferris wheel." Not a lie. Entirely.

"I see. Is that all?"

"The rest is me getting ahead of myself, but I know better than to tell you about that."

Kate laughed that sexy and easy laugh that had Sutton's heart beating faster than it should. "I'm sorry you're not going home with me tonight. Or, rather, that you will, but then you'll have to leave."

It was probably for the best that Kate believed her thoughts were on sex. And, again, not entirely a lie. Her mind never wandered too many steps away from that where Kate was concerned. "If I get that kiss, I imagine I'll survive."

"Speaking of, though..."

Kate trailed off, but Sutton couldn't conjure where she was going. "Speaking of what?"

"Sleepovers," Kate said.

Oh. "What about them?"

"My second cousin is getting married next weekend and Harper is one of the flower girls and already has plans to spend the night with the other flower girl."

She should appreciate that Kate was thinking ahead, trying to arrange it so they'd have some time together. But a tiny part of her couldn't help but be disappointed that was the extent of it.

"I mean, no pressure, but if you want to be my date to the wedding, too, I wouldn't say no."

"That might be the most backdoor invitation I've ever gotten." Which was easier to joke about than the way her heart leapt at the idea of going to a wedding together.

Kate made a show of cringing. "Sorry."

"I'm totally saying yes, but I feel compelled to give you a hard time."

Kate grinned, but then her smile softened. "Thanks for saying yes. I can't remember the last time I had a date to a wedding."

That fact shouldn't make her happy, but it did. "It would be my pleasure."

Kate explained who exactly was getting married and where, who Sutton would probably know. As seven o'clock approached, they packed up Kate's booth and tucked the bins under the tables. Kate stuffed the money and her iPad in her bag and slung it over her shoulder.

It was still hot out, but the humidity had given way to a breeze, making the evening almost pleasant. They got crawfish pies and boudin balls from one of the stalls, along with a pair of beers. Since the surrounding picnic tables were occupied, they wandered over to the stage area where the next band was warming up. They sat on the grass, knee to knee, sharing the food and watching the crowd. When the music began, folks started to dance. Mostly traditional two steps, but there was some freestyle thrown in and plenty of kids doing their own thing.

"Do you have much occasion to dance in the big city?"

Kate's question snapped Sutton from her reverie. "Not much, sadly."

"Does that mean you're too rusty to spin me around?" Kate asked.

Like most kids in south Louisiana, she learned to dance almost as early as she learned to walk. And though she'd not had many chances to lead, she'd done plenty of practicing in her bedroom, imagining Kate in her arms. "I might not impress, but I think I can manage not to embarrass myself."

Kate grinned. "Good enough for me."

Sutton pushed herself to her feet and extended her hand. Kate took it and let Sutton haul her up. They tossed their trash and made their way to the makeshift dance floor. They joined in at the start of the next song, and stayed for the slow dance that followed. Between the lingering daylight and casual clothes, the sounds and smells of the festival all around them, it shouldn't have felt romantic. But with Kate in her arms, complete with a relaxed smile on her face and her hand on Sutton's shoulder, she would have been hard pressed to complain.

When the music shifted back to something fast, they continued their meander of the fairgrounds. She offered to win Kate a teddy bear, but managed to be gracious when Kate trounced her at whack-a-mole, even agreeing to carry said bear around. Of course, Kate picked out a bright pink one she thought Harper would like, but that was okay.

They bought tickets and joined the line for the Ferris wheel just as dusk settled over the sky. By the time they got on, the stars had come out and brightly colored lights bathed the entire festival site. "At the risk of sounding sentimental, I wasn't sure we were ever going to do this again."

Kate looked at her, eyes shining. "It's okay to be a little sentimental."

They rounded the top and started their first descent. Although she meant what she'd said to Harper about liking it, that first flip of her stomach got her every time. Or maybe it was Kate, looking at her with desire mixed with something more than friendship. "Thank you for today."

Kate smiled. "I'm pretty sure I should be thanking you. Again." She shook her head. "It isn't like that."

"No? What's it like?"

A reminder that life can be so much more than work and token jogs in overly manicured parks? A glimpse into the past she tried so hard not to remember? A hint at what the future could look like? "I needed this. Today, but all the days before, too. The time I get to spend with you, the time you let me spend with Harper. It's all helping me realize what I want my priorities to be."

Kate narrowed her eyes briefly, but then she smiled. "I'm glad."

And because the universe was smiling on her, the Ferris wheel came to a stop, right at the top. Kate quirked a brow, all the invitation Sutton needed. She leaned in and closed her eyes, felt the brush of Kate's perfect mouth over hers. And she was happier than she could remember being in a long, long time.

CHAPTER TWENTY-FIVE

W ell, there's a heartbreak waiting to happen." Mama lifted
her chin in the direction of Harper—barefoot but still
in her flower girl dress—standing on Sutton's feet as they danced a
rather lopey box step to "My Girl."

"I'm not getting my heart broken." Kate turned to face her
mother.

Mama angled her head slightly. "It's not your heart I'm talking
about."

She'd had that thought herself. From the day they'd brought
over tacos after Albin's surgery, Harper was smitten. At first, she'd
figured they wouldn't see enough of each other for any real feelings
to take root. But then Sutton kept showing up—at the store, at her
house. And then she and Sutton had gone and slept together. She
couldn't very well keep Harper from seeing her then. And now?
Now Sutton felt like a part of their lives and Kate found herself
hoping for things she had no business hoping for.

Mama looked her up and down. "Although maybe I should be."

Kate shook her head. "You don't have to worry about me."

"Worrying about you is my prerogative. Same goes for Harper.
Hasn't motherhood taught you anything?"

Despite not liking the current turn in the conversation, she
smiled. "I know."

"How in love are you?"

She lifted a shoulder. "Slightly less than Harper?"

"Why do I get the feeling that isn't saying much?"

"Harper is attached. But I talk with her all the time about Sutton moving back to Atlanta when her daddy is better. She knows what it's like when a friend moves away." That it was okay to be sad, but it was a part of life and not the end of the world.

Mama nodded slowly. "And you?"

"It's not like before. I was a naive kid then." She'd learned her lesson the hard way, but it meant she didn't intend to learn it more than once.

"And you're world-weary now? Aloof and untouchable?"

There were times in her life when Mama's flair for the dramatic drove her up a tree. But she'd gotten better at taking it with a grain of salt. She'd gotten better at taking a lot of things with a grain of salt. This thing with Sutton—whatever the hell it was—included. "Crusty old crone, that's me."

The song ended and another, faster one began. Harper skipped over to where she stood. "Come dance with us, Mama."

Even if she wasn't inclined to dance, she was happy to get pulled away from her mother's probing questions and the teasing that was only partially teasing. She stuck out her hand and Harper grabbed it, pulling her to the dance floor and to Sutton. The three of them bopped and bounced. She swayed her hips and shimmied her shoulders, letting the worries about what was next fade to the background. They'd be waiting for her when the music stopped.

When it did, a tried and true slow song followed. Harper, along with several of her cousins, groaned and made faces before running off to raid the dessert table. Kate watched them go. Mushy promises of forever notwithstanding, she really did love weddings.

"May I?" Sutton eyed her hopefully.

It was one thing to slow dance with Sutton at the Sugarcane Festival. It was another to do it at a family wedding. There were the curious gazes, of course, especially from relatives who hadn't seen them together since they were teenagers. There was also the whole matter of it being a wedding. But she'd asked Sutton to be her date. Doing that and then refusing to dance would be silly. "Please."

One of Sutton's hands clasped hers; the other settled at her waist. She'd rolled up the sleeves of her baby blue button-down, but she still had that polished look that could make Kate's knees go weak. Sutton guided her back and forth, nothing fancy, but it made her feel like a princess anyway. Mama's words echoed in her mind.

What was a little heartbreak, anyway? A reminder that she was taking chances and living, that's all. Something she hadn't done enough of lately. Or maybe it was something more than that. Maybe it was a fleeting moment of joy. A kind of happiness she'd stopped feeling and lost track of along the way.

When the song ended, Sutton stood still and she realized her eyes had drifted closed. She opened them and, if the look Sutton gave her was anything to go on, her feelings were written all over her face. She cleared her throat. "One more drink before they close down the bar?"

Sutton gave a knowing smile. "Sure."

They headed to the bar, then stood together on the side of the dance floor. She sipped her seven and seven, happy for something to do as much as the way the cool liquid quenched her thirst.

Sutton took a slow swig of her beer. "I'm not going to lie, I love weddings."

She smiled in spite of herself. "You would say that."

"I'm a romantic. I've made peace with that."

"And you're saying I'm not?" Most days, she'd say she wasn't, but for some reason it didn't sit well tonight.

Sutton didn't miss a beat. "You can be anything you want to be."

"All right. I'll show you romantic. You want to get out of here?"

The suggestive tone got Sutton's attention. "I'm at your disposal."

"Give me two minutes." She downed the rest of her drink and went in search of Harper. She found her with Macy. Laurie had them collecting their shoes and baskets and other flower girl paraphernalia before leaving. She kissed Harper good night, kissed Macy for good measure, and thanked Laurie again for hosting the sleepover. After finding her own shoes and purse, she went in search of Sutton. Kate found her exactly where she'd left her, looking relaxed and confident and sexy as fuck.

Sutton set down her bottle. "Ready?"

She had a second of questioning whether her plan was really the best one, but shoved that worry aside. She had a point to prove, after all. "Ready." Out in the parking lot, the night air was heavy and smelled of honeysuckle. It reminded her so much of that summer before Sutton left, even more than being on the Ferris wheel together had. "I have an idea."

"Why do I get the feeling it's something that could get me into trouble?"

She shrugged. "Trouble is relative. Are you game?"

Sutton hesitated, but only for a second. "I am."

Kate looked around before grabbing Sutton's hand. Not afraid that someone would see them, exactly, but sinking in to the covert nature of what she had in mind. "Come on."

If Sutton was surprised to be led in the opposite direction of her car, she didn't show it. They crossed the street and walked along the east side of the library, skirting the fenced off practice fields of the high school. When she took a right, Sutton stopped dead in her tracks. "Wait."

She turned around, feigning innocence. "What?"

"Are we—"

"Yep."

Sutton shook her head. "We are way too old."

She poked a finger into Sutton's chest. "We most certainly are not."

"How about too mature. Are we too mature?"

"I'm pretty sure that's a sub-category of too old."

"No, no. One can have maturity regardless of age."

"Are you scared?" It might not be a fair button to push, but she knew it would do the trick.

"Kind of, but only because I'm a sane and law-abiding adult."

Kate let go of Sutton's hand. She planted her hands on her hips and cocked one of those hips to the side. "So, that's a no?"

The hesitation lasted more than a second this time. In fact, so many seconds ticked by, she expected Sutton to bail. But when Sutton finally blew out a breath, her smile was wide. "I said I was game. I'm not backing out now."

"Good. You're sexy when you're brave." She winked at Sutton, grabbed her hand, and kept walking.

❖

After wiggling through the same gap in the fence they'd wiggled through as teenagers, Sutton found herself staring up at the Duchesne water tower. How could it look taller now than when she'd been a kid? And how had she let Kate talk her into this again?

Oh, right. It was where they'd had their first kiss. And Kate had made that comment about showing her romantic. She didn't stand a chance.

Without hesitating or waiting to see if she'd follow, Kate started to climb. The fact that she was doing so in heels and a dress filled Sutton with a mixture of fear and awe. "So, I need a little guidance here. Is it completely skeevy of me to look up your skirt? Because I'm not sure how I'm supposed to resist."

Kate stopped climbing. She looked over her shoulder and down at Sutton with an expression of pure mischief. "I think I'd be offended if you didn't look."

The playfulness, laced with a trace of challenge, reminded her so much of the times they'd done this before. Kate—fearless and always up for adventure—coaxing Sutton to let go, to be brave. "If I fall and crack my skull open and die, know that I died happy."

"You aren't going to die. Unless you tell Harper we did this. Then you'll be dead because I'll have killed you." Kate grinned and resumed climbing.

Sutton couldn't help but smile. It was such a Kate thing to say, both because it was hyperbolic and because she had no doubt Kate meant every word. She gave herself a few seconds to appreciate that, along with the view of Kate's perfect legs and the flashes of red under her skirt. Then she started to climb.

About halfway up, she paused and made the mistake of looking down. She closed her eyes and froze. "Holy fuck."

"Come on, you can do it. The view is worth it. You always said so."

She had always said so. "Yeah, but my frontal cortex wasn't fully developed back then."

Kate stopped and once again looked down. "We don't have to. If you're scared, we can go back."

It was the line she'd used back then. More effective than a taunt or a dare, it tapped into Sutton's deep-seated desire not to disappoint people. Especially people she cared about, people she loved. Especially Kate. "I'm coming."

For some reason, the rest of the climb passed in a blur. She hoped the descent would, too, when the time came. She'd worry about that later.

Before long, they sat perched on the narrow walkway, feet dangling and arms hooked over the railing. She had Kate's thigh pressed against hers and the entire town spread out before her. And the sky. She was pretty sure there wasn't a sight more beautiful than the night sky from the top of the water tower. Well, except maybe the woman sitting next to her.

Yep, worth it.

Sutton pulled her eyes from the skyline and focused her attention on the view up close. Kate had a faraway look in her eyes and a relaxed half smile that made her features seem almost ethereal. Or maybe it was the moonlight. "Thank you for this."

Kate turned to face her. "I haven't been up here since you left."

It was hard to believe, though Kate would have no reason to lie. "You haven't?"

"Wait." Kate raised a finger. "I did come once, right after you left for college."

"But not since. Why not?" She had no business hoping it was for sentimental reasons, but she hoped for it nonetheless.

"That first time made me miss you so bad I wasn't sure I'd be able to get myself down."

She let herself put a hand on Kate's leg. Did she get to offer reassurance about that now? "I'm sorry it was so hard. I'm sorry for everything."

Kate shook her head and let out a small laugh. "I was eighteen. I was a giant bundle of feelings."

"But you were my bundle and I made you feel that way." Probably pressing her luck now.

Kate shook her head. "I made you feel some pretty awful things, too."

That heartbreak felt so insignificant now, with the rest of their lives laid out before them. But before she could say as much, Kate continued.

"And then I was pregnant and at least had the wherewithal not to take stupid risks." She shrugged. "And then I had a baby and not five minutes to myself, much less hours upon hours to disappear."

She'd been so caught up in her own anger and grief, she hadn't spent a lot of time thinking about what Kate's life looked like after they broke up. "I'm sorry you had to face all that alone."

"I wasn't alone. My parents were amazing and Bryce stepped up big time. Keeping Harper was my decision, but it was a family effort. I couldn't have done it without them."

What if, even with the pregnancy, she and Kate hadn't broken up? "But you should have had me, too."

Kate bumped Sutton's shoulder with hers. "You're getting sentimental on me."

Sutton smiled. "Guilty as charged."

"Guilty as usual, you mean." Kate's tone was teasing, but it struck a nerve.

"I've become much more jaded, I'll have you know," Sutton said.

"Have you, now? How so?"

"Well, I have a stuffy career and have been neglecting my passions. So much I'm not even sure I have passions anymore. If that's not jaded, I don't know what is."

Kate frowned. "I'm sorry if that didn't come out the right way. I wasn't trying to make you feel bad."

Sutton blew out a breath. "You're making me feel lots of things."

She winced. "Sorry about that, too?"

"Don't be." Sutton shook her head. "You made me realize I've been operating on autopilot."

"There's nothing wrong with that. I mean, a lot of people settle into a routine that makes them happy, and that's not a bad thing."

"Hey, I said don't be sorry. I mean it." Because even if it was fine for some people, it wasn't fine for her. At least, she didn't want it to be.

"Fine. I take back the apology."

Sutton grinned and this time bumped her shoulder to Kate's. "I've missed your needling."

"Okay, okay. You don't need to mollycoddle me."

"I love that you aren't afraid to ask hard questions, Kate. It's one of my favorite things about you." One of so many.

"Well, no more hard questions. I promised romance and I intend to deliver." Kate bit her bottom lip slightly and leaned in.

They'd kissed already. They'd done a hell of a lot more than kiss. And yet there it was. That crazy jolt of electricity that stole her breath and left her shaky. Lightning in a bottle, she used to call it. Magical, but rare. But she felt it with Kate, every damn time.

This time, any pieces of her heart still in her possession went tumbling. And when the kiss ended and Kate rested her head on Sutton's shoulder, she knew there was no going back.

After a long while of sitting like that—staring at the town, staring at the sky—Kate lifted her head. "Do you want to come back to my place?"

"Is it wrong to say I thought that was a foregone conclusion?"

Kate chuckled. "I still feel like I should ask."

She knew she was being overly serious and she didn't even care. "Kate, I will be with you every chance you give me."

She expected a comeback, or at least a gentle tease, but Kate merely nodded.

"I—" The trajectory of her thoughts was interrupted by the realization they had to get back to the ground before they could go anywhere.

"What? Having second thoughts?"

Sutton shook her head quickly and stood. "I was just thinking about who was going to go down first."

Kate's eyes got huge and a small squeak escaped her.

The double meaning of her words registered. Making her laugh. Making her brave. She angled her head. "The ladder."

"Right. The ladder."

There was something to be said about keeping Kate on her toes. She'd have to remember to do that more often. She bowed. "Ladies first."

Chapter Twenty-six

They made it up the porch steps, but before Kate could unlock her front door, Sutton pushed her up against it. She threaded her fingers into Kate's hair and pulled her into a kiss. Just as intoxicating as before. Maybe more so now, given they were safely back on the ground and mere feet from Kate's bed.

Kate made this soft moaning sound, and it took all of Sutton's self-restraint not to slide a hand up her skirt right then and there. Surely, giving in to the heat between them had to be safer than the feelings threatening to swallow her whole.

Kate fumbled with her keys. "You have to let go of me long enough to get the door open."

"Or I could take you on the porch." Sutton's mouth was at her ear, the words barely a whisper.

"I'm sure Miss Picou would love to peek out her window and see that."

Sutton chuckled. "I don't suppose that's how to foster good neighborly relations."

"Considering she still goes to Mass every day, I'm going to say no."

As desperately as she wanted Kate, Sutton didn't want her like this. She stilled her hands and forced herself to pull back. "Sorry."

Kate's eyes danced with laughter. "Sorry for what you were doing or sorry for stopping?"

"Sorry for doing what I was doing on your front porch like a horny teenager with no restraint."

Kate laughed. The sound managed to be both sensual and edgy. "There's something to be said for no restraint."

"I want to worship you, Kate, and to do that I'm going to need to take my time."

Kate angled her head slightly. "You're not going to get all precious on me now, are you?"

In spite of her feelings—her deep, vast, threaten to drag her under like a rip tide feelings—Sutton laughed. She'd always been the more emotionally intense one. It proved oddly reassuring that part of their dynamic hadn't changed, even now. "I won't. Promise."

"Good."

Kate stuck her key in the lock and opened the door. She grabbed Sutton's hand and pulled her inside. When she closed it behind her, she was the one pushing Sutton against it. She gripped the front of Sutton's shirt and pulled her into a kiss that was hot and hungry and anything but precious.

She happily let Kate take the lead. She'd turn the tables eventually, but for now, the intensity of Kate's desire drew her in like a siren song. She didn't care what happened, she just needed more of it, and to get as close as humanly possible.

Kate took her hand once again. "My room. Now."

She followed Kate down the narrow hall, past Kate's studio and Harper's room, and into Kate's. Kate flipped a switch and a lamp next to the bed came on. Though she'd been in Kate's room several times, something about tonight felt different. She found herself paying attention to the details: antique four-poster bed, coverlet splashed with bright red anemones. So much more sophisticated than Kate's room when they were young, yet so very Kate.

"What?"

Sutton smiled. "Just admiring your space."

"It's not your first time here."

"I know. But I'm thinking how it's all grown up but still you."

Kate pointed at her and made a little circle with her finger. "You're being precious."

She laughed because it was such a Kate thing to say but also because it was true. "I'm not. I swear. Here, let me show you."

Kate smirked then, that sexy little smile with a hint of challenge behind it. It somehow managed to make her even sexier. Sutton closed the distance between them and pulled Kate into a kiss. Really, just picking up where they'd left off on the porch. Because whatever deep feelings had been stirred up in that moment on the water tower, desire was front and center. At least for now.

They continued kissing and Sutton worked the hem of Kate's dress up her thighs. Her fingers grazed the smooth skin, sending her already racing libido into orbit. She slid the dress higher and higher, over Kate's torso and up the arms she'd extended over her head. "You are so beautiful."

"I'm not eighteen anymore," Kate said, almost shy all of a sudden.

"No, you're not." Sutton shook her head slowly. "You were amazing then, but still a girl. We both were."

"And now?" Kate's voice held the same hint of challenge as her smirk a moment before.

"Now, you might be the most beautiful woman I've ever known."

Kate opened her mouth but Sutton pressed a finger to her lips.

"I'm stating the facts as I see them. Nothing less, nothing more."

She threaded her fingers into Kate's hair and resumed kissing her. The tangle of their tongues drove her mad, as did the scrape of Kate's nails along her skin under her shirt. Without breaking the kiss, Kate managed to unbutton Sutton's pants and send them to the floor. Sutton's shirt was next.

They tumbled onto the bed, limbs entwined and hands seeking. Kate, who'd sort of landed on top, straddled Sutton's thighs and sat up. She circled her hips a few times, grinding into Sutton in the most delicious way. At the same time, she reached behind her back and unhooked her bra. She slipped it off and tossed it aside.

Kate's breasts—pale and full and perfect—proved irresistible. As always. She snaked her hands up Kate's torso to take them in each hand. Kate moaned and threw her head back, never stopping the slow undulations of her body. She didn't want to be the sort of person who sat in awe of the woman she was about to make love to, but that's exactly what she was.

When Kate leaned down and kissed her, her hair fell forward, making a curtain around their faces. It gave her a flashback to high school and the days when they would make out for hours and hours in Sutton's bedroom, after school and before her dad got home from work. It was so vivid, she could practically smell the strawberry shampoo Kate used to use.

No longer haunted by the past but wanting to ground herself in the now, she grabbed Kate's wrists and sat up, rolling them over and switching their positions. Kate's smile might not be surrender, but it felt a lot like it. Not the bad, defeated kind, but like she was maybe, finally, letting herself feel even a fraction of what Sutton felt.

Kate sank into their newly reversed positions, arching her back and watching the play of emotions on Sutton's face. Definitely wanting, arousal. But something more. Something that made her go all soft on the inside, but hot and needy at the same time. "Mmm."

Sutton's fingers encircled her wrists again, this time pinning them over her head. "Mmm, indeed."

She tested Sutton's grip, then relaxed into her hold. Damn, it felt good.

"I like you like this."

Kate bit her lip, even as her body instinctively arched. "How is that?"

Sutton's gaze threatened to set her on fire from the inside. "Completely at my mercy."

She gasped, her body responding even as her brain tripped.

"Does that bother you?"

It should. She wasn't in the market to be dominated. And yet. And yet a part of her yearned to let someone else take over, do the thinking and the worrying and the sorting out of what should happen. And how. And when. More pronounced than the night in New Orleans, more than just sex. She didn't have the words to express that, so she merely shook her head.

"I don't take that lightly, you know. In fact, I take it very, very seriously."

It felt like maybe Sutton was talking about more than that moment, but Kate kept herself in the present. In this moment, she could let go. Let Sutton take over. "Yes."

"Yes, you know, or yes, you're okay with that?"

She smiled. "Yes."

Something in Sutton's eyes shifted. Like she'd been holding back, or maybe, waiting for permission. She shifted so that she straddled one of Kate's thighs instead of both of them.

Kate opened her legs in invitation. Sutton let go of one of her wrists, grazing her fingers down Kate's torso and over her. Her body bucked and her clit threatened to explode with nothing more than that single touch. But, as though sensing how turned on she was, Sutton shifted her hand. She slid her fingers up one side and down the other, avoiding her center and teasing her, coaxing her higher.

"I'm sorry, but I really need to taste you."

Kate nodded dumbly, unable to formulate more of a response.

Sutton let go of her other wrist, but nodded toward her hands. "I'd like you to leave those right there, though. Do you think you can do that for me?"

Another nod.

Sutton shifted again, this time settling herself between Kate's legs. She took her time going about it, wrapping an arm around each of Kate's thighs and pressing a flurry of tiny kisses everywhere but where Kate needed her the most. "You are perfection."

She let out a ragged laugh. "I'm dying is what I am."

Sutton chuckled, but didn't leave her hanging. She pressed her tongue into Kate and sent her tumbling right over the edge.

"Fuck."

Sutton eased away, but only far enough to say, "I hope you aren't done with me."

Kate shook her head.

"Oh, good."

As Sutton's tongue continued its exquisite torture, her grip on Kate's thighs tightened. She felt her arousal ratchet up once again.

But it was no longer Sutton's mouth she needed. As if sensing that—reading her thoughts or reading her body—Sutton's fingers joined her mouth. But like before, it was a tease, leaving Kate clenching at nothing.

"Please. I'll beg if I have to."

"Please what?"

She groaned.

"I need to hear you say it."

"Please be inside me."

Sutton shifted. Kate thought she might tease her more, make her wait. But she didn't. Sutton's fingers plunged into her with a force that matched Kate's longing, with a possessiveness that took her breath away.

"Yes. More. Please." It was her voice, but she barely recognized the raspy desperation.

Sutton obliged, adding a third finger and putting more force behind her thrusts. Kate arched. She moaned. Not unlike the times before and yet somehow different. Like Sutton knew all her secrets now, knew every touch to send her body—and maybe her heart—over the edge.

She came, and she came again after that. Sutton was relentless. And when Sutton locked eyes with her and said, "One more, for me," she did.

When Sutton finally eased away, she was fairly certain she'd never catch her breath again. Aftershocks rippled through her, shudders that made her whole body tremble. Sutton held her, stroking her hair and making little hums of pleasure.

"I don't...I can't..."

Sutton kissed the top of her head. "I know."

It wasn't even about the sex, though, fuck, the sex had been amazing. No, they'd gone beyond sex tonight. Way beyond. She sort of already knew this, had known it since that night in New Orleans, but she'd set it aside, not wanting to weigh down the fun with the very real truth that she was falling for Sutton Guidry all over again.

And now? Now there was no denying it. For better or worse, she'd opened her heart and Sutton wasted no time taking up residence. Like that's what she had been waiting for all along.

As the reality of being in love with Sutton took root, she couldn't help but wonder what it meant, what she would do about it. Much like that initial attraction, ignoring it or wishing it away would be futile. So, for tonight at least, she could enjoy it. Bask in Sutton and feelings she hadn't felt in a long time.

And since she was one of those people who believed actions spoke louder than words, she went about showing Sutton in the best way she knew how.

Chapter Twenty-seven

S utton walked into the house, though she might as well have been floating on air. Neither of them had said it out loud, but last night had been a turning point. No way were they friends with benefits anymore. Not that she ever really considered Kate that. Now, though, it was mutual. She knew it with as much certainty as she knew the sky was blue.

Dad sat at the kitchen table, drinking coffee and reading the paper. The sight of him, not fully recovered but so much closer to his old self than he'd been in months, years maybe, only added to the aura of bliss. "Good morning, old man."

He peered at her over the top of his reading glasses. "What's got into you? Why do you have a goofy look on your face?"

"I'm happy. Is there a crime against being happy?"

He folded the paper and set it down. "We need to talk."

The tone alone took her mood down a couple of notches. The seemingly innocuous phrase—that never was—dampened it more. "What's wrong?"

He scowled. "Nothing's wrong. We need to talk."

"No one says that when they're delivering good news."

"It's not bad news. It's, well, do you want coffee?"

This was going from bad to worse. "Do I need coffee? Do I need something stronger than coffee?"

"Everyone needs coffee." He picked up his cup. "I need coffee."

She took the empty cup from him and refilled it from the pot, then poured a cup of her own. She joined him at the table and braced herself for whatever not bad news bad news he'd been stewing over. "What's going on?"

"Are you still thinking about sticking around? About moving back here?"

"I haven't made any decisions, but I am thinking about it." She hadn't said as much to Kate, but based on last night, she felt a hell of a lot more confident about their chances for a future.

"Then there's something you need to know."

Her brain raced ahead, flinging out possibilities of what he might say. Reasons he'd cooked up why it was a bad idea. Reasons she and Kate shouldn't be together. "What? What do I need to know?"

He looked at her, then down at his coffee. He'd never been one to hesitate sharing whatever he had on his mind, so the pause, the hesitation, sent her anxiety into overdrive. "Back when you left for college, I didn't want you to come home."

"What?" Not only did she have no idea what he was talking about, she couldn't fathom why it was relevant now.

"I wanted you to make something of yourself, to see there was more to the world than this podunk town."

He'd said as much at the time, if more gently. "I knew how much you sacrificed for me to go to school. I knew how important it was."

"But you had one foot stuck here."

He didn't use Kate's name, but she knew deep down that's what—who—he was referring to. "I missed home, sure. I missed you and Kate and my friends. Homesickness is pretty standard fare in college."

He shook his head. "It was more than that. I knew you wouldn't neglect your studies, but I worried you'd wind up here, taking some job that was beneath you and never realizing your potential."

"But that's not what happened. You can't think wanting to come home now is that."

"No. You've grown up and made me more proud of you than I can say. What you choose now is your decision."

"Okay." So far, none of this was much of a revelation. Was he trying to make her feel better about whatever she decided, in the most awkward Dad way possible?

"But if you're going to choose here, if there's a chance you're going to be with Kate, you deserve to know the truth."

It was as though her rib cage had a trap door. It swung open and her stomach fell through. Heart, too, and maybe her lungs. She'd already weathered what felt like the biggest betrayal possible. What could he possibly have to add?

"I told Kate you were happy."

"Like, recently?"

He let out a sigh that sounded like the weight of the world sat on his chest. "No, then. I told her you'd made friends and loved everything about being at school, that you talked about coming home like it was something you needed to do more than wanted. That you were making this incredible life."

"I don't understand." She hadn't been utterly miserable, but she'd not been any of those things, either.

"I wanted that to be true, convinced myself it was only a matter of time before it was. I wanted her to start to see that, to understand. So it would be a gentle letdown when the time came."

It should make her feel better that he wasn't dishing dirt on the woman she loved, that he wasn't trying to undermine them. But the weight of his betrayal settled heavy in her chest. "You lied to her. And to me."

"I was trying to make it easier on you both in the long run. It didn't feel like lying or meddling at the time. And I wasn't aiming to get her to sleep with that boy, but I think I may have played a part."

Oh, God. Even as he'd attempted to explain, that part of the equation hadn't entered her thoughts. Now that he'd put it out there, it expanded, taking up every nook and cranny of her mind.

"When you came home for Christmas and she was pregnant, I felt terrible. But, maybe, also that it was for the best."

"But I loved her. I loved her more than anything."

"You were kids. It was puppy love."

She shook her head slowly. "Kate was, is, the love of my life."

"I was wrong. I was wrong about so many things and I'm sorry." He looked at her with tears in his eyes.

It occurred to her she'd never seen him cry, not once. As much as a part of her—the young, devastated, and brokenhearted part of her—wanted to rage at what he'd done, what had happened as a result, she couldn't bring herself to. Kate might have made the choices she made regardless. And even more importantly, if she hadn't made those choices, there wouldn't be a Harper. "Thank you for telling me."

He looked at her with confusion. "That's it?"

"That's it." What good would being hurt or angry do now?

He thrust both arms in the air in seeming frustration. "Jesus, I thought you'd yell or storm off or something."

She wasn't quite able to muster a laugh, so she let out a sniff. "Sorry to disappoint."

His arms dropped. "You're really not mad?"

How could she explain? "I'm disappointed, hurt. But I feel like things happened the way they were supposed to."

"Huh."

"Don't get me wrong, I'm not letting you off the hook because your heart was in the right place. You had no right to do that to either one of us."

He nodded. "You're right."

"I was devastated." And so blinded by anger and betrayal that she didn't even give Kate the chance to apologize, or explain. If that was the one thing she could go back and change now, she would. God, she'd wasted so much time.

"I get it if you want to tell her."

Did she? She couldn't think clearly enough to know that yet. All she knew, the only thing reverberating in her mind clear as day, was that one thought. She'd wasted so much time. And that stopped right now.

❖

Kate had just finished stuffing Harper's booksack for the first day of school when Sutton's cryptic text came through. Something about good news, and wanting to deliver it in person. But not when Harper was around. The only thing she could think of was some kind of promotion that meant she needed to leave sooner rather than later. Which would be good for Sutton, even if she had a hard time mustering enthusiasm for it.

Harper's bus is at 7:45 and I don't have work til 9. Is that enough time?

Despite the apprehension brewing, Sutton's response—*I forgot it was the first day of school! Can I come over early enough to wish her luck?*—made her smile.

I'm sure she'd like that.

She opted not to tell Harper, wanting her focus to be on the start of school and not Sutton. The resulting surprise managed to dispel Harper's nerves just as they were starting to get the better of her. She couldn't have asked for a better send-off, and said as much to Sutton as they headed inside.

"Thank you for letting me be a part of it. I hope I get to be part of all sorts of little moments with her. And you. And big moments, too, for that matter." Sutton's smile seemed almost coy.

"You're being weird. What's going on?" Whatever it was, she could handle it. She would handle it.

"What if I didn't leave?"

Even as part of her knew what Sutton meant, she hesitated. "What do you mean? Like right now? I thought you were staying to talk. Wasn't that the point?"

"I mean, after my dad is all better. I've been thinking about it, and us, and I want to stay."

"I don't understand." She searched Sutton's face for meaning, but it didn't clarify anything about what she was saying.

"I've asked my company to move to a fully remote position. I'll still have to travel quite a bit, but I'll be based here instead of Atlanta."

"And you can do that?" She knew Sutton was a bigwig at her job, but this was beyond even that level of fancy, at least in her book.

"I mean, New Orleans isn't a hub, so it's more complicated to fly out of, but I don't mind that. And my company sure as hell isn't going to nickel and dime me about the cost." Sutton smiled. She seemed almost giddy. It made Kate question her own confusion and rising ambivalence.

"That's what you want? To be here permanently?"

"Yes." Sutton took her hand. "I want to be here. With you."

If a tiny part of her heart leapt with joy at the prospect of Sutton staying, the much larger part went into fight or flight mode. "But this was going to be temporary. You were going to leave."

"And now I'm not. I want to be with you, Kate. It's not a sacrifice to relocate if that's what you're worrying about."

It was definitely on the list. Along with worrying about where Sutton was going to live. And what it would be like trying to navigate a serious and long-term relationship. What that would mean for Harper and the life and the routine they had together. "It's not that. Or at least not just that. This is a big step, Sutton. One I guess I thought we'd discuss before you started making decisions."

That seemed to get her attention. Sutton's face went from buoyant to deflated in about two seconds. "I'm not trying to rush things. Or pressure you, for that matter. I know we just got back together."

Back together. It wasn't like she hadn't thought the phrase. Bryce had sure used it enough. Even Mama, yesterday morning, had asked if all the lovey-dovey romantic time with Sutton meant they were getting back together. "But we didn't talk about it like that. Not with all that weight, all the implications."

"I know, I know. You know me, always a few dozen steps ahead. But I did think we were on the same path."

Part of her wanted exactly that. She'd started to fantasize about it, and not just in the abstract. She could see what a future with Sutton might look like. But something about Sutton putting it out there made her a little dizzy. Like having too much to drink, it was the kind of feeling she was tempted to go along with, but knew she'd regret come morning. "It's complicated."

Sutton took a deep breath. She resisted the urge to pace and tried to ignore the first licks of panic swirling around in her chest. She laughed, but it sounded forced, even to herself. "It's never a good sign when you're telling me something is complicated."

Kate didn't respond and the panic spread.

"Are you—" She stopped, needing to know even as she dreaded the answer. "Are you not in love with me?"

"I…" Kate paused. Seconds ticked by. The silence blew through awkward and landed squarely in torture. She looked at her feet. She sighed. Eventually, she looked into Sutton's eyes. "I don't know."

"Oh." For the second time in her life, the ground seemed to give way from beneath her and her entire being—body, heart, soul—tumbled into free fall.

"I'm not saying that I'm not. It's just, this isn't what we agreed to."

The truth of Kate's statement cut her to the bone. They'd agreed to be friends, with benefits. They'd agreed to have fun and have sex and have a summer of shaking up the routines they'd found themselves in. They hadn't talked about feelings or whether or not they had a future. Not once.

But just like she had a tendency to spin out worries and what-ifs, she let herself spin an entire life. One in which she and Kate finally got their happily ever after. Where she and Kate and Harper got to be a family—so different from what she'd dreamed about but so perfect in its own way. Where the mistakes they'd made didn't matter anymore. "My Dad told me what he said to you."

Kate looked at her, once again, with confusion. "What? When?"

"When I left for school. He told me he made it seem like you were holding me back from making something of myself." And even though they'd hashed it out and shed a few tears, the idea of it still made her stomach coil.

It took a second, but realization dawned and Kate blanched. "Sutton—"

She lifted a hand. "I didn't know. I swear to God I didn't know until yesterday. He had no right. And what's more, if I'd known, I wouldn't have reacted the way I did. I would have forgiven you."

The paleness made the flush that crept into Kate's cheeks all the more dramatic. "And what? You'd have offered moral support and taken the night feedings over school breaks? Dropped out of college and taken some minimum wage job to help support us?"

She hadn't thought the logistics through because it was pointless to now. She'd thought Kate of all people would see it that way. "I don't know. I, well, I wouldn't have abandoned you. I know that much."

"But you did." Kate's tone was matter-of-fact, without even a trace of anger.

"And you'll never truly forgive me. Is that it?"

"It isn't about forgiveness."

"No? Because from where I sit, you decided to forgive me enough to sleep with me but not enough to consider making a life with me. I didn't realize there was a chart or I would have asked for it sooner." She could hear the irrationality in her voice, but the ship of sound judgment had sailed.

"Don't you dare make it seem like I'm the unreasonable one here, that I'm making you jump through hoops to earn my attention. Or affection. Or whatever you think I'm withholding. I spent the last ten years building a life without you. Ten fucking years, Sutton. That doesn't vanish because you decide to change your mind about what you want."

Sutton opened her mouth, but no words came out. She tried again. "I've always wanted you."

Kate closed her eyes and took a long, slow breath. When she opened them, they were glassy with tears. "You could have fooled me."

Kate's words were like a punch to the gut and a kick in the chest at the same time. The combination left her winded and queasy and unsure how a moment that was supposed to be so perfect could go so horribly wrong. Like Christmas break her first year of college, when she spent thirteen hours on a bus ride home wanting nothing more than to curl up with her girlfriend and not think about coding classes or frat boys or her work study job in the dish room for three whole weeks. When the girlfriend she'd missed for four excruciating months told her she was pregnant.

Just like then, it somehow felt like her fault. Like she'd made the wrong decision and managed to set off a chain reaction that sent her whole life up in flames. And just like then, the humiliation of thinking she and Kate had something they didn't threatened to consume her.

"I should go."

Kate shook her head. "No, you should stay so we can talk."

She shook her head, too, but for a very different reason. "I need to go."

"Well, I'm not going to beg you to stay. Not this time." Kate lifted her chin. Gone were the tears. In their place, a kind of defiance that broke Sutton's heart even more.

Sutton fled. She got into her car, cranked the ignition, and drove. Through town, past field after field of sugarcane and soybeans, up to the interstate. She got as far as New Orleans before reason began to set in. And yet, she couldn't stop driving. Without any of her things and without Hugh. Into Mississippi, across to Alabama. She stopped for gas and to text Dad she wouldn't be home. And she just kept driving.

Chapter Twenty-eight

Sutton let herself in the front door and stepped inside. The living room sat as she left it: couch and the club chair she'd indulged in angled to face the television and gas fireplace. She'd picked out everything in the room, from the throw over the back of the couch to the art hanging on the walls. Yet, it felt like a stranger's house.

She walked past her home office and dining room and into the kitchen, flipping on lights as she went. Everything was tidy and, again, hers but not hers. Was this normal? She'd been gone close to three weeks once or twice, but returning never gave her this unsettled feeling. Maybe it was because, on those trips, she stayed in hotels. Home would always feel like home after such generic spaces.

Maybe it was because she'd left everything so neat and put away. She wasn't a super cluttered person, but there were usually bits of her life scattered about—dishes in the sink or mail on the counter or something. And Hugh. Maybe she hadn't thought about how much Hugh made things feel like home.

Or maybe it was none of those things. Maybe spending three months at home had reminded her that Duchesne never stopped being home and everything about her life here was a placeholder. Maybe she'd spent the last decade biding her time without even knowing it.

The truth of that revelation landed heavy. Despite the hours and hours of driving, she pulled out one of the stools from the breakfast bar and sat. Had she wasted the last ten years of her life?

No. That was both dramatic and untrue. She'd built a career. One she liked, that gave her stability even if it didn't always stir her soul. She'd also gotten distance and perspective. She and Kate would never have gotten a second chance if she'd moved home after school. And never leaving in the first place? Well, for all the times she'd questioned that decision, it was nice to finally put those doubts to rest. If she'd never left, Harper might never have been born and she'd never be able to wish for that.

Okay, so her home felt like anything but. Now what?

As if on cue, her phone rang. Dad. As usual, he didn't bother with a hello. "What the devil's gotten into you?"

It was hard to tell if he was worried about her or irritated with her. "I don't know what you're talking about."

"Kate stopped by earlier looking for you. I told her I thought you were with her."

Just the mention of Kate's name made her pulse trip. That Kate had come looking for her? To argue more? To make up? She didn't even know what to do with that.

"Sutton, where the hell are you?"

She looked around, suddenly feeling like a fool. "You don't want to know."

"I damn well do want to know. Are you in trouble?"

She laughed at the question. Aside from that one time she and Kate got caught up on the water tower, she'd not been in trouble a day in her life. And yet, here she was, sitting in a pool of trouble of her own making. "Not the way you're thinking. I'm at my condo."

"In Atlanta? What the blazes are you doing in Atlanta?"

Being an idiot. Running from my problems. Instead of saying either of those things, she settled on the bigger truth. "I'm not sure."

"Did you two have a fight? Is that what this is about?"

Did they? Parts of the conversation were a blur at this point. She remembered telling Kate about her plan, about wanting to stay. Everything went sideways from there. And when she asked Kate whether she loved her, Kate hadn't answered. Everything after that was adrenaline and despair and a need to escape. "Maybe."

"So, you drove across three states to blow off some steam?"

"You don't have to try to make me feel stupid. I already do."

"I'm not calling you stupid. Not in your right mind, maybe, but not stupid."

She rolled her eyes. "Gee, thanks."

"I told you what I told you to make things better, not worse, you know. If I'd known you were going to run over to Kate's and have a fight about it, I would have kept it to myself."

"That's not what we fought about." At least not really.

"So you did fight." His voice held the grim satisfaction of being right about something bad.

"I told her I wanted to stay and it didn't go well."

"Well, what did you say? How did you say it?"

Was she really having a relationship conversation with her father right now? "I don't know. I was excited. I wanted her to be excited, too."

"You steamrolled her, didn't you? You were twenty steps ahead and you threw it all out there like a done deal."

Had she done that? Maybe a little. "I asked her if she was in love with me and she said she didn't know." Saying it out loud made her chest ache.

"Mm-hmm. Was it a question or an accusation? Did you tell her you loved her?"

For a guy who'd spent the last twenty years of his life as a bachelor, he sure was asking a lot of pointed—not to mention on point—questions. "She has to know how I feel. I basically threw myself at her feet."

"You're smarter than that. You know it doesn't work that way."

Ugh. How could a day that was supposed to be so good turn so very, very bad? "I've ruined it, haven't I?"

"You're being dramatic. Kate came here looking for you. She wouldn't have done that if she was done with you."

Even though Kate hadn't called or texted, Sutton wanted to believe him.

"What are you going to do now?"

She looked around, suddenly entirely sure. "I'm going to spend a couple of days packing and getting ready to put this place on the market. And then I'm coming home."

Her declaration was met with silence.

"You think I'm being rash, don't you?"

Another pause. "Are you doing it for her or are you doing it for you?"

What a loaded question. One she might not have been able to answer weeks, days, or even hours before. "I want Kate. I want to be with her more than I have words to express. But I'm doing it for me."

"That's the right answer. I know you think I probably don't give enough credence to love, but I don't think you can take care of someone else until you've got your own self sorted."

She wondered how much he spoke from his own experience. He never spoke ill of her mother and was always quick to say he hadn't been the best husband. "I love you, Dad."

"I know, I know." Even from afar, the sentimentality creeping into the conversation clearly made him uncomfortable.

"And I'm not coming home for you, but I'm glad it means I'll be closer by."

He mumbled something she couldn't quite make out, then cleared his throat. "I guess you want me to feed your damn cat."

She laughed and felt some of the tension in her neck and shoulders, her ribs and her stomach, ease. "I think it's the least you could do."

More grumbling, then, "You gonna call Kate?"

She took a deep breath. "Just as soon as I figure out what I'm going to say."

"You know, sometimes showing up is more important than the words."

Kate's last words to her echoed in her mind. The part about staying to talk and the part about not begging Sutton to stick around. "When did you get so smart?"

"I have my moments. I have moments of being a complete idiot, too."

"Well, I guess we have that in common."

"Keep me posted, okay?"

"I will. Oh, and, Dad?"

"Yeah, buddy?"

She looked around her condo again. "Can I live with you until I find a place?"

His laugh did more to dispel her anxiety than the conversation had. Well, except maybe the part about Kate looking for her. "We'll discuss your rent when you get back."

"Deal."

They hung up and she got up to wander her space. Should she sell it furnished or try to take things with her? She'd just as soon leave most of her furniture behind, a feeling that drove home how unattached she was to her life here.

Despite the long, not to mention emotional, day, she was wide awake. And suddenly starving. She pulled out her phone and put in an order at her favorite Vietnamese place. Might as well enjoy it while she could.

She pulled up her text thread with Kate and started at least half a dozen messages. Every attempt fell flat. Maybe Dad was right and showing up mattered more than the words. She couldn't do that tonight, but she'd do it soon enough. And, hopefully, Kate would give her the chance.

❖

Kate drummed her fingers on the kitchen counter. She so didn't want to be having this conversation. For the briefest of moments, she considered not telling Harper, at least not yet. But she'd probably find out in short order and hearing it from someone else would only make it worse. Kind of like hearing about Sutton's departure from Albin.

He'd been apologetic, to be sure, though it was hard to know if that had more to do with Sutton leaving or knowing she knew about his dishonesty all those years ago. He tried to convince her it was temporary, but this time, she didn't believe him. On top of that was the fact that Sutton had bolted once again and couldn't even be bothered to tell her in person.

No, Harper deserved to hear it from her, sooner rather than later. Because it was the right thing to do. And because she didn't run away from conversations just because they were hard. Unlike someone she knew.

She headed to the living room, where Harper was sorting a box of imperfect beads Kate had given her to make bracelets with. "Honey, can we talk for a minute?"

Harper looked up, blissfully ignorant. "Sure."

She dumped the handful she was holding back into the pile and Kate perched on the arm of the sofa. "Sutton had to go back to Atlanta."

The first thing to pass across Harper's face was confusion. "Like, for a little while?"

"I think for good."

Harper shook her head, confusion giving way to disbelief. "I think you're wrong, Mama."

"I don't think I am." She almost said she wished she wasn't, but didn't.

"But she's coming to my birthday party next week."

She closed her eyes and, for a second, contemplated throwing Sutton under the bus. But nothing would be gained from that, other than a moment of her own self-righteous indignation. "She said she would if she was still in town. I don't think she's going to be."

"But she promised."

Whether or not Sutton had actually promised was almost beside the point. "I think she promised to try."

Harper got up from the floor and planted her fists on her hips. "Why would she leave without even saying good-bye?"

"I don't know, honey." Not the truth, exactly, but not entirely a lie.

Harper paced back and forth, the look on her face morphing from confusion to suspicion. "Did you do something to hurt her feelings? Is that why she left?"

If she wasn't going to throw Sutton under the bus, she sure as hell wasn't going to do it to herself. "I think it's more complicated than that."

"It's not fair." Harper punched her hands down at her sides and stomped a foot.

"Harper." Even though she knew Harper was hurting, she used her warning tone. In part because she instinctively did when Harper seemed on the edge. In part because she didn't think she could handle a full-blown tantrum today.

"Well, it's not. Sutton said she wanted to stay and you made her leave."

"I didn't make her leave." She knew better than to engage in this type of argument with an emotional almost ten-year-old, but the retort came out before she could stop herself.

"Then why did she go?" Even though she asked, Harper's eyes held accusation. Well, maybe accusation and condemnation rolled into one.

"Because even if she wanted to stay, her house and her job are in Atlanta." She took those things seriously, even if Sutton didn't seem to.

"But people move. You said so yourself. She wanted to move here and you said something so she couldn't."

She tried for a calming breath. With it, the will to resist defending herself or her actions. Not only did Harper not need to know the specifics, painting Sutton as the bad guy wouldn't accomplish anything. Though, God, it was tempting. "I'm not arguing with you about this."

"I thought you were friends again. What did you do to make her so sad?"

She closed her eyes this time and prayed for patience. "I didn't do anything."

"You did. I know you did. You're so mean." Harper fled the room then, a flurry of arms and legs propelling her down the hall.

When her door slammed, Kate let out a shaky breath. But rather than loosen the tension in her chest, it left her hollow. She tried to breathe normally, but she couldn't get her lungs to fill the right way.

Damn it. Damn her for being reactive and stubborn. Damn Sutton and her cowardice. Damn the whole damn thing.

At least she was thinking damn instead of fuck. That had to count for something. She laughed, but the sound was brittle. She went to the sofa and collapsed, suddenly exhausted.

Harper didn't have tantrums often. She was lucky in that respect. And when Harper did, Kate was usually decent at keeping a level head. Why hadn't she been able to do that this time?

Because even without Harper's involvement, she had enough of her own anger at Sutton that, if she let herself sink into it, she could barely see straight. Because even though Sutton professed to love her, she didn't care enough to stick around and work on it. Because she'd promised herself from the beginning she wouldn't end up in this position and here she was. Again.

Fucking A.

Chapter Twenty-nine

Kate had no sooner gotten Harper on the bus when Bryce showed up bearing large iced coffees and a box of donuts. He angled his head in the direction of the porch swing. "My first meeting isn't until ten, so we have time. Talk to me."

She took the coffee and sat down sullenly. "She left."

He gave her a look that hovered just this side of pity. "Tell me everything."

She did. Every excruciating detail.

When she finished, Bryce folded his arms. "So, you were mad that she wanted to stay and now you're mad that she left."

"When you say it like that, it makes me sound completely unreasonable."

His gaze didn't waver. "You are being unreasonable."

She scrubbed her hands over her face. "It's not as simple as you make it seem."

"I thought your mantra was that things were usually simpler than people made them out to be."

She did say that. A lot, unfortunately. She stood by it, but it made her current stance more tenuous than she'd like. "She thought she could just decide to move here and pick up where we left off and act like the last ten years never happened and live happily ever after."

"It's presumptuous. I'll give you that. Especially if you hadn't talked about where your relationship might be going." He nodded slowly.

Kate narrowed her gaze. "There's a but in there. I can tell. And I'm pretty sure I'm not going to like it."

"But she wasn't asking to move in with you or get married. It kind of seems like she was asking for a chance."

"But she didn't ask." That was the part she kept going back to. That Sutton had her epiphany or moment or whatever and that was all that mattered in her book.

"Did you let her?"

She generally prided herself on being a patient person, but this wasn't shaping up to be one of those moments. "Why are you taking her side?"

He lifted both hands. "I'm not. I'm on your side. No questions, no hesitation. Always."

"Well, you sure are asking a lot of fucking questions." She grumbled the reply, but her irritation with him was already waning. He had her back and she knew it. Even when she wanted to ring his neck, he knew her as well as she knew herself and his prodding always came with her happiness in mind.

"Honestly, I'm just trying to understand."

She blew out a breath. "Okay, fine. Understand what?"

He lifted his shoulders, then let them drop. "Understand what you want."

"Like, do I want to get back together with Sutton? Do I want to see if we can have the life and the family we dreamed of when we were kids? I don't know, Bryce. That's the problem."

"Those are big things. I think it's okay not to know the answers yet."

She grabbed his shoulders and made a show of pretending to shake him. "Then why are you asking?"

"Technically, I asked what you want. That's a very broad category of things. You decided to take it in that direction."

"Okay, then. I want a drink. How's that?"

"Maybe let's wait until afternoon. You never did do well with day drinking."

"Prude." Being facetious got her to crack a smile, so that counted for something.

"I'm serious, though. You have to have some clarity somewhere and you have to want something you don't have. Otherwise you wouldn't be in such a foul mood."

She flipped him off on principle, but let his words sink in. "I want to be able to talk to Sutton without the stakes feeling so high. I want to move slowly and not rush into something we might regret."

"Completely reasonable. Did you tell her that?"

She rolled her eyes. "She didn't give me the chance."

"Ay. There's the rub."

It was a signature phrase of his, ever since he had to recite Hamlet's "to be or not to be" soliloquy in high school. And him whipping it out usually meant they were getting to the heart of the matter. "I want her to stick around and not run the second things get hard."

The playfulness left his face and he regarded her with pure compassion. "Yeah."

"Fuck." She'd spent pretty much the entirety of her adult life convincing herself she didn't need Sutton, that she was over her. And suddenly it felt like all she'd been doing was pretending and Sutton had the power to break her heart all over again. "I'm fucked."

He squeezed her hand and gave her a stern look. "I wouldn't go that far."

"No? Didn't I just admit I've been hung up on her all along? That I've been lying to myself this whole time?"

"Absolutely not." He spoke with enough force that she almost believed him.

"You have a different explanation?"

"Look, you have feelings for her. Pretty strong ones."

God, she did not like where this was going. "Fine. I do."

"You hadn't decided what to do with them yet, or if hopping on for another go was worth the risk."

"I don't like that you make it sound like a ride at the Sugarcane Festival, but I'll concede the point."

"Thank you." He bowed slightly. "But things were moving along and you were letting yourself wonder and then Sutton strolled in and dropped her little bomb about moving back."

"Yes, and I like that analogy much better." It certainly had felt like a bomb dropping in the moment.

"She jumped the gun and didn't give you a chance to get there on your own."

She lifted a finger. "Or decide if I wanted to get there in the first place."

"Exactly. And when you put the brakes on, she freaked."

Kate scowled. "Freaked and bailed."

"None of that means you've been pining or that you didn't get over her the first time."

He did make it sound perfectly logical. "I want to believe you."

"You should. I'm smart. We've been over this before."

She rolled her eyes and laughed. "You're the smartest and bestest brother a girl could ask for."

"I know. I keep trying to tell you." He leaned in and elbowed her lightly. "So, what are you going to do?"

Right. Because even if she felt slightly better about the state of things, they were still a mess. And she'd not heard a peep from Sutton for the last two days. "I don't know."

"You'll figure it out. You always do."

"Oh, my God." She hadn't even told him the rest.

"What?" He looked at her with alarm.

"I was so focused on being mad at Sutton, I didn't tell you the biggest part."

"Bigger than her wanting to move home and play house with you?"

"Okay, maybe not bigger than that." But still pretty big. "Sutton had a whole thing with her dad about what he said to me that fall she left."

He regarded her with confusion. "Huh?"

"All that stuff Albin said about Sutton making something of herself, doing better than this town. About her finding her people at college. You know."

"Oh." He let the word hang.

"Yeah." It had been that conversation, paired with missing Sutton so much she could barely stand it, that made her extra susceptible to Randy's attention, his assertions she was the smartest and prettiest girl he knew. "She didn't know."

"Like, at all? Even when everything blew up?"

She shook her head. "Apparently not. And seeing us together now got him feeling sentimental—"

"Guilty is more like it."

"That, too."

"Wait, so what does that mean?"

She'd been mulling it over, but hadn't come up with anything solid. "I don't know. In some ways, it doesn't change anything."

"But?"

"But I think it makes Sutton feel worse about what happened."

"Worse like maybe you never would have slept with Randy in the first place or worse about acting like chicken shit when she found out?"

"I'm pretty sure the second. She adores Harper and basically said she couldn't bring herself to wish Harper didn't exist."

Bryce made a face.

"In a good way, I mean. We were having a moment."

"If you say so."

That, at least, she didn't doubt. Sutton's affection for Harper was so obvious, there was no way in hell she could be faking it. Still, did that mean she wanted to be a parent to Harper? And, maybe more to the point, did she want Sutton in that role—for Harper or for herself? "I trust that she loves Harper. What I don't know is what that would or should look like if she were to stick around."

"And where do we stand on that front, again? I'm confused."

So was she. "What front?"

"The sticking around one."

Oh. "Honestly, I have no idea. Albin says she's coming back in a few days, but I haven't heard from her. Not a word."

He frowned. "And you're too proud to call or text her first."

"It's not about being too proud. I went to her house, for Christ's sake, and she was already gone." Her voice had gone up a few notches, so she took a breath and continued more quietly. "I asked her to stay and talk and she refused. I think it has to be her call if she changes her mind."

"You are a stubborn one."

"That's not fair." And she prided herself on being rational and reasonable.

"Okay, fine. You have a point. But I go back to my original question: what do you want?"

Her original answer reverberated in her mind. "I want to talk."

Bryce shrugged. "Is that more or less important than who talks first?"

He'd effectively backed her into a corner. "It's more."

"I'm not saying pick up the phone right this minute, but don't lose sight of that in being all stubborn and right."

She laughed because it was a more appealing reaction than to cry. "I won't."

"Good. Now I have to go to work or my boss is going to fire me."

She glanced at her watch. "Shit. Me, too."

They stood and he put a hand on each of her shoulders. "You're going to be okay. However it works out, you're going to be okay. You know that, right?"

She nodded. She did know. The problem was, she'd started to set her sights on being so much more than okay. And that was the part she didn't feel at all certain about.

❖

Sutton was taking a chance showing up at Kate's house in the middle of the afternoon. There was every possibility she was at work. Or that she was home, but Harper would be getting home from school any minute. But she'd spent the last nine hours driving and she didn't want to wait a second longer than she had to to tell Kate how she felt.

Kate's red hatchback sat in the driveway, so at least she was home. Sutton got out of her car and climbed the porch steps. She shifted from one foot to the other, thinking vaguely she must look like she needed to pee. She took a deep breath and planted both feet firmly on the welcome mat. And then she knocked.

Kate opened the door, giving her the once-over in lieu of a greeting. "What are you doing here?"

Kate looked suspicious but also maybe a little happy to see her. Was she imagining that? She hoped not. "I was hoping we could talk."

Kate didn't break eye contact, but her expression remained impassive—a cool assessment if ever Sutton saw one. "All right."

"All right, we can talk?" Only in that moment did she realize how afraid she'd been Kate would simply slam the door in her face.

"Yes. Harper's due home from school in about half an hour, just so you know."

"I'll talk fast." Her gaze dropped to her feet, but she forced herself to look back into Kate's eyes. "I'm also hoping to do some listening."

Kate gave an almost imperceptible nod and swung the door wide. "Come on in."

"Thanks." She stepped into the living room and looked around. She'd probably been there more than a dozen times, but it sort of felt like she was seeing it with new eyes. Ones that recognized it was Kate's home, one she built for herself and for Harper with no help or input from her. She wiped her sweaty palms on her shorts and tried to relax.

"Can I get you something to drink? Iced tea? Something stronger?" A hint of a smile played at the corner of Kate's mouth, but it seemed more rueful than anything else.

"I'm good, thanks." She didn't have to own that she wasn't sure she could keep anything down.

Kate gestured to the sofa. "Sit, sit. You don't need to wait for an invitation."

Sutton perched on the couch, but didn't lean back. Kate looked like she wanted to say something, but she didn't. Instead, she sat in the chair kitty-corner to the opposite end of the sofa. Pretty much the spot farthest from her without leaving the room. She took that as her cue. "First, I owe you an apology."

"Okay. What, exactly, are you apologizing for?" The question wasn't antagonistic, but it wasn't conciliatory, either.

"Well, a lot of things. But first, for running out on our conversation last week. It was immature and, worse, cowardly."

Using the word cowardly seemed to get Kate's attention. "Thank you. It was difficult to not be able to talk about what you were suggesting."

"It's no excuse, but I was afraid."

"Afraid of what?"

"Afraid I'd overplayed my hand. Afraid I'd rushed things and ruined any chance we had." She paused, desperately not wanting to say the rest. But Kate deserved the truth. "Afraid of being way more in love with you than you are with me."

Kate nodded slowly, as though digesting Sutton's confession. "Is that why you ran away the first time?"

"The first time?"

Kate's gaze didn't waver. "Ten years ago. When you came home and found out I was pregnant."

The weight of the question—and everything it implied—hit her. She'd wrapped herself up in feeling betrayed, used it as armor against the real fear. The one that ate at her and left her with nothing. "Yes."

"Are you just now realizing it or finally getting around to admitting it?"

She swallowed. "The first."

"Sleeping with Randy was stupid and impulsive, an attempt to make the loneliness go away, even for a minute." Kate heaved out a sigh. "And, since we're doing this whole honesty thing, the fear."

"But what were you afraid of? That I wouldn't come back?"

"Maybe a little. Or maybe I was afraid that you'd come back for me but give up this whole amazing life you were supposed to have and eventually resent me for it." She shrugged. "Not that I could have articulated that at eighteen."

Of all the dark and destructive thoughts that haunted her those first few months away—or the months and years after, for that matter—that had never been one of them. "All I ever wanted was to be with you. I convinced myself you didn't feel the same."

Another half smile. This one, though, seemed genuine. "I guess it's good we finally cleared the air."

Sutton nodded. It was. But that wasn't all the air that needed clearing. "When you weren't immediately thrilled with the idea of me sticking around, I guess all that came crashing back."

"I get that. I swear I do. But I hope you can see how it did the same thing to me. Things got hard and you disappeared."

Her heart sank. "And you can't forgive me for that."

Kate let out a groan. "I never said that. Why do you always jump to the worst-case scenario?"

Why did she? Maybe because if she anticipated the worst, anything that wasn't the worst wouldn't hurt quite so much. She'd always been a worrier, but had she really become that person? "I'm not sure."

"Well, you should do some therapy or something because it's freaking annoying."

For some reason, Kate giving her a hard time did more to give her hope than the moment of understanding they'd shared the moment before. "Point taken."

"Good. So, now what?"

That was her Kate—cut through the bullshit and get right to the point. "Well, I listed my condo and I'm going to rent a house here."

"What?" The look of complete surprise on Kate's face would have made her smile, if it didn't scare the crap out of her.

"I know, I know. It's kind of a rash move. The thing is, I want to be here. Yes, I want to be with you, but it's more than that. The last few months have made me realize how much I miss being home."

"Wow."

"I'm not trying to steamroll you, but I'm also making it clear that I'm planning to stick around."

Kate narrowed her eyes. "Did Bryce get to you?"

She laughed. "No, but a certain otherwise crotchety old guy helped me see it was time I put my money where my mouth is. Or maybe where my heart is."

"Okay, then."

Excitement and uncertainty buzzed through her, making her almost dizzy. "Atlanta isn't for me. Duchesne is. That much I know. I also know I'm not going to be that thirty-year-old woman who lives with her dad while she tries to build a new life."

Kate chuckled. "I respect that."

"Of course, I'd be lying if I said my end goal wasn't to be with you. I'm hoping you'll give me the chance to try."

"You know, if you hadn't run out of here like your hair was on fire, we might have gotten to this part of the conversation a whole lot sooner."

She cringed. "I really am sorry for that."

"I know. And I'm sorry I freaked out in the first place."

"I should have talked to you before getting carried away."

"Maybe we both learned our lesson this time."

"Oh, I've learned. I swear." Sutton stood. "So, does this mean we're made up?"

"I'm not sure we were technically fighting."

Sutton skirted the coffee table and grabbed Kate's hand, pulling her to her feet. "Yeah, but if we're making up, that means I get to kiss you."

"I see."

"So, does this mean we're making up?" She was part being playful, part wanting to make it clear Kate got to be the one to decide that.

"Yes, I suppose it does."

Relief and joy and a whole host of things she didn't have words for swirled around her. Instead of trying to articulate them, instead of apologizing more or trying to explain, she pulled Kate into her arms and did her very best to show her.

They'd kissed enough in the last few months that Kate's body, her mouth, felt familiar. And yet, something about this kiss felt entirely new. Full of promise and potential, but grounded in reality, in the moment. It managed to thrill her and give her a sense of calm she hadn't realized she was missing.

At the hissing sound of air brakes outside, Kate broke the kiss. "That would be Harper."

"Is it okay that I'm here?" Sutton wanted to see her, but that needed to be Kate's call, too.

Kate quirked a brow. "Depends."

"On what?" She'd do pretty much anything Kate asked, but was curious.

"Are you planning to be at her birthday party Sunday?"

In the roller coaster of the last week, she'd forgotten Harper's birthday was this weekend. "Am I still invited?"

"Do you really have to ask?"

Before she could answer, the door swung open. "Sutton's car is in the driveway. Is she back? Is she here?"

She'd yet to let go of Kate—which she realized with a surge of joy Kate hadn't objected to—so she did then, turning toward Harper and opening her arms wide. Without a second of hesitation, Harper ran right to her. She gave Harper a big, long hug, booksack and all. "Hey, Harper."

"Hey, Sutton." Harper let go and gave her a knowing smile. "I knew you'd be back. Mama wasn't sure, but I knew."

She glanced at Kate before looking back at Harper. "I wasn't sure, either. I guess that makes you smarter than both of us."

Harper shrugged, looking every bit the put upon tween. "Obviously."

"Can you stay for supper?" Kate asked.

It was a simple invitation, but it held all the promise of the kiss a moment before. "I'd love to."

Harper hugged her a second time. "I missed you."

"Missed you, too." More than she could ever say out loud.

"You're not leaving again, are you?" Harper eyed her with a trace of suspicion.

She looked at Kate again. "Nope. I'm home and I'm not going anywhere."

Kate didn't say anything, but the look in her eyes told Sutton everything she needed to know. They had a chance to make things right, to make them work in ways that didn't exist their first time around. It wouldn't be easy all the time, and it definitely wouldn't be storybook perfect, but it would be theirs. And she wouldn't trade that for anything.

Chapter Thirty

One year later.

Sutton pulled the covers over her head, but the knocking only got louder and more insistent. She rolled onto her back and groaned. Why did every muscle in her body hurt?

Moving. Right. As the fog of sleep lifted, her brain came into focus. Well, soft focus at least. They'd spent the last two days moving all of Kate's, Harper's, and her possessions into their new house. And even with the help of family and friends, it was a lot.

The knocking continued, but Kate didn't stir. She hesitated, then gave Kate's shoulder a gentle shake. "Kate."

"Huh? What?" Kate lurched forward in the bed, clearly startled. "What's wrong?"

"Sorry, sorry. Nothing's wrong." Now she felt silly. "I think Harper is knocking on the door."

"Oh." Kate blinked a few times, then looked at her with confusion. "Did you tell her to come in?"

"Not yet. I just…She's never seen us actually in bed together." She'd certainly stayed over plenty in the last few months, but she and Kate were always up first. Or Harper occupied herself until they emerged.

Kate's eyes narrowed. "Is that a problem for you?"

"No. Of course not. I wanted to make sure you were okay with it."

"You're so weird." Kate didn't even pretend not to laugh at her. "Come on in, honey."

The door opened and Harper bounded into the room. "Good morning."

Her chipper voice had Sutton smiling even as she felt like an idiot. "Good morning. I'm sorry we didn't answer right away."

Harper rolled her eyes. "Y'all have been snoring for hours."

"It's because we worked so hard yesterday," Kate said without missing a beat.

Sutton flashed back to the night before. They'd showered off the grime of moving and stayed upright barely long enough to make the bed. But the exhaustion hadn't stopped her hands from wandering or need from bubbling up. It only seemed fitting to christen their new bedroom—the first that was truly theirs—the first night. The memory made her smile. Well, the memory along with the relief of remembering they'd pulled pajamas back on after.

"I wasn't going to wake y'all up but I'm starving and there's no food."

Harper was prone to hyperbole when it came to the options available—or not available—to her. In this instance, though, she was pretty sure Harper spoke the truth. They'd boxed up a few pantry items, but it was mostly of the pasta and canned good variety. "I could go out and get something."

Kate groaned. "Maybe, but not yet. Harper, come cuddle."

It was all the invitation Harper needed to pile into bed with them. For as uncomfortable as she'd been a moment before, everything about this felt completely natural. And utterly perfect.

Harper settled herself into the middle and Frances, who'd wandered in behind her, jumped up to join them. The only one missing was Hugh, but he and Frances were still feeling each other out, so it didn't surprise her.

It didn't take long for her imagination to wander to what it would be like to do this with a baby, or a toddler. Hopefully, they'd luck out and have a couple of years of family cuddle time before Harper hit her teens and became too cool for such things.

The wedding wasn't for a couple of months still, but they'd already found a donor and were just waiting for after the honeymoon to start trying.

It still caught her sometimes how perfectly everything had fallen into place. Between how much time had passed and all the missteps along the way, they'd found their way back to each other. And what they'd built was so much better, so much stronger, than anything her eighteen-year-old self could have imagined.

"This is nice, but seriously, I'm starving." Harper's assertion broke into her reverie.

Her instinct was to feel bad and then problem-solve, but Kate groaned again. "Come on, we're trying to have a moment."

Harper flung her head back with all the drama of a teenager. "Fine."

"Let's see what we have, then we can strategize." Sutton dragged herself from bed, barely resisting the urge to groan as her muscles protested.

Kate watched Sutton pad from the room, Harper right behind her. She lingered for a moment, not so much wanting to stay in bed, but enjoying the image and sounds of Sutton and Harper discussing whether the animals had been fed and what they should do for breakfast. It was such a simple thing, and yet it made her heart flip over in her chest with almost the same force as the day Sutton proposed.

Or the day they walked through the house and fell in love with it. She'd started crying like a baby and Sutton held her, petting her hair and telling her it would be okay. They both wound up crying and laughing before it was all said and done, much to the amusement of their real estate agent. It was one of those cheesy things she'd spent most of her life swearing only happened in movies. And yet here she was.

She climbed out of bed before her emotions got the better of her and headed to the bathroom. A minute later, she found Harper perched on a stool at the kitchen island and Sutton opening and closing cabinets with almost comical speed.

"Nothing here," Sutton said.

Harper giggled and pointed to the pantry. "What about there?"

Sutton opened the door and stepped inside. "Hello?" She repeated the "o" to mimic and echo, then emerged. "The cupboards are bare."

The silliness of the exchange made her heart swell.

"What should we do, Mama?"

"I knew I should have done a grocery run when we returned the moving truck." They'd been so exhausted, though, they picked up a pizza instead. "I guess we'll have to go out."

Harper looked to be on the verge of cheering, but then dropped her hands. "Wait. Out to eat or out to the store?"

She laughed. "I think out to eat might be in order this morning, then to the store to stock the fridge."

"Yes!" Harper's happy dance seemed to be getting less graceful rather than more. Perhaps it was the growth spurt. Fortunately, she seemed to be leaning in to being awkward and nerdy, something Sutton deserved most of the credit for.

"All right." Sutton planted her hands on her hips in a perfect imitation of Harper. "Where shall we go and do I have to put on pants?"

Another giggle from Harper. She went for exasperated, if only on principle. A knock came from the front door. She looked at Sutton. "Are you expecting someone?"

Sutton shook her head. "Are you?"

"It's nine in the morning on a Saturday. Who would I be expecting?"

Sutton shrugged. "UPS?"

She anticipated they'd be getting plenty of deliveries in the upcoming weeks, but she'd held off on ordering stuff until they'd moved in. "Will you get it? You can get away with not wearing a bra much better than I can."

Harper looked back and forth between them and rolled her eyes. "What is with y'all and doors? I'll get it."

She ran off in the direction of the front door. Sutton followed and Kate hovered behind her out of view. The door opened to a flurry of excited voices. Albin came in first, followed by her parents and Bryce. Everyone held something—a bakery box, a jug of milk, one of those to-go totes of coffee, a package of paper plates and a stack of cups. "Special delivery," Mama said.

It was hard to say what thrilled her more—the prospect of coffee and donuts she didn't have to leave the house for or the fact that their families had clearly conspired to surprise them. "How'd y'all know how desperate we'd be this morning?"

Albin laughed. "We saw y'all at the end of yesterday."

Mama nodded. "We figured y'all hadn't managed to get groceries or unpack anything."

They filed into the dining room and each took a seat, nearly filling the table. The box of donuts made its way around, followed by the jug of coffee. Conversation never stopped and no one bothered waiting for anyone else to dive in. She imagined hosting Thanksgiving here, something her other house hadn't been large enough for, at least not comfortably. And Christmas—a big family dinner but also a cozy Christmas morning with stockings and wrapping paper strewn everywhere.

It wasn't that she hadn't given any of those things thought before, but it was only in that moment they hit her as real, not some vague or far-off fantasy. Maybe it was her tendency to be rooted in the moment, so rooted she didn't let herself ever really imagine the future. Or maybe it was because she'd spent so many years believing she and Sutton weren't going to happen that it was still sinking in.

Whatever it was probably didn't matter. She had a now and a future and more happiness than she knew what to do with. The universe had given her a second chance. She hadn't realized she wanted one of those, but it was so much better than she could have asked for. And, in some ways, it was just the beginning.

About the Author

Aurora Rey is a college dean by day and award-winning lesbian romance author the rest of the time, except when she's cooking, baking, riding the tractor, or pining for goats. She grew up in a small town in south Louisiana, daydreaming about New England. She keeps a special place in her heart for the South, especially the food and the ways women are raised to be strong, even if they're taught not to show it. After a brief dalliance with biochemistry, she completed both a BA and an MA in English.

She is the author of the Cape End Romance series and several standalone contemporary lesbian romance novels and novellas. She has been a finalist for the Lambda Literary, RITA®, and Golden Crown Literary Society awards but loves reader feedback the most. She lives in Ithaca, New York, with her dogs and whatever wildlife has taken up residence in the pond.

Books Available from Bold Strokes Books

A Fae Tale by Genevieve McCluer. Dovana comes to terms with her changing feelings for her lifelong best friend and fae, Roze. (978-1-63555-918-7)

Accidental Desperados by Lee Lynch. Life is clobbering Berry, Jaudon, and their long romance. The arrival of directionless baby dyke MJ doesn't help. Can they find their passion again—and keep it? (978-1-63555-482-3)

Always Believe by Aimée. Greyson Waldsen is pursuing ordination as an Anglican priest. Angela Arlingham doesn't believe in God. Do they follow their vocation or their hearts? (978-1-63555-912-5)

Best of the Wrong Reasons by Sander Santiago. For Fin Ness and Orion Starr, it takes a funeral to remind them that love is worth living for. (978-1-63555-867-8)

Courage by Jesse J. Thoma. No matter how often Natasha Parsons and Tommy Finch clash on the job, an undeniable attraction simmers just beneath the surface. Can they find the courage to change so love has room to grow? (978-1-63555-802-9)

I Am Chris by R Kent. There's one saving grace to losing everything and moving away. Nobody knows her as Chrissy Taylor. Now Chris can live who he truly is. (978-1-63555-904-0)

The Princess and the Odium by Sam Ledel. Jastyn and Princess Aurelia return to Venostes and join their families in a battle against the dark force to take back their homeland for a chance at a better tomorrow. (978-1-63555-894-4)

The Queen Has a Cold by Jane Kolven. What happens when the heir to the throne isn't a prince or a princess? (978-1-63555-878-4)

The Secret Poet by Georgia Beers. Agreeing to help her brother woo Zoe Blake seemed like a good idea to Morgan Thompson at first…until she realizes she's actually wooing Zoe for herself… (978-1-63555-858-6)

You Again by Aurora Rey. For high school sweethearts Kate Cormier and Sutton Guidry, the second chance might be the only one that matters. (978-1-63555-791-6)

Coming to Life on South High by Lee Patton. Twenty-one-year-old gay virgin Gabe Rafferty's first adult decade unfolds as an unpredictable journey into sex, love, and livelihood. (978-1-63555-906-4)

Fleur d'Lies by MJ Williamz. For rookie cop DJ Sander, being true to what you believe is the only way to live…and one way to die. (978-1-63555-854-8)

Love's Falling Star by B.D. Grayson. For country music megastar Lochlan Paige, can love conquer her fear of losing the one thing she's worked so hard to protect? (978-1-63555-873-9)

Love's Truth by C.A. Popovich. Can Lynette and Barb make love work when unhealed wounds of betrayed trust and a secret could change everything? (978-1-63555-755-8)

Next Exit Home by Dena Blake. Home may be where the heart is, but for Harper Sims and Addison Foster, is the journey back worth the pain? (978-1-63555-727-5)

Not Broken by Lyn Hemphill. Falling in love is hard enough—even more so for Rose who's carrying her ex's baby. (978-1-63555-869-2)

The Noble and the Nightingale by Barbara Ann Wright. Two women on opposite sides of empires at war risk all for a chance at love. (978-1-63555-812-8)

What a Tangled Web by Melissa Brayden. Clementine Monroe has the chance to buy the café she's managed for years, but Madison LeGrange swoops in and buys it first. Now Clementine is forced to work for the enemy and ignore her former crush. (978-1-63555-749-7)

A Far Better Thing by JD Wilburn. When needs of her family and wants of her heart clash, Cass Halliburton is faced with the ultimate sacrifice. (978-1-63555-834-0)

Body Language by Renee Roman. When Mika offers to provide Jen erotic tutoring, will sex drive them into a deeper relationship or tear them apart? (978-1-63555-800-5)

Carrie and Hope by Joy Argento. For Carrie and Hope loss brings them together but secrets and fear may tear them apart. (978-1-63555-827-2)

Death's Prelude by David S. Pederson. In this prequel to the Detective Heath Barrington Mystery series, Heath discovers that first love changes you forever and drives you to become the person you're destined to be. (978-1-63555-786-2)

Ice Queen by Gun Brooke. School counselor Aislin Kennedy wants to help standoffish CEO Susanna Durr and her troubled teenage daughter become closer—even if it means risking her own heart in the process. (978-1-63555-721-3)

Masquerade by Anne Shade. In 1925 Harlem, New York, a notorious gangster sets her sights on seducing Celine, and new lovers Dinah and Celine are forced to risk their hearts, and lives, for love. (978-1-63555-831-9)

Royal Family by Jenny Frame. Loss has defined both Clay's and Katya's lives, but guarding their hearts may prove to be the biggest heartbreak of all. (978-1-63555-745-9)

Share the Moon by Toni Logan. Three best friends, an inherited vineyard and a resident ghost come together for fun, romance and a touch of magic. (978-1-63555-844-9)

Spirit of the Law by Carsen Taite. Attorney Owen Lassiter will do almost anything to put a murderer behind bars, but can she get past her reluctance to rely on unconventional help from the alluring Summer Byrne and keep from falling in love in the process? (978-1-63555-766-4)

The Devil Incarnate by Ali Vali. Cain Casey has so much to live for, but enemies who lurk in the shadows threaten to unravel it all. (978-1-63555-534-9)

His Brother's Viscount by Stephanie Lake. Hector Somerville wants to rekindle his illicit love affair with Viscount Wentworth, but he must overcome one problem: Wentworth still loves Hector's brother. (978-1-63555-805-0)

Journey to Cash by Ashley Bartlett. Cash Braddock thought everything was great, but it looks like her history is about to become her right now. Which is a real bummer. (978-1-63555-464-9)

Liberty Bay by Karis Walsh. Wren Lindley's life is mired in tradition and untouched by trends until social media star Gina Strickland introduces an irresistible electricity into her off-the-grid world. (978-1-63555-816-6)

Scent by Kris Bryant. Nico Marshall has been burned by women in the past wanting her for her money. This time, she's determined to win Sophia Sweet over with her charm. (978-1-63555-780-0)

Shadows of Steel by Suzie Clarke. As their worlds collide and their choices come back to haunt them, Rachel and Claire must figure out how to stay together and most of all, stay alive. (978-1-63555-810-4)

The Clinch by Nicole Disney. Eden Bauer overcame a difficult past to become a world champion mixed martial artist, but now rising star and dreamy bad girl Brooklyn Shaw is a threat both to Eden's title and her heart. (978-1-63555-820-3)

The Last First Kiss by Julie Cannon. Kelly Newsome is so ready for a tropical island vacation, but she never expects to meet the woman who could give her her last first kiss. (978-1-63555-768-8)

The Mandolin Lunch by Missouri Vaun. Despite their immediate attraction, everything about Garet Allen says short-term, and Tess Hill refuses to consider anything less than forever. (978-1-63555-566-0)

Thor: Daughter of Asgard by Genevieve McCluer. When Hannah Olsen finds out she's the reincarnation of Thor, she's thrown into a world of magic and intrigue, unexpected attraction, and a mystery she's got to unravel. (978-1-63555-814-2)

Veterinary Technician by Nancy Wheelton. When a stable of horses is threatened Val and Ronnie must work together against the odds to save them, and maybe even themselves along the way. (978-1-63555-839-5)

16 Steps to Forever by Georgia Beers. Can Brooke Sullivan and Macy Carr find themselves by finding each other? (978-1-63555-762-6)

All I Want for Christmas by Georgia Beers, Maggie Cummings, Fiona Riley. The Christmas season sparks passion and love in these stories by award winning authors Georgia Beers, Maggie Cummings, and Fiona Riley. (978-1-63555-764-0)

From the Woods by Charlotte Greene. When Fiona goes backpacking in a protected wilderness, the last thing she expects is to be fighting for her life. (978-1-63555-793-0)

Heart of the Storm by Nicole Stiling. For Juliet Mitchell and Sienna Bennett a forbidden attraction definitely isn't worth upending the life they've worked so hard for. Is it? (978-1-63555-789-3)

If You Dare by Sandy Lowe. For Lauren West and Emma Prescott, following their passions is easy. Following their hearts, though? That's almost impossible. (978-1-63555-654-4)

Love Changes Everything by Jaime Maddox. For Samantha Brooks and Kirby Fielding, no matter how careful their plans, love will change everything. (978-1-63555-835-7)

Not This Time by MA Binfield. Flung back into each other's lives, can former bandmates Sophia and Madison have a second chance at romance? (978-1-63555-798-5)

The Dubious Gift of Dragon Blood by J. Marshall Freeman. One day Crispin is a lonely high school student—the next he is fighting a war in a land ruled by dragons, his otherworldly boyfriend at his side. (978-1-63555-725-1)

The Found Jar by Jaycie Morrison. Fear keeps Emily Harris trapped in her emotionally vacant life; can she find the courage to let Beck Reynolds guide her toward love? (978-1-63555-825-8)